A TURN IN THE AIR

WICKED MOVES

BOOK TWO

A H. CUNNINGHAM

Content Warning

Please scan the QR code or click on it, for the most updated content warnings. I'm always updating them based on reader feedback, so if you have anything you recommend to add, please email me at:

ah@ahcunninghamauthor.com.

I want the reader experience to be safe and consensual!

Foreword

Dear Reader,

If you don't like prologues and/or third-person omniscient point of view, the first couple of pages might be annoying... but I promise it's worth it.

PROLOGUE

MEN AIN'T SHIT.

That was the prevailing thought in the woman's mind as she crossed the street toward the diner. Nerves coursed through her, her mouth dry as she scouted the restaurant one last time. She wasn't familiar with this town outside of what she had investigated online.

What she knew was plenty.

The diner was at its busiest from seven to nine in the morning. After that, their patrons slowed down to a trickle. This was the type of eatery where the staff knew each other from elementary school, but they were used to strangers coming through as they were right off a heavily transited highway.

It was the perfect location to meet someone incognito and avoid being tracked, and if someone tried to trail her, they'd have difficulty connecting the dots. She was no spy, but the mission before her compelled her to take this leap. This fell right in with her goals in life: do the work she loved, be a supportive friend, and make sure no woman that sought her help ever took an L because she'd fallen in love with a narcissistic user of a man.

Goal number three had a deep-rooted hold on her. Once upon a time, she'd been that naïve girl in love putting all her trust and resources into a relationship with a man who proved untrustworthy.

After putting the pieces together from the devastation he wrought, she also put her considerable skills to good use, and Oriole Hood was born. Oriole was supposed to exist only behind the screen, but here she was, stepping out from behind her laptop to do the work she was born to do.

Gathering courage, Oriole took a deep breath and strolled into the establishment.

A quick scan and she recognized the person she was here to meet, a short, petite, light-skinned Black woman with blond locs and flawless makeup wearing a princess cut maxi dress. She cautiously approached the booth, aware that her nerves paled compared to the woman waiting for her.

"Geneva?" Oriole whispered, using the code name they'd agreed upon.

"Oriole? Oh shit, girl, I was so nervous, I turned back twice before I finally decided to walk in here," Geneva said, swiping her blond locs off her shoulder and furtively surveying the room.

Geneva took a mental inventory of Oriole, the person who was supposed to get her out of the hell that was her life—two years wasted on a man that didn't love her. On a man that was supposed to protect her and cherish her. She'd given him everything—her body, her heart. Geneva had shunned friends who told her that something wasn't right with him. She'd helped him with anything he asked for and kept his money when he required it. She'd jeopardized her livelihood doing some dirty dealings at her job for him.

He'd never told her his hustle, and she'd never dared to ask. Not until that fateful night she arrived home to find him stashing dope in the apartment he paid for. Fear had flashed cold through her. How naïve had she been to believe his good-guy persona? His lifestyle was so incongruous with what she was seeing that she'd faltered on the threshold of her apartment, realizing he was on the phone and not expecting her yet. That's when she heard him say the words that put all of this in motion.

"Listen, we ain't gonna get caught, love. Why do you think I moved all this shit to her apartment? If they come for me, I'll redirect the evidence to her. She can take the fall. I'll ensure the evidence is enough to convict her but not have her rot in jail for long. After all, I do have feelings for her. This is just a necessary evil to get the heat off us."

That was a month ago. Geneva had pretended for a month that all was well while plotting how to get away from him and this life she no longer recognized. She slept next to him at night in fear of what came next. Every woman needs an exit strategy, and Oriole became hers.

Geneva studied her, searching for the woman she'd thought she'd meet. Oriole looked like a plus-size model with sandy brown skin, long shiny brown hair, and the cutest face. Her hair was probably a wig, but that shit appeared to be growing off her scalp. She had on the most flawless makeup and could pass as one of those cutesy cartoons with her full cheeks and cherub looks. And she was dressed in a tight black ensemble that showed her ample curves.

This wasn't who Geneva had expected. Every encrypted message sent was no-nonsense, guiding her through how she could erase all traces of her moves and clean whatever money she "collected" from her man before her exit. Oriole was an expert. She'd expected no frills, and here she was a whole baddy.

If you were abused, crushed, or taken advantage of, Oriole ensured you got paid from the same money your man controlled and earned off your back—*and* she did it in a way that ensured you could never be found out. Geneva didn't understand all the details, but she trusted her.

Risi, one of the girls at the salon Geneva went to, had recommended Oriole, who'd "obtained" fifty grand from her older sugar daddy. The man had kept Risi home, pampering her and her new baby, with the excuse of severe jealousy before she found out he had three other baby mamas. When Risi left and asked for child support, he ghosted her. Come to find out, his whole identity had been a front. Oriole had hacked his accounts and siphoned the money to Risi while she rebuilt her life.

Geneva's story had several similarities with Risi's.

Older boyfriend? Check.

Both had thought they knew their man? Check.

And now, with what she'd learned right before finding her man trying to frame her...

"Did you follow the instructions? Did you change cars and then take the agreed-upon public transportation?" Oriole asked her, making Geneva cringe. She hadn't followed all the instructions. Changing cars seemed like overkill, so she'd stuck to her blue Lexus till she got to the bus stop they'd discussed—no need to tell Oriole, though. She didn't plan to be caught.

Ever.

"Yeah, I did," Geneva lied.

"Do you have the money? Do you think it's marked?"

Oriole asked, squinting at Geneva and Geneva gave a jerky nod.

Oriole had never done an in-person exchange. All her dealings in the past had been done through encrypted systems, with money obtained through hacking and transferred through an account offshore to land in the victim's accounts clean via legitimate payments as influencers or other means. If anyone tried to track Oriole or the money, they'd get lost in a maze of steps that would never end.

When Geneva contacted her and explained her predicament, she'd also explained the only access she had to her man's funds was the money he'd stashed in her house.

She had been leery of dealing with actual cash, but she also knew Geneva was close to getting framed for things she didn't do. The thought of how Geneva's man had used her made Oriole's blood boil enough to lower her suspicions and move forward.

"Ok, I'll swap once you leave. Remember, now that you took the money, you can't go back."

"I ain't going back."

"And you and I won't have direct contact; you'll get your money as promised in a month. Make sure to use this cash for anything in the meanwhile. The worst thing you could do is use your man's cash and learn we were wrong, and it is marked." Oriole slipped an envelope under the plate of grits in front of Geneva.

After the tense exchange, Geneva made a big show of getting up, paid her bill, then left.

A few minutes later, Oriole retrieved the money hidden in the diner's electrical room, just as planned.

She walked out, seemingly unbothered, heart racing with every second she carried the cash.

A forty-minute ride on the bus took her to one of the

busiest gyms in the city, where she powered through the doors, heading to the dressing room. She retrieved a bag, got in a stall, and twenty minutes later emerged with a head of waist-length brown braids, wearing a jumpsuit with a convenient hood to hide her features.

She worked out for two hours before leaving the gym to hop in her car and drive to her friend's dance studio. When she left that night, Oriole vanished to leave Sal Blackwell, software engineer, video game developer, occasional hacker, and anime lover behind.

The perfect plan to go undetected had only one flaw—someone had followed Oriole until she arrived at the studio.

ONE

TODAY's tendinopathy therapy session robbed me of all my usual equanimity. I stood in the waiting room of the Sports Therapy Center, wincing as my tendon's soreness reminded me of all I'd accomplished today. It hadn't helped that I'd had shitty sleep these past two weeks. The nightmares that still haunted me had returned for a new go around my brain, making things even more challenging to navigate.

"Devon, my man, this was a good day. I know you feel sore, and that's to be expected, but I'm telling you, you're more than ready for more relevé work and jumps. You're sustaining your relevés well, and it's time to try more," John, my therapist, insisted as he walked out with me.

After almost a year of therapy, all signs indicated a full recovery, but whenever I pushed myself, a chasm opened up in my stomach, reminding me of what was at stake.

My reality was dance. Dance had always been my solace, my everything. What if I pushed and realized I wasn't the same as before?

I approached the door with a slight smile on my face. John meant well and burdening him with my worries was not something I ever planned to do. Optimism begets results, so I pushed my fears aside for now.

"I hear you. Next session, let's start," I said, ignoring the roiling in my belly.

"Good." John clapped my back, his large hand heavy on my shoulder. The weight of his belief bolstered me, and I shoved my concerns aside.

I'd been in a waiting stage for most of this year: waiting for my tendon to heal after surgery, waiting for my feet to move the way they should again—and for me to gain the courage to do the work I knew I could do.

The visceral need to get back on stage, back to my art, reminded me of when I was twelve years old and my grandmother took me to see a rendition of Oscar Wilde's *Salome* in ballet form. All of the cast had been Black, and the power, grace, and style they commanded on stage mesmerized me. I remembered the wonder that overtook me. The lead male dancer moved with an unleashed precision that spoke to me. His muscles showcased strength with every movement, every leap, and every turn. I left the show wishing I could be on that stage. The arts had always called to me; I played the guitar and sang but hadn't thought of the possibility of dance until that day.

The next day I told my parents I wanted to join a dance school. The common misconceptions and prejudices followed. My parents worried about my sexuality, livelihood, and mental state. I'd been young but confident that ballet was my calling. My usual easygoing nature disappeared, and arguments and recriminations flew like missiles in my home.

It took my big brother visiting from the States to advocate for me.

As the family's primary provider, Delroy had sway over our parents, and he paid for dance school and took me to my first class. I never looked back.

The vibration in my sweatpants pocket shook me out of my reverie.

"I gotta take this." I dapped John up and rushed out of the studio, not wanting him to hear this conversation.

"Devon, hon, how are you?" the dulcet tones of Marisa Martinez, artistic director of the Miami Ballet, greeted me. I knew not to fall for the cheeriness in her voice.

"I'm good, thanks. Walking out of therapy," I said, not betraying my inner turmoil.

"Oh, wonderful! Can you come to the center? Mike and I want to talk to you." Mike was the Executive Director who'd personally reached out to me to move to Miami a year ago before my tendon decided to give up on me for good during a routine practice. I'd dealt with tendon issues on and off most of my professional career but had done the proper conditioning to keep myself away from the surgery table.

That day, when I landed after a double tour en l'air combo, I knew I wouldn't walk out of that studio. My left tendon seared me with speech-impeding pain, leaving me gasping for air. Fellow dancers swarmed around me, trying to be helpful, but nothing could help the damage to my left foot. I'd limped out of the studio, my world rocked at the precipice of desolation. Although debilitating, the pain in my foot wasn't what I remembered the most. The sensation of emptiness gnawing in my gut, the fear of never dancing again, would be one I'd never be able to shake. That same emptiness rushed in at Marisa's words, washing away all the optimism from my therapy session.

"Yeah, sure thing," I agreed, getting into my car, knowing the meeting would change the course of my day.

———

"Baby bruh, look dem locs! Bloodclat, I'm tryna get like yuh when I get outta here. Yuh fresh."

Delroy's embrace was just what I needed after my meeting at the ballet. His arms enveloped me even though we were the same height, both being the tallest in our family. But where I was all lean strength from my dancing, Delroy was all brawn.

"Wa gwaan?" I asked, doing a quick scan of him. I was greeted by a face that could pass as mine, with pensive eyes, long eyelashes, deep brown skin, a broad nose, and thick lips surrounded by a trimmed beard. Delroy was looking good. I basked in the relief of finding him healthy and in good spirits. He might be the older brother, the family provider, but I ensured Delroy was good here until he was free again.

The calm facade Delroy put on for the world was like my equanimity. It came from a similar place. We'd learned early to protect ourselves from hurt by not giving nor expecting too much in return.

People had proven to us time and time again that they only saw the exterior. With him, people saw the ruthless big-time weed dealer brought down by one of his trusted friends. With me, they saw the ballet dancer and all the stereotypes attached to my profession. People tried to define us, put us into neat boxes as any Black man. The difference was even some of our loved ones did the same to us.

"Nothin' much. Just counting dis days."

"A year, mi seh. No more. I'll rest easy then." I nodded, knowing we were both counting on when he'd go free.

"Yuh and I. Listen, can yuh send di money to Britta for di month?" Delroy asked the question he asked me every time I visited as if I'd ever forget to send money to his ex-wife.

"When yuh gon' accept yuh love fah di woman?" I asked.

He kissed his teeth, leaning back on his chair, while I relaxed my legs in front of me, the twinge of pain greeting me still.

"Yuh was in therapy dis morning?" Delroy asked, ignoring my question. I'd let it stand. I wasn't one to push him.

"Yeah, man. That shit don't get easy, but I'm doin' betta. Di therapist thinks I can go back on stage dis season." The familiar pang clanged in my chest.

"That easygoing face don't work on me. Why yuh worried?"

Now it was my time to kiss my teeth. "I'm good, D. Yuh talking nonsense, man."

"Right...so what was that worried face yuh walked ina di here, then? Are the nightmares back?"

He didn't miss a thing. This was why I needed him out of here. Delroy was the only person in the world that understood me well. I wouldn't get that with anyone else; I needed my brother out of this prison.

"The ballet call me fah meeting."

"Rass."

"Yeah, man. The clock running outta time."

Delroy rested a closed fist on the table in between us. I could see his strain; if we were out of here, he'd pound his fist hard enough to rattle the table. But here, he couldn't let all his feelings show. That way lay troubles he didn't need a year closer to his freedom.

"If Winston and Cleo weren't stubborn back then, we'd fix di problem ourselves."

"Moms and Pops didn't want to move here to the States. Yuh couldn't make them do it even if yuh threatened to take yah support away," I reminded him, unwilling to go down this 'what if' rabbit hole. I was in the United States under a work visa. My whole stay here I'd been going from work visa to work visa, sponsored by the companies I danced for. Delroy had always disliked the uncertainty of me depending on other people, but he couldn't claim me through our sibling connection, and our parents refused to go through the process. Deep down, I believed it was out of spite to me, and Delroy probably agreed.

"Bloodclat, I'm sorry, bruh. I should have applied for my citizenship as soon as Britta told me to, y'know. I dragged mi feet, and now..."

"Yuh good." I shook my head, another conversation we'd had many times. This was not Delroy's first time in prison. He'd had two more minor incidents when he was younger that prevented him from applying for citizenship for fear he'd be denied due to the good moral character requirement.

"So...why don't yuh try something like I did with Britta back ina di day? Ain't yuh tight with that dancer who gave yuh di studio job?"

"Who, Aisha? Nah, she got a man." I didn't want to marry anyone. There was a level of trust required to pull off something like that...and I didn't know many people I could trust with my livelihood. It would require someone to take things as seriously and have as much stake as I did. No one around me fit that description.

"Oh...how about them two girls yuh always chillin' with?"

"Who? Mila? Sal?" I chuckled. Mila wasn't about that life. I'd gotten to understand her enough to know her familial ties would pull at her. She couldn't stand lying to her people, and I wouldn't ask her to do that. And Sal? Yeah, right. She'd stab me in the balls first if I asked her to marry me for papers.

"Nah. Mila, she's too tight to her family. That wouldn't work. If I were to do dis, it would be need-to-know. I can't risk fucking up my future here to get dem papers. Rass! I need to get on stage and do this damn dance. I can do it."

Delroy's eyebrows came together, and I knew what was coming.

"Don't you go out there hurtin' yourself again to get on stage for dem people. Then you fuck up your career to get 'em the headline they want. Don't let dem pressure you if you nah ready."

"I won't."

"Alright then, you gon' have to figure something out fast before dem people take away yuh work visa. How long yuh have?"

"Till the end of the year. If I can't be on stage by July, they won't renew my paperwork...I'm fucked."

"Nah, ya need to get someone to marry yuh. Like I did with Brita. And get some pumpum. Yuh need some. Help with the sleeping." Delroy shrugged, smiling.

I knew this day would change with that call, but I hadn't realized to what extent. Now I needed to figure out how to stay in the States while doing what it took to get back on stage. Because even if I did figure out my papers situation, if I didn't manage to get better, I didn't know if I'd recognize myself ever again.

Two

Sal

The comfort of my home could not be replicated anywhere. My three-screen setup where I worked and created was almost as essential as my friendship with my two best friends, Aisha and Mila, which was why I endured working from the back of this reception desk on the days Aisha's ballet and dance studio was busy and her new receptionist needed help.

The reception was a large space separated by a white desk for people to check in. The area had a bit of privacy, which I loved, with a door restricting access to the rest of the space. I had a habit of sitting in the corner closest to the door, where I was hidden.

Helping my friends was in my nature, but with that came pockets of annoyance—like now, as my online friend and partner Patrice told me she was sending the animation for the next storyline in my hentai RPG.

I checked my Signal app and saw the latest message in our three-person chat. My IRL friends were my strength and my support system, whereas my online friends were my soundboard and partners in crime. *Literally.*

> Patrice: Hey, check out the storage link. The animators finished the latest scene. Is hot af.

> Cora: Girl, hot AF is an understatement. I can't wait to publish an interview with you once you release your second game. The fandom is gonna go wild!

My fingers tingled with the itch to dive in and code the next scene. After a few years of mourning the loss of the magic I'd created with my first video game, I realized I needed an outlet for all the ideas that percolated in my brain and the unfulfilled needs coursing through me. Then *Alix, Slayer of Sex Demons*, my new video game, was born.

The commotion of children departing from jazz class washed over me. My friend Mila, who taught the jazz courses, said goodbye to the children and chatted with the parents. The new receptionist, Athena, helped parents with tuition and other administrative questions.

> Sal: I'm @ the dance studio helping out because Athena has to leave soon for her college classes. So I can't look at it yet.

> Cora: Oh, don't you go opening that file. This scene is all about Alix almost succumbing to the sex demon Horix. I don't understand how you come up with these storylines, but they are so good! I can't wait to play it and showcase you in the magazine.

> Patrice: mhm, it's gonna be good.

> Sal: Thanks, y'all. BTW can you please tell me when the envoy hits the stacks?

The codes for *money* and *bank* were so ingrained in our every day, Patrice immediately confirmed receipt of the money once I asked her about the stacks. We really thought we were something with our code words.

I wanted to ensure Cora could transfer the funds to Geneva sooner rather than later, knowing she would need it soon. My stomach seized up at the thought of Geneva, her predicament, and the risk I'd taken to meet her in person.

> Cora: Ok, later, I'm about to go read my Z.J. Grousant ARC

> Patrice: You lucky hoe…I heard this new novel is even spicier than usual, and Zac did some extra x-rated illustrations for a special edition.

> Cora: oh yeah…I got that special ed. Later!

Damn!

Lucky Cora. The new graphic fantasy novel was getting much hype in the Black indie creator world, especially with those of us who loved anime but were looking to see ourselves represented.

It didn't hurt that the author duo were two fine-ass Black men who were so nice and accessible to their fans even after they'd blown up over the past couple of years with their debut series.

Cora, Patrice, and I always lamented how we wanted more Black characters for cosplaying. While there were some, what Z.J. delivered to the fandom was special. Though I had stopped cosplaying a while ago, they both still did it all the time, so we all appreciated Z.J. and their real ass Black characters. This was why Patrice and Cora were my online ride-or-dies, Blerds who'd found each other in a cosplaying forum and never looked back.

When I started doing my Oriole work, Cora, Patrice, and I were in the process of creating an International Business Company to protect our assets as we each evolved in our respective industries. The Bajan powerhouse Patrice owned an animation company that employed Black creators. A straight shooter, Patrice was hard as nails, jaded from life just as I was. Cora, the eternal optimist, always falling for a new partner, ran a popular digital publication and blog, highlighting Black creators in the arts and technology. And I had my burgeoning software development company.

With Cora's connections with banking in Seychelles, we created a holding company that protected our funds. Through that, we could transfer offshore funds and make transfers to the women I helped without worry. They had offered their aid without an ounce of concern. We even had a process for those who wanted to relocate and leave the States for whatever reason.

Sometimes I wished they both lived here, but each of them resided in their respective Wakandas.

As I typed my thanks to the ladies, the flow of easy noise morphed into a hum of tittering and murmurs as Athena buzzed someone in. I didn't bother raising my eyes from my laptop, already knowing the only person who could make a gaggle of students and their moms go into a tizzy.

Devon.

"He's too fine," Mila whispered to me and Athena as Devon greeted the parents and students.

"Wa gwaan, ladies?" The smooth molasses voice

commanded my attention as I worked on my laptop. I wouldn't bother looking up; I just gave a brief nod and kept typing away. There was an urgency inside me with the knowledge that my next scene was waiting at my apartment. If I could finish this commissioned app for my newest client, I'd have the entire evening to code my next video game scene.

"Oh, hi, Mr. Reid," Athena simpered, and I held my breath, avoiding my physical annoyance at the ridiculousness of people's reactions to Devon. I guess an easygoing, sexy-as-sin dancer would create that type of response in people. Having to deal with it day in and day out when in the studio grew old real quick, though.

"Hey, colleague, how are you?" Mila said. The flirtatious note meant nothing more than a passing attraction, something I'd learned long ago. I thought Mila had feelings for Devon for a while, but she'd confessed to me that she just liked lusting at him from afar. She had no wish to entangle herself with anyone now. Few people understood how determined Mila was about her business—and how messy her love affairs could get.

"No troubles bothering me today," Devon said in his lilting accent, and without looking up, I knew he was full of bullshit. His voice might sound calm to the unsuspecting, but a thread within it unsettled me.

Damn this man for making me like him.

In less than four months, he'd inserted himself into our friend group, and I considered him a friend too. I had zero space in my brain for new alliances, but he'd managed to wedge himself in with his equanimity, protectiveness, and good humor. A man who didn't put his ego first on the table was as rare as a black diamond, but somehow Devon pulled it off seamlessly.

I'd seen him in action, teaching the children, dancing, and witnessing his brilliance, but he made you think he was just the boy next door with his gorgeous smile and easy charm. And everyone tripped over their feet trying to bask in that brilliance he tried to mute. Fools, all of them.

The coding for the app I was creating for my client was simple enough that I could work and keep an ear out for the conversation between Devon, Mila, and Athena.

"You went to rehab today?" Mila asked him.

"Mhm," he said in the way Jamaican people had of saying a whole sentence with one sound.

"Mr. Reid, you're doing the last class of the day?" Athena asked as if she didn't know the answer. She had the schedule Aisha sent us all at the beginning of the month, and on top of that, it was tacked to a board right above her.

Fucking annoying. The urge to shake my head was strong, but I restrained myself and kept typing.

"Nah, I just came to hang out with the ladies. You got class today, right?" he asked Athena, and she made a noncommittal sound as if she was considering skipping. She better not; I'd rearranged my day based on Aisha's request for help.

"Awww, you hear that, Sal? Devon came to hang out with us!" Mila tried pulling me into the conversation. She knew better.

"Yeah, I heard," I said without looking up.

"What you working on, Sal?" Devon asked. His genuine curiosity pulled at something dormant inside of me. Aisha and Mila knew all about my work but were so used to my taciturn nature they didn't push me too much with mundane questions about my day. However, Devon always figured out ways to check on me even if I wasn't the type of person who needed that. And for some reason, I always reacted to his attempts.

I considered answering with a single word and continuing to work, but that thread of something in his voice made me look up. The protectiveness I felt for my friends extended to this man, whether I liked it or not.

He stood next to Athena, resting against the inner desk in the reception room. Tall, with a lean strength that spoke of his daily work in the gym to stay fluid and muscled. His rich mahogany skin was so smooth I wondered if he bathed in lotion instead of soap. His open expression was as familiar to me as Mila's winks or Aisha's serene smiles.

He grinned at me, and I felt my lips twitching to match the gesture, but I contained myself. He had his locs loose today, and dark strands and a black beard gleamed under the fluorescent light.

"That app, for that client," I responded and looked back at my computer.

I felt the force of his regard as I returned to my coding.

"Oh, that's right. Is that the man that wants the app for his bar? I thought that was a wicked concept," Devon said, and now I felt Mila and Athena's eyes on me too.

"Yeah, it lets you do your mixes, put in your bar order, and request them via the app."

The fact that he remembered lit a warm, heavy glow in my stomach—or that could be the burrito I ate for lunch sitting a little heavy, one of the two.

"I've seen what you do with your apps. I'm sure you're gonna kill it, adding more functionalities and—"

"Who's that?" Athena pointed to the door camera.

"Not sure." Mila shook her head.

Their voices faded as I focused back on coding, the warm feeling easing out of me. The door chimed, and a grating voice greeted us. From the corner of my eye, I saw a brooding Black man around forty, with a light-skinned complexion similar to mine and looks that some would describe as handsome but that I would categorize as overrated.

"Good afternoon. Sorry for disturbing y'all, but I'm a bit desperate. I'm searching for a woman that might work here. She's one of those 'more to love' broads with long brown braids. Medium brown skin. A bombshell of a woman, thick as fuck, even if she's a bit heavier than how I like them. She was spotted walking in here two weeks ago. I wish I could describe her face, but I don't have that info."

The description made my hands shake over the keyboard of my laptop. A sour taste flooded my mouth, and my despisement for men bum-rushed me.

"There are a lot of parents and people that come into this establishment. May I ask why you're looking for this woman?" Devon asked, and I had never heard him sound so...dangerous. As if he knew ten thousand ways to hurt someone with just a look.

"Yeah, man, of course. You don't want to just be sharing any info, I get it. Nah, see, my cousin's broad?" The man whipped out his cell phone and showed a picture of Geneva.

A cold hand ran from the top of my back all the way down to the bottom of my spine. A manufactured anguish transformed the man's features. "His wife, she's missing. We're desperate. The police ain't doing much, talking about she left on her own. We're doing our own search. The woman I described first, we think was the last one to see Juniper. You know, Juniper wasn't well up here, and we wanna make sure she has the support she needs."

Every word the man uttered enraged me while my heart

hammered. So, this was the story Geneva— *Juniper's* boyfriend was going with? I hadn't realized I'd closed my fist until Mila's hand ran softly over my whitening knuckles. I took a few cleansing breaths knowing that showing any emotion right now would be dangerous.

Thank God for my mama and sisters for raising me to be a chameleon. I never thought I'd be grateful to them for teaching me how to transform myself to please the male gaze, but my gold-digging diploma under their tutelage had finally borne some fruit. It was the only knowledge I'd taken to heart in their lessons.

"Oh, that's horrible! Of course, we want to help, but that description doesn't fit any of us, as you can see. Not the owner and her man, either. We're the only ones that work here."

The man's eyes roved over all of us, and I probably wasn't the only one feeling the glint of danger that came with the look. Then his face transformed again, and I could have sworn I imagined the malice.

He nodded, satisfied that Mila was telling the truth. After all, I wasn't close to what he described. No wig meant my natural coils didn't touch my shoulders, and without body makeup, my skin was the shade of "I can almost pass" that my momma loved reminding me of to my ever-living annoyance. And the lush curves the man waxed poetic about were all enhanced that day by shapewear and corsets. No one would describe me as thick; I was fat, nothing wrong with that.

"Yeah...you sure, though? That description don't ring a bell? We think the lady lives close by here. Before arriving at the studio, she also went to a gym a few exits away. If y'all hear anything, please hit me up. Here's my number." He pulled out a card, which he handed to Athena with a wink.

He'd probably deciphered she was the weakest link in the group.

The chime went off as he strolled out of the studio, the pressure changing as he departed.

"Oh, that's so sad. I really hope they can find that lady. You know how the cops are, when it's one of us, they don't wanna help. I'll mention it to Aisha in case it's one of the parents you might not know," Athena said. She was the only one oblivious to how the air had emptied out of the space while the man was here.

The code on my laptop swam, my eyes incapable of focusing with everything in my mind.

Two sets of eyes bored into me, the insistent nudge of their concern filling me with anxiety.

Without lifting my gaze, I breezed out of the reception to Aisha's office in the back. If I walked fast enough, they wouldn't see me lose my ever-living shit. Cora had warned me not to meet Juniper code-named Geneva, that this was too much, that I might be in over my head.

I needed a plan to shake this search off the studio and my friend's business.

THREE

DEVON

THE SENSE of unease stuck to me like wet dumpling dough on my hands, refusing to let go. Both Mila and I knew that man had been describing Sal.

We were both here closing the studio that night when she walked in looking like every red-blooded straight and bi man's fantasy with some body makeup making her bronzed. But all the adornment detracted from her quiet beauty. She didn't need any embellishment, and I had wondered why she'd dressed up like that, but now things were making some sense. I'd wanted to ask Sal what was happening, but Mila had stopped me.

I wasn't privy to all of Sal's comings and goings. No matter how close I'd gotten to Mila and Sal as friends, I was acutely aware there was some shit she did for a living that she kept tight to her chest. I hadn't worried much about it; after all, our friendship was in its infancy, and there would be a time she'd deem me trustworthy enough. Besides, I had some shit I kept tight to my chest too. But this last month or so, she'd started relaxing more around me, engaging me in conversation similar to Aisha and Mila, and I relished the accomplishment.

Sal was the type of person that kept her affection, her energy, and her regard under lock and key. She refused to give more to people that weren't in her circle and was unbothered by the social niceties that dictated politeness to make them comfortable. I envied that shit; I loved how she could be what others considered rude but was only being herself while still having a draw on people around her. Because her goodness always shined through. Sal wasn't nice, but she was *good*, and that shit was worth its weight in gold.

These past four months as a teacher at Mrs. Brown's Dance Studio had been a gift to me. When Aisha, my old friend from New York, called me to ask if I wanted to teach kids, I jumped on the opportunity to be immersed in my art without the pressures of performing. What I hadn't expected was to be adopted as the fourth member of Aisha, Mila, and Sal's group, which had been invaluable to me on days like today when bad news over bad news rained upon me. So even though I was worried as fuck about my visa being revoked at the end of the year, the knot in my stomach wasn't for my troubles; it was for Sal.

That dude was up to no good, and there was knowledge at the edge of my brain that niggled, insistent but irretrievable. I couldn't shake the feeling I'd seen the man before, but where?

"Hello!" Aisha walked in, followed by her partner Knox. The two traveled a tumultuous road at the beginning of their relationship but had now settled into a perfectly synced partnership. They were opposites in many regards but managed to bring out the best in each other. I wondered if I would ever find someone I could let in the way these two did. I doubted it. People usually just wanted the surface and weren't interested in exploring the depths.

"What's up?" Knox asked as he stood behind Aisha. He had a besotted look on his face as he stared down at her.

"Nothing much. A guy just came looking for his cousin's woman. She got lost, and I guess they think whoever saw her last is one of the parents here—sad business. Well, I gotta run to class. See y'all tomorrow!" Athena said, emerging from the back with her backpack and sprinting to the door.

"What? What woman is missing?" Aisha asked, perplexed, staring at the door that Athena had just closed.

Athena had missed every single undercurrent of that conversation, but that was for the best.

"Someone is after Sal," Mila stated bluntly.

Damn. I hadn't wanted to put it in those simple terms in my brain, but Mila wasn't far off from my concerns.

"What is happening?" Knox's deep voice rumbled in the studio, and I knew this shit could get contentious real quick if we didn't have an actual conversation about it. I explained what had transpired with the man, leaving aside my suspicions about who he could be. I'd been around my brother and the business enough to know some key players, and I suspected that might be where I knew this man from.

"So they are saying the woman is missing? But maybe it's true, and she tried to play Sal? I mean, it could happen?" Aisha said, reluctance to discuss the matter dripping from every word she said.

"Has Sal ever failed in her assessments?" Mila asked, uncharacteristically serious.

Aisha shook her head, wrapping her arms around her. Knox immediately put his arm around her shoulder.

"I think we need to talk to Sal first," I said, nodding to them. Of all of us, I probably knew the least about her business, but I had a sense of trust that I couldn't shake away. She would let us know the level of concern.

"True. She would slaughter us all if she knew we were over here having a whole conversation about her."

"All facts." Aisha nodded, them she trained her eyes on me and frowned. "What's wrong?"

"Nothing." My calm demeanor was firmly in place.

"Nah, something is up with you. You were weird even before that dude arrived." Mila squinted her eyes at me.

These women, always in my business.

I grinned.

"Nothing that can't be fixed. I gotta figure out how to extend my visa with the ballet. They're asking me to perform for the summer showcase, but I'm not sure I'll be ready. So, I gotta find an alternative solution, that's all." I shrugged my shoulders, brushing off their concern. This wasn't something they needed to worry about. The summer showcase was months away.

Mila and Aisha had been nagging me about a long-term solution to my status in the country, and I always managed to dodge the conversation. Sal would oddly always have my back, telling them to leave me be. Where was she when I needed her?

"I've been telling you, you need to get hitched to someone trustworthy and keep it moving." Mila rolled her eyes at me and then winked. For all her winks, she wasn't offering herself, which was why I knew she couldn't pull it off long-term. Her family dynamic was essential to her, and it would probably complicate her life. I had figured out she was trying to leave behind the mess of previous relationships. I could respect that.

"Maybe I could help? I mean, we could pull it off. Just do it for the time you need—" Aisha's offer was cut off by an animal sound emerging from Knox.

I stifled a grin, knowing my relationship with Knox was tenuous. A while ago, when things were uncertain, his possessiveness would get the best of him sometimes. I always brushed it off; I was never a threat to him, but Knox had missed that important fact in his single-minded regard for Aisha.

"What? I mean, it wouldn't change things for us. We would just have to pretend..." She looked up at Knox, who pierced her with a hard stare.

"Ok...ok," Aisha murmured, rising up on her tippy toes to kiss his cheek.

Mila snorted, and I winked at her. Inside, though, worries for Sal and me made my gut contort in knots. How could I help her? I couldn't shake the sensation that this situation was more critical than we thought.

"Maybe we should go check on her." I moved toward the hallway leading to the back just as Sal emerged with her laptop in hand.

"Are you alright?" I asked. As always, she wasn't giving too much away with her facial expression.

"Why wouldn't I be?" Her eyebrows knitted, and annoyance emanated from her in waves before her face cleared, and a gentleness shined through. "Oh, about that guy? I'm going to figure out who he is and neutralize the threat." She nodded.

I wondered if she meant it as it sounded.

"Um...how are you planning to do that?" I asked.

Whatever she saw in my face made her brown eyes crinkle at the corners. That's as close to a smile as I could get from her, but lately, I was getting a couple of crinkles a day. I'd been collecting them avidly.

"Not what you think, but I like that you think I'm that dangerous," she said, a deadpan expression in place.

"Oh, I know you're dangerous enough."

"I am," she said, face completely serious. Then she kept walking, and I wondered if I was worrying in vain.

Four

Sal

A BLACK CAR was parked by the entrance of my apartment complex. That same car had been loitering around the studio the past few days. The man had returned two more times with more information about the person he was looking for. Even Athena had picked up on the weird vibe. And now, my apartment was compromised. The palpitations of my heart were so loud in my vehicle that it could stand in for the beat of the song on the radio.

Rush hour meant a long line of cars was trying to get through the gate, facilitating a discreet turnaround. Checking my rearview mirror, I left my apartment complex and dialed the ladies.

"What's up? Can't you get enough of us? Already calling us?" Mila said in greeting.

"No. That dude is parked outside my apartment complex," I whispered and immediately got upset with myself. *Why am I whispering?*

"Oh no! Athena told me he was asking more questions

about each of us that usually staff the desk. Then he also told her how he found out the woman that saw Juniper last was single and lived alone, so not a parent. He's trying to narrow things down."

"Fuck." I pounded my fist on my steering wheel, heading toward Mila's apartment.

"Have you heard from her?" Mila asked. I was glad I had told Mila and Aisha that night about what I'd done. I had been a bit shaken up after all the sleuthing and confessed that it was my first time meeting one of the women I helped.

"No, that's out of protocol. We break contact before they receive the money; I can deny I know their location because I have no idea. She's safe now. If not, they wouldn't be trying to trace me."

"That's probably true, but I don't feel comfortable with him going to your apartment like that. I think you need to come to stay with me, or maybe you and Mila...." Aisha said.

"Nah, shit is crowded as it is at Mari's. I'm just waiting for my apartment to finish the repairs on the roof to move back," Mila reminded us.

"Right, fuck. So where can I meet y'all?" I asked. I redirected again, the nerves making me forget Mila was staying at her sister's for the next couple of weeks.

"Come through Mari's. We can chat here."

———

MILA'S SISTER'S home was a beautiful four-bedroom house surrounded by palm trees and greenery, further north than where I stayed. Mila opened the door and pulled me in. I breathed easier now that I wasn't alone, the simmering anger at being put in this position by Juniper's deadbeat of a boyfriend lowering a bit.

"Sal, I haven't seen you in a minute!" Mariana hugged me. Her warm belly pressed against mine, and I pulled back to admire her.

"You're huge," I said.

"Oh, Sal, I love your charm." Mari's musical laugh tinkled in the living room.

"But you are. I mean, not you, but your belly." I nodded, keeping the rest of my thoughts in my mind.

"Oh ho, nah, don't you go lying to me now! I know my ass is huge," Mari said, shaking her head.

"Ain't nobody told you to get knocked up by your two men." Mila shook her head, then plopped herself on the sofa.

"Are we talking about Mari's ass? It's our favorite subject." Mason, Mari's boyfriend, sauntered toward us and stood beside Daniel, their other boyfriend. The sense of family and support surrounded me and gave me a measure of peace while my mind raced with what could come next. I'd tried to find the man that kept coming to the studio through his vehicle's license plate, but I'd continuously run into roadblocks. I was going to have to search some of the police and government databases that I usually tried to avoid.

The name he'd given us was clearly fake, and all the dead ends were making me uneasy. I didn't like feeling out of control. I needed a plan.

"Ugh, the three of you are about to have kids, and you still act like it's the first time you fucked. It's a little too much, a'ight?" Mila complained.

"Aww, lil' sis, don't be jealous; your person will soon

come. So, to what do we owe the pleasure, Sal?" Mason asked.

"Nonya, Mason," Mila retorted.

"Huh, last I checked, this was our house," Mariana reminded her.

"It's private," I said, not wanting to entangle anyone else in this mess.

Everyone stared at me for a minute, telling me my words probably sounded harsher than I intended. Shit.

"You heard the lady; they need privacy. We'll be in our room if you need us." Daniel nodded at me, ushering a protesting Mari and Mason away.

"Sorry, girl, those three want to be in everyone's business," Mila said when the coast was clear.

"It's ok. So...I don't think I should go back home tonight," I said, a sigh escaping me at my predicament. I kept breathing deeply to keep the anger and anxiety at bay. How had my life spiraled into this weird alternative reality? I knew that dude was dangerous. I'd clocked his gun the second time he'd come through, and nothing about how he approached the situation told me he was concerned about Juniper.

"Yeah, I don't think you should. I would offer you stay here, but..."

"Yeah, it would be a bit crowded." I nodded.

"I don't think Knox would be too keen on bringing any of this to their doorstep—" I paused when I heard the doorbell. Mila jumped up from the couch and hurried to open the door.

"I got it!" she yelled across the house.

"My house is not a train station, Mila!" Mari's muffled voice replied.

"Mcht!" Mila waved the words away as she opened the door, and Devon walked in.

Gentle eyes with a kind smile greeted me, and the room felt cozier and comfortable with his calming presence. I unclenched my jaw and nodded at him, then stared at Mila, who managed to ignore my gaze.

"What gwaan, ladies?"

"What are you doing here?" I crossed my arms over my chest, annoyed at his presence. Did he think he needed to come here and fix my problems? I felt more than capable of figuring it out. This was probably the work of Mila. I seared her with a nasty look and rolled my eyes when she ignored my annoyance.

"I'm here to talk to you."

"About what exactly?" I asked, eager to get whatever advice he had out of the way so that I could figure out my next steps.

"About your situation and how we can help each other out."

"Alrighty then, I'm gonna run to the guest room and let you chat." Mila jumped up as if the hounds from hell were chasing her and practically ran out of the living room.

"Whatever this is, I'm probably not gonna like it, am I?" I asked Devon, who just shrugged and grinned.

"We'll see."

FIVE

DEVON

SHIT. Sal was as closed off as ever as she sat in the armchair, legs crossed, and I needed her in the most agreeable mood possible right now. I'd visited my brother yesterday and showed him a picture I'd snuck in of the man that kept coming to search for Sal. Right away, my brother identified him, confirming my concerns. I gingerly sat across from her on the sofa opposite her seat, every movement calculated to set her at ease.

Sal was taking this whole situation too lightly, and she needed support. Today's run-in at her apartment was the perfect example. Mila and Aisha had called during my drive home, asking on behalf of Sal if she could crash at my place. That ask ignited the final spark for an idea that had been percolating in my brain since I'd seen Delroy after I found out about my visa. I had some less-than-altruistic reasons for my visit; I'd figured out how Sal and I could help each other out while keeping her safe. Now I only had to convince her.

"First, I know who that dude is coming to the studio."

Her expression blanked out, her mouth tight in a straight line. Damn, but she could shut a man out with just a look. I pushed through. Opening my legs, I rested my arms on them, my entire being open to receiving anything she had to say.

"Don't frown. I know you tried to look too, but this guy is probably a phantom online, or at least whatever persona he presented to us is. He's the second-in-command to one of the biggest and most dangerous dealers in the city. And that dealer...no one knows his face or true name," I further explained.

One dark brown eyebrow raised in challenge. I didn't know if she was impressed or mad, but I was prepared to withstand the heat of her gaze. Sal had dealt with so many people she could just shut out, but she wasn't ready for me.

"Oh, really? How do you know?" She crossed her arms over her chest, and I fought the urge to let my eyes wander. Whatever she'd gone through in the past, she was very distrustful of men's advances. I'd seen it plenty of times while out with the ladies. Men would approach her and she'd shut that shit down immediately. I'd promised myself I wouldn't make her uncomfortable ever.

"I know you looked into me." I nodded, a slight smile escaping me. "You probably checked up on me that first day I walked into the studio. I don't play any games, so I would have told you this regardless, but my brother was also a dealer. Weed only, but he was one of the biggest distributors. He purchased large amounts from growers and supplied most of South Florida."

"Was?"

"Fair. He's trying to clean up his game. He was in the parking garage and adult entertainment businesses when one of his homeboys ratted him out. Even pointed out his latest shipment location to the feds, but we found out about the snitch on time to at least move the shipment. He was charged with conspiracy to distribute."

"He's in his last year, right?" She nodded, her shoulders lowering, lips softening as we continued our conversation. Good, I needed her to be receptive to my overall message.

"Yes. He can't wait to be out. *I* can't wait for him to be out. I miss him."

Her gaze went from challenging to gentle, and it soothed something inside I didn't know had been hurting. I missed Delroy; he was the only person that truly understood me.

"Were you involved?"

I knew the question would come. I paused, trying to say the right thing.

"He entrusted a lot to me in the past... But he understood that life wasn't for me." How did we end up with me in the hot seat?

"Mhm. I think you'd be good at it. You have an edge to you...but you hide it well. But I can see how you have the talent but not the disposition." She nodded, assessing me. Her observation was spot-on, making me shift in my seat. People usually didn't see me that clearly. But Sal...

"Did Mila tell you about my visa problem?"

"Yeah, those fuckers. Why would they press you to dance if you ain't ready?" Her outrage for me was appreciated, but the reality was that the Ballet needed to move on if I couldn't perform anymore. The knot in my stomach contracted at the possibility of never performing again.

"Nah, they're not doing anything not stipulated in my employment agreement with them." I shrugged.

She nodded along expectantly. I grew warm, the speed

of my circulatory system accelerating under the pressure of her gaze. Here goes nothing...

"I want to propose..." I coughed and started again. "I want to propose a partnership. Marriage for support." I was going to say 'protection,' but I knew that would be the wrong thing to say to her.

Sal uncrossed her arms and mirrored my pose, thick thighs open, arms resting on them. Her anime t-shirt strained against her breasts, and still, I kept my eyes on hers.

"So you want to marry me for your papers? What's the support about?" she said, eerily calm.

"My brother will be out in a year, but that doesn't mean his influence and reach have diminished. He's not violent and rarely resorts to that, but he is highly respected. While you figure out how to chase away the tail of this drug dealer, you can be in my apartment with its enhanced security and my added company. And as you continue to do your work, you'll have my backup—*our* backup. It doesn't hurt to muddy the trail for them. You getting married and living with me would be something that will confuse them for a while."

"Yeah. I don't know how much they know, but one of the things about the O— my other persona is that it's well-known that I hate men. Don't trust them."

"Only your other persona?" I asked, noting she refused to answer my proposal. I relaxed against the sofa, crossing one leg over the other. Her eyes flickered before the calm returned.

"Well, you're proposing marriage to me, so tell me, Devon, do I hate men?" She sat back in the armchair, crossing her lush thighs and propping her head on a hand.

"I think you're selective with your trust." I'd been nervous about proposing this arrangement to her, but now I felt a different current between us. Maybe the awareness of what we could be if we took this step affected both of us. I couldn't miss how her nipples strained against her T-shirt. I'd noticed she rarely wore bras but had kept that knowledge tucked in a space far, far away in my brain.

"Same with you. You can be this happy-go-lucky dude, but you manage to keep things on lock." She taunted me with her observation.

"I'm an open book, Sal. Ask what you want to know."

"Why me? Why not Mila?"

"I just told you why; I want it to be mutually beneficial."

"You don't want to be in a position of powerlessness. I get it. I would hate that too. But yet you ask me, the one person that could fuck it all up for you with a few clicks on my laptop?"

"Is this you warning me not to mess with you?"

"No, I'm making sure you understand what you're offering. You're right; I don't trust easily. Right now, I'm vulnerable, but I'm not one to be taken advantage of. For some odd reason, I trust you, but I want you to understand what you're getting yourself into with me if I say yes."

She was right. I hadn't wanted to take this route before because it left me in a very unbalanced position. The trust required for someone to marry you and keep your secret for more than three years was precarious at best.

And I had many secrets.

People's loyalties changed, and here I was, trusting someone I had met just a few months ago. But I knew in my gut this was the right thing to do. My grandmother, may she rest easy, always said to me, *"There ain't nothing more powerful than your instinct."* It worked for Delroy and Britta, even though I suspected Delroy was in love with her.

But that wouldn't be my luck. I'd protect my heart while ensuring Sal had all the protection and support she needed. We would keep our friendship intact after this. That I vowed.

"I understand, Sal." I stood up and walked in front of her, going on one knee. She eyed my progress warily, her chest rising and falling with deep breaths. I held her cold hands, supple and delicate, and gazed into her brown eyes. From this close, I could see the freckles adorning her nose and cheeks, and something inside of me froze in recognition.

"Will you be my wife?"

"I...um... Yeah. But do you need to be this cheesy with it?" she replied, breaking the tension of the last few minutes. I cracked up at her agreement. I stood up and pulled her with me, draping her with my arms. Sal tensed, then her softness melded with my hard planes, and my breath hitched. She smelled sweet, so incongruous with her personality, and my mouth watered as her breathing matched mine.

Shit, an untimely erection threatened to grow inside of my sweatpants, so I awkwardly disengaged, patting her shoulder to remind both of us this was transactional. A friendly partnership.

But why couldn't I fight the urge to gather her in my arms again?

Six

DID I just agree to marry Devon Reid?

I must have lost all sense of reason in the past few hours. I'd been doing this work for three years now, but never had I been close to any real danger. I was talking a big game with Devon and the girls, but deep down inside, I wondered if I had overexerted myself with this last exchange.

Juniper had been in danger, her freedom about to be compromised by a good-for-nothing man, and I couldn't just disengage because I was afraid. I'd done my research on her; she worked in a jewelry store in Brickell and kept to herself a lot. Had a few boyfriends in the past but nothing serious. Her finances were all wonky, but when I'd asked, it was because she had been siphoning money on behalf of her boyfriend from her job. The boyfriend was where I ran into the roadblocks. The name he gave her was false. No address matched. He slept in her apartment a few nights a week, but she could not share what he did the other nights.

I needed to figure out how to get information on this

guy after me and make sure he had more to lose than I did. I'd always done that work before, discovering the indiscretions of the men I took money from to help their exes, but I hadn't been able to do it with this mark. Now I was paying for my sloppiness. The mark was so careful, she didn't even have a picture with him. Two years, and not one picture to show. She said he was very reserved and hated photographs and social media. Juniper should have known at that moment something was off.

I'd been prepared to refuse Devon, hysterical laughter threatening to escape me as he knelt before me. I was poised to say no when an image of my video game heroine flashed in my mind. What would Alix do? Alix was brave, fighting sex demons, following adventure after adventure, and here I was poised on the precipice of a life-changing decision, and all I could think was *what would Alix do?*

Words were tumbling from my mouth, and Devon was whooping and embracing me, and just for a second, I let myself enjoy the feeling of complete trust and safety that surrounded me as he hugged me. Never had a hug meant so much to me, an assurance that things would be ok, that he and I would manage to keep a good partnership. And he felt so good. His arms were sinewy around me, his heart beating so fast against my ear, telling me he was as affected as I was by the moment. His embrace felt and smelled like sitting by the ocean with a lemonade, and I discreetly took a whiff of him.

Then he was disentangling himself from me and patting me on the shoulder, and I'd never seen him as awkward as this. I didn't know if he thought I was catching feelings with one lowly hug, but Devon could rest easy; I wasn't looking to fall for him. I was incapable of trusting men. He was right about that.

If only I could divest myself from lusting after them. If only I'd been blessed with attraction to any or no gender, but no, I needed to be saddled by the curse of heterosexuality. This might be my only problem, so we needed some fences.

"Alright, before we say anything to anyone, can we discuss parameters?" I nodded for him to sit down again. All his lean muscles, scent, and presence were becoming too much to handle. My mouth went dry as he relaxed in his seat.

"What are the parameters?" he asked, his lips quirking in the corner. I followed the line of his mouth and wondered what those lips could do.

Oh damn, this was the part where I said something.

"We keep it a hundred with each other. No lying. No subterfuge. There will be times we're not ready to share something, and that's ok. But no outward lying."

"You don't even have to tell me that, regardless of our arrangement. Please know that I'd never lie to you," he said with an intensity that made me break our eye contact.

"Same. Well, I can be secretive, but...I don't lie. I know you want me to live with you because this dude is after me, but after that, I'll return to my apartment." Right away, he started shaking his head, his locs brushing his shoulders in movement.

"No, we need to be in the same place till I get the green card. We'll need to do interviews and speak about our life together. We must keep this as simple as possible, live together, and learn our tendencies."

There was a skip in my chest that I didn't recognize. Maybe a hiccup?

"Ok, that makes sense; we live together until the green

card goes through. But not the whole three years, right?" I asked.

"If you prefer not to...then no. I know of people that kept their finances together on paper but lived separately and divorced after the citizenship approval and the three years."

If I *prefer not to?* What would he prefer?

"The whole thing is for me to support your endeavors. Wouldn't it make sense to happen with both of us under the same roof?" he asked, taking me out of my thoughts.

Three years of living together, seeing this man with no shirt on, deep mahogany skin gleaming after showers, his scent permeating my senses...

"I think we should reevaluate after the papers come through." I crossed my arms under my chest, and Devon looked away from me, then back with a nod.

"Ok, that makes sense." Did he look disappointed? What was this?

"Who do we tell?"

"The fewer people that know the truth, the better. On my side, besides Aisha and Mila, only my brother will know. My parents will think I found my girl."

"Your parents?" *His girl.* That chest hiccup didn't feel too good right now. I rubbed between my breasts to ease the discomfort, and as always, Devon's eyes stayed on me, but did I imagine that slight widening?

"Yeah, they're still in Jamaica. Didn't you find that out?"

"I did; you're right. I don't plan to tell my mom or my sisters, either. They'll be happy to think I snagged a rich dude." I rolled my eyes at the fuckery that would ensue when I told my mom of my upcoming nuptials. Actually, I didn't plan to say anything until I had no choice. I kept my communications to a minimum with them and shared very little.

"You don't get along with them?"

"What would make you think that?" I asked him.

He nodded toward my chest, and I realized I had crossed my arms again. I let them go, uncomfortable with my tell and with the fact he'd clocked it.

"Alright, so we don't tell anyone but the ladies. Everyone else will think we just, what? Fell in love?"

"Why do you say it like that? Is it not plausible?" His lips quirked up again.

"Have you met me, Devon?" I spread my arms wide, shaking my head at him.

"Oh, I have. And I also know that for all you put a wall up between any man around you, you left a window open in our wall. So...I'm patient. It would have been plausible." He shrugged and ran his index finger up and down his bearded chin. And I stared at those lips of his, almost pink against his darker skin, until a smile bloomed between them.

"Whatever, tell yourself that. So, should we get Mila and call Aisha?"

"For sure."

His deep, honeyed voice eased around me, making me believe in fairies and dragons but just for a minute. I gathered my wits and turned my back on him because there was no way in hell I would fall for Devon Reid.

My future husband.

SEVEN

SAL

AFTER THE TENSE exchange with Devon, I needed a reprieve. Mila took one look at me and proposed I stay one last night with her. We agreed to go to my apartment the following day, hoping the guy wasn't around, to get my things before moving in with Devon. Devon and I also made tentative arrangements to get our marriage license at the courthouse, a thought that made my skin break into hives.

I lay next to a snoring Mila, staring at the sun creeping up through the blackout curtains, the light inevitable. That's how things felt right now; yesterday's decision felt predetermined in a storyboard I hadn't fully approved.

After my ex-boyfriend robbed me and my talent and a few other mistakes, I painstakingly ensured I was always in control of my life. I detached myself completely from my mother's influence, and her move to Jacksonville with my sisters was the last nudge needed for our dysfunctional relationship to be something I could manage from afar. I put my finances and talents on deck and started a freelance software company. I strengthened my friendships with the people most important to me.

Then three years ago, after hearing from a friend of my sister's who was in town, commiserating about how her baby daddy had stopped working legit jobs to rob her of her court-appointed child support, something inside of me snapped. Even though I'd bounced back, many like me couldn't. So, I started Oriole then and there.

I never imagined it would lead me to marry someone to protect myself and mine. I wasn't dense; one of the main attractions of moving in with Devon was the fortress he lived in. I assumed the apartment was a gift from his brother. He lived by the beach in a ten-story building with the tightest security I'd seen in a minute.

I had tried hacking their security system last night after Mila fell asleep, and I had trouble just getting into the preliminary outer infrastructure. After my unsuccessful fifth try at breaching their camera system, I fell asleep, knowing I'd be safe tomorrow.

For all that Devon said he would support me, he meant *protection*. Every time he said the word, the other silently preceded it. I wouldn't take the offer with animosity, but I'd never needed this type of protection before. It bothered me that I needed it now, but I wasn't naïve to assume I understood the game being played by Juniper's boyfriend. I needed to be strategic, and staying with Devon, even marrying him, provided me some additional intel and leeway I didn't have before.

After a hasty breakfast with Mason and Mari, we headed to my apartment. A few drives around the block assured us the black car wasn't present, so we entered the complex through the automated gate.

Even though it was technically spring, the heat and

humidity lay like a blanket over me as we walked toward my little townhome.

"So...staying with Devon. You should break the streak."

I stayed silent. Sometimes that strategy worked with Mila and her horny thoughts.

"Salo—" She stopped when I pierced her with my death stare. "So, are you gonna answer or not?"

"I'm not breaking my streak," I said as I unlocked the door and punched in my alarm code.

"You should, though. What has it been, three years?"

"Two."

"Right. That dude you basically constricted yourself around that day in the bar to just fuck you and stay quiet. But he was such a bad lay, that don't count." Mila breezed into the townhome, looking around. I closed my eyes, wondering why I had shared anything with her.

"I have my toys. They're enough."

"Listen, you know I'm all about toys, so I won't fight you on that; they'd probably do better work than the dudes you occasionally pick up. But honestly, I think you do it on purpose—find the most clueless, cutest guy around, no threat to you, and you pick them up. You know they won't ever challenge your brain, capture your heart, or make your legs tingle." Mila pointed at me, grabbed the bags we'd brought from Mari's house, and strolled into my bedroom.

"I don't pick up clueless dudes on purpose; they just end up being clueless."

"Lies. You do it purposefully, which is why I'm surprised you agreed to Devon, but it's the right thing to do. Are you sure you are ok, sugar cake?" Mila whirled around with concern on her face. My annoyance fled as I saw how worried she truly was. All this blabbering about toys and streaks was to keep herself and me from fretting. Ugh. Only she could make me sentimental.

"No, I'm not ok, but being at Devon's is reassuring." I refused to lie to her; when Aisha, Mila, or I dropped our walls for a second, it was a tacit agreement to match the same with vulnerability. And it felt good to say out loud that I was worried as fuck. I was in a chess game when I thought I'd been playing solitaire.

"Right, ok. Well, let me pack all your toys, so you at least have some stress relief," she said, and laughter fizzled out of me.

"What are you doing tonight? You want to hang out with me at Devon's?" I asked her as she packed up my clothes, and I disassembled my workstation. I needed my Macs, and Devon explained he had a third bedroom where I could set up.

"I'm going to Aisha's. She and Knox are alone tonight."

"Ugh, y'all are nasty," I said, finishing with my hardware and turning to the bathroom to get my toiletries.

"Nah, it's hot! I can't get enough of them." Mila followed me to the bathroom and waggled her eyebrows.

"Y'all better not get your wires crossed and fuck up the friendship," I said, pointing my setting mousse at her.

She plopped on my sink and watched me go around my bathroom collecting items.

"Have Aisha and I ever gotten our wires crossed?"

"No, 'cause you have managed to stay above the fray there. But there's always the first time."

"Nah, Knox is definitely not my type outside of the bedroom. Fucking them is fun, but that's it. It's a friendly fuck arrangement." She sighed in contentment.

"Hey, if it's working for you." I shrugged and turned around to get my bath bombs, then my stomach plummeted.

What if Devon didn't have a bathtub? Without much thought, I pulled out my phone and shot him a text.

> Sal: You have a tub?

The three dots showed almost immediately.

> Devon: Well, hello to you, Sal. I do have a tub in your room.

> Sal: Good, that is how I destress. It would have been a problem.

> Devon: I would have let you use the one in my bathroom if needed.

Thoughts of me relaxing in Devon's tub materialized, a whisper in the back of my mind telling me it would be good for my streak to let that happen.

"See? I'm telling you, you should break your streak with Devon. Do as I do with Knox and Aisha, keep it friendly. It doesn't need to be messy," Mila said as she peered down at my screen. I put my cell phone away.

"I'm not fucking Devon." I threw the bath bombs into my duffle bag and power-walked out of the bathroom, ignoring Mila's taunts.

I had two large pieces of luggage and three smaller ones to take with me. Anyone that saw me would think I was moving out of my apartment. And still, my closet was full of sweatpants and anime merch. Maybe I should purge before moving back. My cozy townhome would be hard to leave, but I'd manage.

With a last glance at my things, I walked out of the door, greeted by a warm, humid wave of air and Mrs. Marshall from next door. Mrs. Marshall was always in my business, trying to converse with me whenever I was in or out of my home. I tried to be polite for the sake of her age and overall respect, but sometimes, like today, I needed to cut her short.

"Sal! People have been coming to see you, but you were away. Where you going?"

"Hello, Mrs. Marshall, I'm donating some stuff," I said, walking by her. She was such a busybody, and I had no time for her right now.

"Mrs. M, who came for Sal?" Mila asked, sidling up to Mrs. Marshall, who immediately leaned over to impart her gossip. Ugh. What was Mila doing?

"Well, first, this man was light-skinned and handsome. If I were ten years younger, I'd try to go for a ride. But he was a bit hard-looking too. He was snooping around, so I asked him what he needed. He tried to ask me things about you, Sal, but you know I'm a tomb."

Which translated to she'd told him everything she ever knew about me. Great. Mila and I exchanged looks. The man with the black car seemed to have made it through the gate.

"Then another man came through. Whew, chile, he was handsome! He reminded me of you, Sal, for some reason." She gestured at me.

"What did he want? And why did he remind you of me?" I said, and Mila's eyes widened. Oops, I probably barked that. Mrs. Marshall sniffed but couldn't help but give us the tea.

"Well, he just wanted to talk to you, he said. Gave me a number to share with you if I saw you." She whipped out a smooth black card from her cleavage and handed it to me. I shuddered but accepted the card. Why couldn't she just put it in her pocket? Why? Her caftan had pockets; I could see them from here. I turned the card and read it.

Xavier Souza, followed by a cellphone number engraved in white.

"A new person?" Mila's alarm was evident.

"Why did he look like me?" I zeroed in on Mrs. Marshall.

"Didn't want to talk much, rude just like you..." Mrs. M said, and I rolled my eyes, ready to book it, but then she continued. "But also, his eyes, nose, and ears were similar. You know I'm observant. If I hadn't met your mom and sisters, I'd think he could be your brother or cousin or something." The fact that Mrs. M knew I didn't have cousins or brothers was something I wouldn't ponder too much today.

Another player, but *why?*

Were they trying to lull me into lowering my guard? This was getting more complicated by the minute. I stared at Mila, who schooled her worried expression and smiled at me. She shrugged, and I shrugged back, acknowledging there was not much we could do now.

"Thanks, Mrs. M! See you later!" Mila waved, and we left her behind.

We walked to the SUV and packed up the large pieces, then turned around and went back to get the smaller bags, uncharacteristically silent after what we had learned from Mrs. Marshall. I had two suspicious people looking for me in a week, and I didn't like that. The things I did for the people that approached me needing help existed in a grey area that meant I kept my business private. I couldn't afford strangers trying to track me down. My stomach roiled as I pondered how to protect myself from these men. I ran to my bathroom to get my night face cream, head hazy, when I heard my doorbell ring.

"Stay there," Mila said with urgency.

I eased my way to my bedroom, where I had a better view of the entrance as Mila opened the door.

"Hi! How can I help you?" Mila asked with false cheeriness.

A medium brown-skinned man of average size and great looks stood in the doorway. Something about his aura was closed off, and I immediately went to my distrustful place.

"I'm looking for Sal Blackwell."

"Oh, well, she's not here." Mila gestured to the inside of the apartment but never moved an inch from the middle of the door frame.

"Damn. This is the second time I have tried. I hope she's not trying to avoid me. I really need to speak with her. I left a business card with her neighbor. Can I leave one with you? Tell her to hit me up; I have some information that she'll consider valuable."

"Oh, ok." Mila nodded and received the card, staring at the guy. I was staring too. Who was he in this farce that was my life now?

The man departed soon after.

Shit. What had I gotten myself into?

———

Devon awaited us downstairs in the lobby of his condo. I'd been here before a couple of times with the ladies to watch movies. The building boasted the latest technology and security, and its overall architectural design showed it. The lobby was surrounded by steel and marble, all smooth lines and minimal color. There was a reception desk staffed not by door attendants but security guards who gave you the impression you were about to enter Quantico.

The elevators were connected to biometrics, and when I asked Devon how guests accessed them, he explained the security guards called the elevators after guests had been screened. To save us all that trouble, Devon always greeted us downstairs and had us pre-screened the first time we visited him so we didn't have to go through these steps each time.

"Every time we come, I wonder who else lives here," Mila said, shucking off her shoes as she walked into Devon's immaculate apartment. I took a second to admire my temporary new place: gleaming wood floors, plush rugs in front of modern white furniture, and Jamaican art on the walls.

I'd been fascinated by the art the first time I visited, wondering what it said about him, but hadn't wanted to ask about it. Each piece was a splash of vibrant color combinations, a mesh of strokes that formed a story on each canvas. One looked like an old house in the middle of palm trees and sand, another a boat full of bananas on the beach. One was of a tall boy dressed in ballet clothes next to a palm tree.

Devon had stood next to me, noticing my interest, and told me his grandmother had created them. His soul twin, he'd called her, the person in his family that had encouraged his love for dance and love for everything artistic. He'd spoken about her with a reverence that made me want to know him better. That was Devon's first crack in my hard shell against anything male.

I stared at where I'd be having breakfast each morning, a state-of-the-art kitchen with stainless steel appliances, a wall full of color with baskets brimming with herbs, scotch bonnet peppers, lemons, mangos, and bananas, and a kitchen island with stools where I could sit.

Three large windows faced Fort Lauderdale Bay, small vehicles whizzing past in urgency down below as I stood by the windows looking around at the large white sectional that faced a giant flat-screen TV against a dark gray wall. Then there were the three large bedrooms on the second floor of the loft-style apartment. Spiral stairs led to them, all facing the bay. I'd never seen them, but now one of them would be mine.

"Mostly, it's government people or c-suite dudebros." Devon shrugged. He stood by the door, his eyes tracking every move I made in the apartment. "Do you think you'll be comfortable here? We can make any changes you need." He spoke to me as if Mila wasn't there.

I tried not to bristle at the offer, an offer he shouldn't have needed to give. Having to be here, dependent on him, was stirring up some old wounds I'd left alone to scab. I didn't need to restart picking at them.

I did not trust men.

No man in my life had proven me wrong. Not my father, whom my mother had to escape because he didn't support her decision to have me. Not my grandfather, who kicked my mother out of their apartment because she was too fast for getting pregnant with me, her third child by a different father. Not my awful ex-boyfriend, who took advantage of my vulnerability, and more men in my past— no man in my life had proven to me I could set an inch of trust in them. And here I was, playing house with this dude I'd only known for a few months.

Twilight Zone.

"I'm not planning to be here for long; no need to make any changes."

I took the stairs as Mila sighed behind me.

"Which one is my room?" I asked without looking back.

"The second one. Mine is the last," Devon said, and I opened the door to the chamber.

The space was expansive, with dark gray walls and a queen-sized bed in the middle with royal blue bedding. Another large screen floated on the wall. Devon had arranged it to be inviting. An armchair sat in the corner next to a coffee table with a night light, and a desk where my screens could fit was next to the nook with a tall gamer chair. I ignored the tingling sensation at the sight of the gaming chair and the thought that Devon might have gotten it for me. I was making no sense. I didn't want this, but mixed feelings arose at his thoughtfulness.

I snuck a peek at the bathroom and gasped at its size. Both the room and bathroom had floor-to-ceiling windows facing the bay, with a standing tub right by the window. My heart pitter-pattered at the thought of taking long baths in there. Then a phantom image of Devon kneeling by my side with his hand in the water made me curse Mila for putting thoughts of streaks and toys into my head. I hadn't masturbated in the week since all this mess had started, and I was long overdue.

Yeah, that was it; I was just horny, not horny *for Devon*. That made complete sense.

I settled my small bags in the walk-in closet. I would have plenty of time to unpack. After another cursory glance of the room, I exited. My curiosity led me to the next room, which was Devon's dance room. The wooden floor also gleamed here, with the wall adjacent to the guest room featuring a full mirror and barre. On the opposite side, I saw a large white desk with another chair, and my stomach did a lazy pirouette.

Had he gotten both setups for me?

Like the guest room, the chamber faced the bay with large, glittering windows. This apartment was beautiful. I needed to make sure not to get used to it.

I turned off the light and went downstairs to find Devon and Mila whispering.

"...and then the guy gave me this business card." Mila slid the card across the kitchen island to Devon.

"Y'all done talking about my business?"

Mila swirled around in the stool to stare at me, then gave me her apologetic puppy eyes, signaling she wasn't trying to argue with me today. I rolled my eyes. I knew she was worried, but she also knew I handled my own business. But who could blame her? Here I was, having to marry a dude to keep my shit protected. *Yeah.*

"Sal, Mila means well." Devon gave me one of his dazzling, reassuring smiles and something uncurled inside me. I batted that feeling away, hardening my core.

"I know, but she also knows I can handle this. That business card is a gift." I pointed to the card.

"Listen, I have to go. Migue has a job for me today, so I can't stay long." She hopped off the stool and came to me, her honey-blonde strands brushing against my shoulders as she hugged me.

"Ok." I let her hug me, and I was thankful for her support today.

"Are you ok, sugar cake?" Mila whispered in my ears, and I just nodded. A knot formed in my throat, and tears threatened to gather in my eyes, but I ruthlessly pushed the feelings aside and Mila away from our embrace.

"Alright, alright. I'll be fine. Nothing this dude can't protect me from, right?" I said sarcastically, but Devon only nodded solemnly. How annoying. Why did he need to be so...so perfect?

"Ok, you better take care of her!" she warned. Then they both exchanged a long look. Mila's shoulders sagged, and she turned to me. "Listen, Sal, maybe until this shit dies down, you just don't go around town alone?"

I stared at her dumbfounded, then back at Devon, whose face was completely impassive. But his eyes... His eyes willed me to say yes. I wanted to refuse out of spite. I wanted to lash out at them both, but to what avail? I had already come to the same conclusion. Until we knew what we were dealing with here, being unaccompanied wasn't a smart move.

I nodded.

Mila sighed in relief and pulled me into another hug. Then she waved us both goodbye, leaving us in the silent apartment.

I stared at Devon, and our eyes locked in a silent battle. I couldn't blink; I couldn't take in enough breath to dislodge the knot in my throat. His locs were loose around his face, and his mouth was set in a soft line surrounded by his beard, and for a wild second, I wondered if those lips could ease the tumult inside of me. As if he realized my thoughts had shifted, his commanding gaze softened into molten lava. I avoided squirming as I stood there. I didn't fidget. Not under any man's stare. But Devon's eyes, usually calm and content, were nothing but daggers full of passion. And I thought I wanted to be pierced by him over and over again.

Down, girl. That way lay problems.

I wrenched my gaze from him, then turned around and went back up the stairs to my room, the heat of his stare following me all the way to my door.

Eight

Sal

When I escaped to my room, I forgot all my bags were downstairs.

There was a soft knock on my door just as I was about to go back to retrieve the rest of my items.

"I brought up all your luggage. I left it outside your door whenever you're ready," Devon said through the door, and I swung it open, annoyed I'd made such a mistake.

"Thanks," I grumbled and saw his lips quirk up at the corner—the asshole.

"I'm going to therapy. Do you want me to grab something to eat on my way home?" he asked, leaning against the door frame. I stared at his arm gracefully braced, coiled in strength, and swallowed. Then I shook it off and nodded.

"Yeah, that would be good."

"Any preference?"

"I love Mr. Chen's."

"Yeah, me too. We'll call it an early dinner." He nodded, a sweet grin blooming, making other lips bloom below.

This was a problem.

I'd always had a healthy libido, some might say an elevated one. I never had an issue being attracted to men. But as a rational human being, I didn't run eyes closed into danger. I stayed away from people and situations that hurt me, so I was adept at fighting my natural response to people I was attracted to. But Devon seemed to disarm me, and I didn't appreciate it. This was how my body betrayed me for letting him in as a friend. He didn't have a danger sign glaring on his forehead, so my pussy clearly thought it was open season. Well, no. She was wrong. I had self-control.

"Sounds like a plan," I said and closed the door. I heard him chuckle as he bounded down the stairs.

———

"Sal! Food is ready!"

Devon's deep voice traveled to my open door, the words sounding so natural to me, and I'd only been in his apartment one day. I'd been productive the hours he'd been away. All my luggage was empty in the corner of the room, and my workstation was set up in the third bedroom. I'd even hooked up an additional screen I'd brought just because I had space in my bedroom and connected my laptop wirelessly to the TV screen. Then I'd made myself comfortable, taking a shower and changing into house clothes.

Devon had arrived earlier but seemed to have retreated to his room while I was setting up my bathroom. I must have missed him returning downstairs.

Making my way to the kitchen, I found a shirtless Devon sorting through paper bags with fragrant food. I caught a whiff of chicken and broccoli and closed my eyes in happiness.

"I didn't know everything you liked, so I might have ordered too much. I got chicken with broccoli and sesame chicken—I *do* know you love that. Some white rice and special fried rice. Lo mein. Steamed veggies. Egg rolls. Dumplings. We can always have leftovers tomorrow." He winked and kept flexing his chest as he pulled container after container out of the bags. My stomach grumbled at the smell of the delicious food as my mouth watered. The watering had nothing to do with the sudden thirst that assailed me at Devon's thoughtfulness. I'd seen him shirtless before at the studio. There was no reason for the sudden rise in temperature inside of me.

"I do love sesame chicken. Text me next time. No need to order all this to impress me," I said, immediately worried it might have come out too harsh. I seldom measured myself with people; there wasn't a reason to present myself as anything but authentic, but I didn't intend to hurt Devon. I looked down, then tentatively searched his face, but there was only an indulgent smile.

"I could have, but I figured you didn't have lunch, same as I, so why not just splurge? Do you want to sit at the dining room table or the kitchen island?"

The island would keep me from staring while I ate, but then he would be awfully close. On the other hand, I could have him across me at the dining room table but would have to contend with the heated gazes I was sure I was imagining between us.

"Let's eat at the table." I pointed at it, and he followed behind.

———

DEVON

When I spoke with Delroy and told him of my plan to propose to Sal, I was adamant I didn't want to muddy the waters with anything beyond friendship. No matter what I wanted to believe about the immediate threat to her, the long-term risk lived on my side. If I slipped up and started thinking with my dick, what exactly would happen to our marriage? So, after many jokes and innuendo from Delroy, I decided to ignore the attraction I had felt for Sal from the day I met her. The embers of that attraction made me hyper-aware of Sal, of all the little details that made her tick, but I'd been disciplined about keeping the interest buried deep down and treated her as a friend from day one.

This is why I could tell Sal was suddenly aware of me as someone beyond the friend she allowed around the perimeter of her life. I didn't know what to do with that knowledge. For now, I'd let things progress as need be. We needed to get married as soon as possible.

We sat down and companionably ate our dinner. Sal was right; Mr. Chen always hit the spot. The warm food settled in my belly, bringing a sense of contentment.

"How was therapy?" Sal asked, surprising me with her question. Usually, I had to initiate conversation between us.

"It was ok. I started doing jumps today."

"How are you feeling?"

"I'm alright. Tender, but at least my tendon didn't give out on me. I felt, though, as if in school again, relearning the best way to move my feet." The contentment in my belly congealed at how tentatively I'd moved today. I was eons away from my usual strength. At this rate, it would be hard to perform in July.

"I'm thinking of adding extra rehearsals here at home.

The choreographer for the summer showcase is coming in a few days to teach it to me."

"Away from prying eyes, I get it. Why expose your underbelly to your fellow dancers when you're not sure you'll be able to perform?" Sal took a sip of her lemonade, piercing me with her observant gaze.

"Yeah, pretty much." I shrugged. Inside, though, the fact I didn't need to explain myself much felt too good to examine.

"Well, I haven't danced in a long time. I sometimes help Aisha with choreography, though, so if you need help?" She shrugged as if this was something she did all the time, but she only offered things like that to Aisha and Mila, and I was honored to be in the same category as them.

"Thanks." I had to cough to clear my throat. Here was the first night, and she offered more support than I gave. "So...the marriage?" *Might as well bring up the subject.*

"Yeah, whenever you want. I read online we just have to request the marriage license from the courthouse, then we can have a notary perform the ceremony. Or we could do it all at the courthouse."

She scrunched up her face at that, and I don't know if she was opposed to the idea of the marriage in general or the location of the ceremony.

"We shouldn't do it at the courthouse. We're trying to sell we're an established couple, right? That we planned this ahead? Maybe I'll ask Aisha if we can do it in her backyard," Sal said and kept digging into her food. My chest tightened at the idea of having an actual ceremony with our friends, regardless of how small. I wished Delroy could come...but why would it matter? In the end, this wasn't real.

This wasn't real. *This. Wasn't. Real.*

"A'ight. I'm good with that."

"Cool." The clink of her fork reverberated in the living area, and I slowed my chewing until I found her staring at me.

"So you know...we forgot one agreement when we decided this." She ran her hand down the middle of her chest, pushing the fabric of her t-shirt inward, and I couldn't help but focus there. She did this whenever she felt strong emotions, and it was such a distraction. I disciplined my gaze and kept waiting for her words. My mouth felt suddenly dry, and I ran my tongue over my lower lip, seeking something I knew wasn't there. Her eyes dropped to my lips, then went back to my face, and red rose up from the neck of her t-shirt.

Goddamn, she was blushing. I tapped my foot in four-count, trying to focus on any choreography that could help release me from Sal's hold.

"If you want to fuck other people, you should. I only ask that you give me a heads up so I can wear my headphones while I code my video game."

The record scratch on the *Don Quixote* Act i finale I'd been playing in my head to keep from pursuing anything with Sal jarred me to the core.

"Excuse me?"

"If you want to fuck—" she started again, staring at me as if I spoke in patois to her.

"No. Stop right there. I don't need to fuck anyone while we are together." *I don't need to fuck anyone that's not you.*

Sal scoffed, then pursed her lips at me.

"So you're going to be celibate for three years?" She raised an eyebrow. The red on her neck had dissipated, and she was entirely in control.

"Let me worry about what I will be for three years."

"Nah, that shit is no good; you can't keep those feelings

repressed. I'm not asking you to." She crossed her arms, and I suppressed a groan. Sal, in her full grumpy persona, seemed to be my new aphrodisiac.

"I know you aren't." I went back to my broccoli, hoping she'd give it a rest.

"For real, Devon, if you need to fuck—"

"All this talk of fucking makes me think I might not be the one with the immediate need." I let my gaze roam over her from the top of her brown curls currently all coiled up and short, the tip of her nose covered with freckles, to the red that had made a return on her neck, down to her full belly and thick thighs displayed by her biker shorts. "If I need to fuck, I think I won't have to look far from home."

"See, here I'm trying to help, and you're trying to run game on me. Listen, if *I* need to fuck, I think I won't have to look far from your home. Actually, I don't think I'll have to ask at all."

And with that, Sal excused herself from the table, leaving me speechless with a growing erection.

Nine

DEVON

WE SETTLED into a routine over the next few days. Sal mostly holed up in her room. However, she granted me her presence during breakfast each morning. I soaked up each minute of it, curious to know more about her now that we had one-on-one time. Rarely had I hung out with her alone. Whenever we had planned something and the other ladies bailed, Sal was always quick to cancel, so now that I had her all to myself, I enjoyed our quality time together.

We went to the courthouse on the second day to request our marriage license. Sal did all the paperwork and hastily thrust the paper at me to sign, her hand hovering on the top of the document. Maybe nerves were getting the best of her, but once we were done, she turned around and dead-panned, "Congrats, one step closer to your green card."

Ok...not nerves.

That had been three days ago. We waited for the obligatory state mandate period, but no more. We were getting married in the afternoon.

No one that saw us this morning would have had a clue, though. We were both sitting at the kitchen island, Sal with her tablet and me with my phone in hand, as we ate the scrambled eggs I'd made for us.

Sal wasn't much of a cook, but without prompting, she'd paid attention to how I liked my coffee in the morning and started making it for me, even though she drank tea instead. I didn't know what to make of the gesture, and every time she thrust a cup of coffee in front of me, liquid spilling a little, that shit made my stomach do a grand jeté.

Just like every morning, Sal grunted and gifted me monosyllabic answers, which for her was as chatty as she could get before ten. The woman wasn't a morning person, and that was ok. After tossing and turning at night, her company was all I needed.

"Were you able to find anything from the dude's business card?" I asked, one of our main topics of conversation the past few days. She'd been frustrated that there wasn't any connection in her findings of Souza with regard to Juniper.

A grunt, then she nodded. I was starting to suspect she had Jamaican in her because she was eloquent with sounds and gestures. I decided to change the subject, the warning of her grunt enough for me to sense her frustration.

"So, what keeps you busy during the day? Did you finish that last assignment?" I tried another route as I enjoyed the cup of Blue Mountain coffee. She kept her head buried in her iPad, but I knew she heard me. Just as I took a sip and smiled, she attempted to sneak a peek, but I caught her. I winked at her; she rolled her eyes.

"I finished that. I haven't gotten a new commission yet, so I'm working on my video game."

Seventeen words. A record for eight in the morning.

"You've mentioned the video game before. Is it anime?" The question wasn't far-fetched; she was wearing a black hoodie with Sailor Pluto on her chest. I'd heard her tell Mila that Sailor Pluto had the crew's best personality. I didn't know much about anime, but I remembered the Sailor Moon fever back in the day while in school, and Sailor Pluto was the grumpy one. Figured.

"Kind of anime," she mumbled, and I frowned. Before I could clarify what "kind of anime" meant, she put her dishes in the dishwasher and then bounded up the steps.

"See you later," she said without looking back.

Weird. I fought the urge to follow her and ask more questions.

Instead, I finished my cup of coffee, then headed to my therapy. John pushed me hard today, hopping on my injured tendon while throwing a weighted ball doing wonders to my state of mind and overall nerves. With my mind in the right place, I arrived at the studio ready to dance.

Classes went by in a blur, and a sense of purpose imbued each of my instructions to my students. Where I would usually be careful with demonstrations of relevés, I leaned into them today regardless of my sore tendon. The dancers fed my mood, enhancing it to a higher level.

Finishing my last afternoon class inspired, I turned on "The Hardest Button to Button" by The White Stripes and let the muscle memory of McGregor's *Chroma* fuse in me. I'd performed the ballet in New York the season before moving to Florida, loving the sumptuous moves. There was something visceral and utterly direct about McGregor's choreography. I loved executing it on stage, the rush in my veins a river with a force that connected me to each person in the theater. Communing with Sal in the mornings, then the wins in therapy and class had my confidence at an all-time high. And if the thought of marrying Sal today made my palms sweat, well, I wouldn't think of that right now.

This was supposed to be a pas de deux, but even without a fellow dancer, my body knew exactly what to do; I went into a trance as my muscles flexed and my feet pointed, and I got lost in the dance, letting all my worries dissipate.

———

SAL

Dance classes ended early because of my wedding. *Our wedding*. Aisha texted me in a panic that she had to close early to get the house in order. I wasn't sure why she was panicking; this wasn't anything special.

I'd come to the studio a bit early with Mila to meet Devon, hoping not to make this a bigger deal than needed.

"Girl, I can't take how smokin' hot you look! I'm so glad I picked you up. I got to ogle those hips the whole way here," Mila exclaimed as we opened the door to the studio. I scowled but couldn't disagree with her assessment. I tugged at my white dress, even though the pencil shape meant the hem was slightly above my ankles. The problem wasn't the length; it was the stretch. I didn't know why I made this purchase a few days ago. It certainly had nothing to do with the breakfast conversation Devon and I had earlier in the week when he mentioned he'd gotten a new suit for the wedding. Nothing at all.

For the most part, I wouldn't say I liked dresses and had thought of wearing one of my palazzo pants and a top, but here I was, feeling myself in this outfit. I'd done a full beat with earthy tones and a red lip. If there was one thing I was glad I inherited from my mom, it was my killer makeup skills; I just didn't need it every day.

But today, I'd been inspired while getting ready. I parted my curls, slicking down one side and leaving the rest of the coils popping on the side and back—basically, no crumbs were left.

But I didn't care one way or the other.

I really didn't.

Now, if my groom could finish working, we could get this wedding rolling. I wanted to return to his apartment early enough to play *Tales of Arise*. I'd been too busy when the game came out two years ago and prioritized other releases. Now that I had a slowdown in commissions, I wanted to dive into the RPG experience, even though Cora had warned me she felt the praise for the game was over-rated. I needed to keep my mind occupied to avoid focusing on how my life had spiraled out of control in the span of a week. I was being pursued, about to marry, and committing a crime.

Well, I was usually committing a crime, so that wasn't new, but still. I realized I hadn't answered Mila.

"Why are you talking nonsense?" I asked as I ran my hands down my hips. I had my mother to thank for all this extra cushion on my sides. And let's not talk about how my ass spread on and on across the mirror.

"You made a *choice* when you bought that dress. And don't try to tell me you had this; I sadly know the state of your closet."

I incinerated Mila with my evil glare, but she skipped away as if she was made of dragon skin—the brat.

I was wasting time chatting it up with Mila. Focusing

on what I came to do, I yanked the dance room open, ready to collect my groom.

I halted when I almost bumped into Devon, wearing tight brown-colored dance shorts, a white tank top, and his ballet shoes. His torso sinuously undulated as his muscled arms extended toward an imaginary ballerina. My eyes focused on the sculpted tautness of his thighs—the beautiful art of his anatomy. Transfixed, I admired Devon's few last movements until he finished in the middle of the room with a bow. When he turned his face to me, his eyes widened in appreciation, then darkened as they ran from my feet to the top of my hairline.

The heat of his gaze touched my draped cleavage, caressing the soft lines of white molding my curves, studying the hidden indent from belly to vulva. I ignited under his admiration. My chest and neck warmed under his appreciation, and I held his gaze in a heated challenge.

"Are you ready?"

"I'll be just a minute." His teeth sank into his lush lip. "You're always fucking spectacular, y'know."

What the fuck was this flapping going on in my belly? I pressed my hand to my stomach, and I don't think any air circulated in my respiratory system for a few seconds. Whatever he saw in my expression pleased him as he strolled away to the opposite door at the back.

Shaken by the brief interlude and the way I reacted to Devon, I glided to the reception area, fist over my mouth, willing my blush to dissipate.

"Oh ho, this is gonna be interesting!" Mila stared up and down at my obvious discomfort—if the waterfall between my legs could be categorized as discomfort. But I didn't intend to fall for the attraction between Devon and me. I was made of stern stock.

Devon

The early evening was kind to us, and a cool breeze rustled the leaves of the plants in Aisha and Knox's garden. String lights crisscrossed above us, and the pungent smell of earth and foliage mixed with the mild scent of my nervous-induced perspiration.

My entire attention was focused on Sal's expressions as we finally stood in front of each other, surrounded by Mila, Knox's parents, Aisha, Aisha's grandparents, and Trinity.

Sal's luxuriant red lips scrunched up in a slight scowl as she stood in the garden for our wedding. Her eyebrows fought to touch each other. Her freckles were close enough to count them. Sal, dressed in white, her sandy luminous shoulders, the plumpness of her chest, her pillowy belly. Her hips were sumptuous sculptures crafted for someone to hold on to. I wanted to hug her and let her softness fuse with me as she pushed her dress up to give me space to get closer between her legs.

Damn, I needed to calm down. My heart performed petit allegro, and I begged my dick to relax.

I held her damp hands as all the attraction I'd tamped down for months flared to life at the primitive but effective ceremony of joining lives. My head and body were in such turmoil that I almost missed Knox's prompt.

"Do you, Devon, take Salome to be your wedded wife, to cherish in love and in friendship, in strength and in weakness, in success and in disappointment, and vow to love her faithfully today, tomorrow, and for as long as the two of you shall live?" Knox asked.

I paused, a warm rumble coasting along my entirety.

Whatever the reason we were doing this, the words rattled in my head, the combination of them becoming a charm I couldn't escape. My throat seized up. I'd never thought I'd say these words, but if I ever did, it would have been to someone that ultimately saw me for who I was. Saw the good and the ugly.

Sal's curious gaze settled on me as she waited patiently for my words. Her hands had dried, and she squeezed mine. I rested my gaze on our hands, then back to her face, and she gifted me with one of those Sal smiles, which consisted of a crinkle of her eyes. Then she mouthed, "I got you," and somehow, even though she meant she got me with getting my green card and all that entailed, I knew it could go beyond that with Sal. And that shit scared me.

"I do," I said, and the telltale red flush crept up from Sal's off-the-shoulder dress.

"Do you, Salome, take Devon to be your wedded husband, to cherish in love and in friendship, in strength and in weakness, in success and in disappointment, and vow to love him faithfully today, tomorrow, and for as long as the two of you shall live?" Knox said, and Sal's eyes grew serious. She pierced me with an intense gaze that was hard to decipher.

In love and in friendship. Now hearing the vows again, I had a clear picture of how this could have been if Sal and I had the time for our friendship to progress naturally, for our trust in each other to grow organically. Maybe we would have voiced our attraction for each other in a few years. Maybe we would have fallen slowly and irrevocably in love. Maybe we would have implicitly trusted each other.

I didn't break eye contact with her. I wasn't naïve; I knew Sal felt it too, but her walls were well-constructed and required meticulous dismantling. But I could hold onto *in love and friendship*. Not all love needed to be romantic, which could be the basis of our agreement. Calmness flowed through me as I squeezed her hands and grinned at her, and her entire face relaxed.

"I do," Sal said.

"I declare you, Salome and Devon, married." Knox's pronouncement had a sense of finality, and our eyes widened in recognition.

Mila flashed her digital camera at us as Sal threw her lush arms around me, and my hands automatically held her hips. It felt like I had been waiting to rest my hands on her like this for my entire life. Her almost-scowl with her glossy lips made mine twitch in desire, and I longed to tease that curve with the tip of my tongue. I forgot for a moment that the pictures and the hug were for the camera. I forgot all of this was for us to have photographic evidence and video of the happy memory.

There was no pretending the groan as our lips sank into each other, the tip of her tongue coming to the seam provoking the swipe of my tongue in retaliation, our mouths meshing in passion. The claps and cheers sounded perfect to my ears, and I allowed my hand to roam up her back, avoiding sliding down to where I truly wanted to be.

We were married!

Just when I was leaning into our kiss, Sal sank her teeth into my lower lip, eliciting a bolt of lust that electrified me, then eased away, her eyes dazed with desire, puffs of her breath blowing against my feverish skin. I wanted to pull her in again, and I could see the taunt in her gaze. Something dormant woke up in me, stretching languidly at her brazen regard.

"Alright." She patted me on the shoulder and disentangled herself from my hold, her chest brushing my torso as she got off her tippy toes. "I'm gonna get out of this dress, and then we can head to your apartment," she announced and stormed back inside.

"Yeah, that went exactly how I expected it!" Mila guffawed, and Knox clapped me on the back as I stood there stunned, wondering if I'd survive Sal.

Ten

Devon

So much had transpired in the day that it felt odd walking out of my shower and putting on house clothes as if I hadn't gotten married today. After Sal emerged from Aisha's bedroom wearing sweats and one of her anime t-shirts, we all had an early dinner cooked by Aisha and her mother-in-law. I hadn't even been able to taste the food, the surreality of it all still lingering with me.

Tonight could be any night, but now I had a cold gold ring on my finger that commemorated my altered state. I flexed my hand open and closed in a fist, trying to get used to the feeling of the jewelry.

A loud boom and floor vibration announced Sal's location. I searched for her, intrigued by the noise and looking to chase away the feeling of her lips on me. Maybe if I found her and she did her Sal thing where she barely acknowledged me, I could return to putting my attraction for her in the box I'd so tightly kept in check. I descended the stairs to find her comfortable in the corner of the sofa, playing a video game.

All I saw was creamy light brown skin as I cataloged each area I'd love to taste. Her shoulders, the tip of her button nose, the middle of her tits, those fucking thighs... But what hit me in the chest was that she'd taken my offer to be comfortable in my home and truly made a space for herself here.

"Feels weird, huh?" she asked without making eye contact as I sat on the opposite corner, and she pointed to my ring finger. When I'd suggested Sal make herself at home, I had no idea what that would entail. The tank top with no bra and tennis shorts might make her comfortable, but not me.

Rass.

"Sorry, what?" I asked her. This was what happened when I let my mind wander.

She didn't answer and kept playing.

"So, what you playing?" I asked, trying to keep the conversation going.

"*Tales of Arise.*"

"Oh, that's what's up. So...what is it about?"

A sigh. This was going well. This was how things usually went between us. I didn't need the complication of a non-reciprocated attraction between us. I kept wavering, but I knew I needed to keep things friendly.

"Do you honestly want to know?"

This woman.

"Yes, why would I ask if I didn't want to know?" I grinned and shook my head.

"Mhm. It's an RPG game set between a medieval world and a highly modernized world. It's cool so far; I'm just starting."

"That's what's up." What else could I say? She had a way of using sentences that closed conversations. It was an art. We sat without chatting while she navigated the game. If she was trying to perplex me, she was unsuccessful; I relished the quiet.

"Do you like video games?" she asked after a few minutes.

"I don't play a lot. I'll play any of the FIFA games with my brother."

"You talk a lot about him," she said, placing the video game on pause, then turned around in her little sofa nook to face me.

"I do. That's my best friend." I smiled wistfully. One year to go.

"One year to go," she said as if I'd telegraphed her my thoughts. Again, I was struck by how obviously she felt at home here and how much she paid attention, even when she pretended she didn't. I was glad for it; even though she was here to keep herself safe, I knew I was asking a lot from her. I'd asked her to lie to her family, even though she readily offered. Still, it wasn't ok.

"That's right—one year. So..." I waited for her to look at me. "Did you call your family?"

She scrunched up her mouth, and her scowl materialized.

"Not yet. I'll probably call them end of this week." She shrugged.

"Do you mind me asking, why are you estranged from them?"

I relaxed, stretching my arm on the sofa back. The space in between us settled as a valley of safety and comfort. Sal propped her legs up under her, and the expanse of skin that her shorts exposed made me second-guess my decision to stay in my corner.

"You heard my full name tonight?" she asked, and I nodded. I didn't know why she didn't like it. It was a gorgeous name.

"Yeah, Salome. My mom named all of us after femmes fatales. My other two sisters are Magdalene and Eve. And Mom's name is Lilith."

"Rassclat, that's very biblical of her."

"If only. Lilith believes to this day that seducing a well-to-do man will solve all her problems. And she raised us to believe the same. She goes about it in a quiet, calculated manner. The sad part is she's mostly been used most of her life, same as my sisters. They don't see how they've made their gold digger beds and slept in them."

"Kinda harsh to call them gold diggers?"

Sal searched around the room for the next words, her silence the pondering kind. Her face was a kaleidoscope of emotions, and I saw disappointment, frustration, sadness, and rejection there. The wall of Salome was down for a moment, and I took full advantage of the opportunity to get to know her better.

"I don't think it's harsh because that's what they are and what they even think of themselves. Proudly, I might add. Their view of men is warped and..."

"But your view of men is healthy?"

Sal's eyes widened, and I shocked myself with the question. I didn't know why, but I wanted to delve into her reasoning.

"I never said my view was healthy, but it's crafted by my experiences, so I take heed of my previous mistakes. I might exaggerate how I feel about the opposite sex, but it's all warranted. I know some men are good. Look at Knox and Aisha."

She paused, hand in the air, and I felt the sting of her silence. I didn't need anyone's acceptance, but it would be nice if my own friend saw I was a good man. Even if I had my doubts.

"You, for what I've observed so far... I don't know how you treat women romantically, but if I let myself be guided by Aisha's recollections, it doesn't seem you're a man whore, at least."

Damn. At least she mentioned me. I didn't know whether to smile or scowl. "But a man could say the same about women, and we would be labeled immature at best, incels at worst."

Sal scoffed but leaned into the middle of the sofa, getting into the conversation. I felt the rush of adrenaline I got from a good debate. I usually tried not to get into these types of conversations with most people other than my brother and a few close friends. That's it. Best let them see what they wanted to see, but with Sal... Well, with Sal, things just went their path, and I couldn't help but go along for the ride.

"Nah, see, those types of men complain about women being independent. Women who put themselves first before wanting to bend over any gendered expectation. Is that what you are?" The challenge was unmistakable.

"At this point, I think you know me better than that, but I'll bite. I don't think women need to bend over backward for any person. I believe relationships are about healthy compromise. No one should have to put forth more of themselves physically or mentally to make the other person happy. Also, you need to be happy your damn self before going into a relationship, ya understand? I might have been hurt in the past, but I've never written off women as a whole, y'know." I shook my head.

"Mhm, but you were perfectly fine marrying me and committing to marriage for three years. That doesn't seem like someone looking for love." Her head tilted to the side in a *gotcha!* gesture I wanted to erase with a kiss. Why was this conversation so invigorating? Fuck, at this point, I was going to have to gather some of those superfluous cushions the lady at the store convinced me to get when I got this sectional and use them as cover just to keep things PG.

"Me not villainizing women doesn't mean I don't think romantic love is for me."

"Mhm, but me saying men aren't for me is me villainizing them instead of you acknowledging romantic love *isn't* for me either?"

"One implies love is not for me because of myself. The other implies love is not for you because of others."

I ran a thumb over my lip, attempting to tamp down the smile that wanted to flourish. Sal followed the path of my thumb and squinted.

"So why don't you think romantic love is for you?"

"Because it's hard for me to open up for people to know me fully."

"So you're unwilling to do the work?" she said, frowning.

"No, I...I... I haven't had high success being fully vulnerable with people in my life, not just women. Family too."

The accompanying ache to my words left me tender whenever I thought of my parents. Of the facade I had to put on anytime I was around them.

"Mhm. Interesting. It seems we both have a similar

problem on opposite sides of the coin." She shrugged, allowing an impasse that surprised us both.

"Oh, so you gonna let this be a tie?"

"I don't debate to win, I debate to stimulate my brain. This was great stimulation. And food for thought too. And I do think you have the ability to be vulnerable. It's just scary as fuck, and it's okay to say that too."

And with those words, Sal left me behind in the living room, wondering why it had been so easy for me to unburden myself like that.

Eleven

Sal

Three more days, and I was swimming in information that did not match up. The ladies had seen the guy's car again by the studio, but he didn't come in to ask questions. The plates on his car came up as an impounded vehicle once I hacked into the local police database. It didn't make any sense, but it was the only path I had to follow.

The struggle to keep my frustration at bay was becoming a physical ailment. Any given day, I'd love to stay in my apartment, work on my video game, or do some sleuthing, but now? Knowing I couldn't be out and about was messing with my motivation.

Leads to Xavier Souza were more promising. He had some online presence, but he clearly had someone good scrubbing anything that wasn't about his profession as a lawyer. I was digging into his past cases to find any connection between Juniper and him, but so far, nothing. He seemed to lead a quiet life, had all his bills paid. I'd hacked into his private social media but there were no pictures there, so I was going through his connections to see if they matched any of Juniper's.

I tried my best not to be a beast around Devon, which meant I kept to myself more than ever. Every morning, he asked me if I wanted to ride with him to the studio, and I declined his offer every time. He, in turn, seemed to be leaving earlier than usual for his therapy.

I'd seen him limping last night and almost asked if he was ok but curtailed the urge. I'd felt tight in my skin since that conversation on our wedding night. Our viewpoints were similar and so opposed simultaneously; the whole conversation made me turn the puzzle over repeatedly in my brain like a Rubik's cube. The desire to sit down and chat with him and hear his thoughts became a distraction when I couldn't afford any.

Then there was my lack of immunity to his shirtless state. I'd seen Devon without a shirt when he rehearsed many times in the studio. While Mila and sometimes even Aisha objectified him respectfully, I'd inured myself to his obvious appeal.

But living under the same roof, even if temporarily, must be rewriting my code because Devon eating breakfast with no shirt on in the morning had become my favorite entertainment. And that needed to stop because my awareness around him was ratcheting up. Soon, I'd have to wear bras around him to prevent my nipples from loudly announcing my untimely attraction.

Thoughts of his bare chest and smooth brown skin aroused me enough to want to explore the next bit of coding I'd finished last night for the next scene in my video game *Alix, Slayer of Sex Demons.*

As I approached the alpha stage, I knew I would soon need another tester, but for now, I enjoyed it being a process for only me. I tested the game out whenever I finished a particular challenge and was almost at the end of the entire design process. In this specific scene, Alix had just defeated two sex demons with the aid of her sidekick, Jax. Jax was a tall, lanky Black character who had to convince Alix he was up to the challenge of being her partner while conquering these sex demons. Where Alix was a no-nonsense badass, Jax tried to fix things with diplomacy and positivity.

For each new trial they'd worked together, I gave the end of the scene a glimpse of teasing tension between them. In this challenge, I was finally having them fuck, with him pressing her down to the floor and giving her head until she came. I'd finished laying the code for this moment in the game, and my palms itched excitedly.

The TV in my guest room was larger than I had at home, but the idea of seeing Alix, Black and beautiful, on the living room screen had been tickling the back of my mind since the moment I moved here. I had plenty of time before Devon was back from therapy and class, and with the decision made, I bounded down the stairs.

Alix appeared on the screen, the last saved session showing her right after she fought alongside Jax. They were standing back-to-back, the avatars swaying as they awaited the player's response.

The imagery and pure colorful beauty still held me enthralled. With the help of other Black illustrators, I'd created this beauty. Alix stood in her combat gear. When I'd initially imagined her, she was a thick badass wearing a crop top and biker shorts because I wanted her to be able to move quickly as she vanquished evil. To look accessible but edgy. To feel relatable. The illustrators took my vision and fleshed it out until I almost shed a tear or two when I saw her in technicolor.

Alix now still wore the black and purple crop top I'd imagined with the classic anime waifu look, but she was Black through and through. Thick, with a few rolls showing beneath the hem of her crop top, lush thighs encased in sculpting shorts, and a tummy. She sported a gurade-style sword. Her face was an ode to Black beauty with a wide button nose, plump lips, sultry eyes, a rampage of brown coils with a side part, and a swoop to the side that curled at the end with an edge. Every time I saw her on the screen, she made me happy.

Beside her, Jax stood slim and tall with mahogany skin and an impish smile that spoke to his easygoing nature. Jax wore black and gray with a splash of purple to denote he was team Alix all the way, a full warrior bodysuit that conveniently zipped open from the front. He had two fined honed spears crossed at his back, which he wielded with precise efficiency. A big afro adorned his crown, and his gentle eyes were framed by sexy, bushy eyebrows.

I started playing the game, immediately switching to dialogue between the two main characters. They told each other how well they'd collaborated to slay the enemy but that they still felt that heightened arousal. Jax confessed that he always felt that arousal around her, and she asked him to prove it. Jax impishly questioned Alix, then the game provided me with an option. I already knew them all.

1. Ignore Jax and skip to the next challenge.
2. Flick open her crop top at the snap that holds her breasts together, or
3. Ask him to unzip his suit.

The two last options led to the same outcome, just a slightly different path. Selecting the zipper option, the frame whirled in a flash of light to transition to a video. The smooth animation of Jax showing Alix his thick length made me tingle.

The sweep of his hand over his dick flowed flawlessly, and I couldn't wait to tell Patrice how well her team had done. I selected the next step, which led to both characters butt naked, with Jax licking and slurping between Alix's thighs.

The swipe of his tongue against her pussy vividly aroused me, wetness surging between my legs. For fuck's sake, my horniness was at an all-time high. I hadn't masturbated since moving in with Devon, and I was long overdue for a wonderful orgasm. It didn't help that I was overstimulated by Devon's easygoing presence and his smooth voice whenever he spoke to me or on the phone with his brother.

Fuck it, I had needs, and Devon wasn't coming back for at least a couple of hours, so I didn't need to move. Taking a risk to rub one out in an open area felt reckless, but my entire situation felt reckless. I might as well continue to flirt with danger.

Throwing caution aside, I yanked down my shorts and panties, the beat of my heart amplifying to my body, the throb of my pussy merging with the speed of my heartbeat.

I could run to get a toy, but absolutely no one had time for that. On the screen, Alix's moans and Jax's slurping came through the surround sound, the vibration enough to stimulate my ears and increase the heat in the room.

With the pad of one finger, I caressed my clit, the wet softness yielding to my touch. In circular motions, I massaged my labia, creating friction against my nub, the tingling upgrading to a tremble. The wet sounds on the TV coincided with mine. Alix's moans became my own as we both chased our inevitable conclusion.

One-handed, I pressed the next command, which showed Alix gobbling Jax's dick while he continued to sip on her goodness, a good ol' 69 pose for the masses. My legs shook as I let go, losing myself in the pleasure, shelving all my worries away, if even for mere seconds.

Release hovered near me as I applied direct pressure to my clit.

"Fuck, oh…"

The beep of the electronic door pad announced Devon's arrival, but my brain was too sluggish to register what was happening.

Slow footsteps behind me, then, "What in the—"

Adrenaline exploded in me, and every lick of sense vanished in the explosion. With speed I seldom showcased, I stood and yanked my pants up in one fluid motion. My wetness seeped through both sets of fabric.

Fuck. No time to worry.

Dreading what came next, I whirled around to notice Devon's mouth gaping open at the display in front of him. I couldn't blame him; I had hentai on the screen and had been starting my bottomless party.

"Forget what you saw," I ordered, pointing a finger at him for good measure. Then I ran for the sake of my dignity.

"What the—? Wait!" he commanded, and something in the tone of his voice made me tremble. The stairs never seemed so far away. I ignored Devon, my loud stomps in the room competing with Alix's keening. Shit, I hadn't turned off the TV. Too late—my chest tightened, and my juices trickled down my legs as I ran up the steps.

The staircase seemed to elongate before me, the landing far away as Devon's footsteps reverberated behind me.

The thrill of his pursuit enthralled me, making the need to escape imperative but the desire to be caught alluring.

Why did Devon get to activate my most profound secret desire?

"Sal, Sal, stop. Let's talk." How the fuck was he not winded? I couldn't get any air in my lungs.

Finally, I got to the top; my room was almost there. I ignored his plea until a hand grasped my waist, the heat and hardness of him pressing on my ass igniting that fight-or-flight instinct so deeply embedded in my kink of choice. Without thought, I elbowed him, and a whoosh escaped him.

I craned my neck to see him, which was a mistake because my legs ceased their normal function, reminding me at the worst possible time of how clumsy I could be. I tripped, my belly swooping as gravity became my enemy. My hands shot out before the rest of my upper body, and I landed knees first, hands second. My ragged breaths resounded in the open hallway. Scrambling to continue, I crawled on all fours, the pain radiating from my limbs slowing the process.

"Why the fuck are you running?" Devon asked, exasperated, his breath fraying. I still ignored him and tried in vain to forget how my body responded to him still stomping behind me. The fact that he was usually light on his feet didn't register.

He'd slowed down to give me space, and for a moment, I wanted to scream at him to take me. Just like this, primal and hard as my juices dripped from between my legs. The throbbing of my pussy had transformed into a raw, intense need to be conquered, and I fought the moan threatening to escape.

"Let me help you get up... I just want to help. You're safe with me. You know that, right?" he pleaded, tentatively placing his hand on my arm closest to him. That was the problem—I knew I was safe with him. Everything in me *knew*.

The need to provoke him overruled my thoughts, and I rolled away into the railing that faced the open lower floor and swept him with my leg. Devon hadn't been ready, and he stumbled forward, landing facedown, the top half of his heavy, delectable, warm build over me.

"What in the—?" he bellowed again like a broken record.

With all my might, I shoved him, the heat of his shoulder and chest seeping into me, making me hungry, making me crave. He barely moved. I might have broken him because he kept repeating the same question over and over.

Devon stared at me as he pulled away, lying next to me on the floor, so close our breaths mingled, the railing behind me digging into my back. The concern in his gaze transformed to wonder. Whatever I telegraphed to him slowly became apparent as his eyes trailed down to my heaving chest, my traitorous hard nipples, and back to my face. My mouth dried, and I ran the tip of my tongue over my bottom lip, then the top. He followed that path and then stared at me again.

The heat and predatory gleam were unmistakable, and I rubbed my thighs together to chase away the response it elicited.

"Oh," he breathed, and I moaned, helpless to hide this from him. He'd caught me when all my defenses were down.

I shoved at his chest again, harder this time, and he took advantage of the movement, air sailing out of my lungs as he rolled us until I fell on top of him.

Him and his hardness.

"I need you to get up. Get away from me and run to your room. Tell me this isn't what I think this is. I need you to state your boundaries loud and clear," Devon said in a deceptively mild manner that ruffled all my feathers.

"Of course, you know what this is. And, of course, you need it to be all perfect and shit and discuss clear consent." And fuck if I didn't crave that from him. The only other man I'd trusted with this side of myself had been my ex, and he was good to me, but then he betrayed my trust in other ways. I didn't gift this to anyone anymore—I just kept it deeply hidden and protected. I'd long stopped wishing I could be with a man I could trust so intuitively we could play like I wanted to play with Devon today. I wanted to be taken, but I didn't want to make it easy for him.

"I don't know if I can do that right now. I'm not..."

"I get it. We're both too worked up; this demands a clear head. So I'mma need you to get up, and I'm gonna take a very cold shower. And we'll talk during dinner."

"Ok." I nodded, then instinctively rolled my hips against his, and a shuddering breath escaped him.

"Sal, I'll never do anything to hurt you. So *please* don't torture me like this."

The plea was what made me finally move. My wants might be significant, but Devon's friendship was more important.

I disentangled myself from him, a sad sigh escaping me as I stood back up. Downstairs, the scene for Alix and Jax kept going as I'd never prompted them to finish, their groans and moans a tempting reminder of what it could be with Devon.

"I'll see you later." Looking at him as he straightened himself to his full height, the thickness between his legs was evident and impressive, and my pussy ached to gain acquaintance.

"Stop staring," he chastised.

"No. I can't," I refused.

In the span of a millisecond, my head bumped against the wall, and all the air whooshed out of my lungs as Devon rammed against me, the force of him calling to my baser instincts.

"Don't play with me, Salome. We talk first...then I'll make sure to make you pay for running away from me today."

My heart sprang from my chest, like recognizing like, and I moaned again in acknowledgment of that edge I'd noticed that he kept so well-hidden. The scent of him, clean sweat, sea salt, citrus, and pheromones, was railing my senses. He separated himself from me and swaggered past me into his room.

Tonight couldn't come soon enough.

———

Devon

Nerves seldom visited me before performances. I'd been on stage too many times to count, and after a while, it became second nature to harness all the adrenaline that propelled me to the stage.

There was only one night that I remember that had me pacing my dressing room, wishing my heart would be calm enough for me to focus on the performance ahead. My parents were in the theater, visiting from Jamaica, and had conceded to come and see me after my brother pushed them to try. Delroy meant well, but mother and father were as stubborn as they got and still had antiquated views regarding my profession, even after all the success and accolades.

Exposing my art and joy to them worried me it would tinge my enjoyment of my profession, and it would remind me of the reasons I left Jamaica and them behind. The recriminations, the lack of understanding, the silent disappointment.

That performance was one of the best of my career.

The nerves I felt today reminded me of that performance, but the flavors of the nerves were different. Safeguarding my corners that remained in shadow, protected from judging eyes, had become my own work of art. Showing Sal one of those corners pushed me to take a run before dinner.

The pounding of pavement under my sneakers served as a constant reminder that I kept this side of my life very private. I participated in kink separately from anyone that knew me; even Aisha and the few other dancers that were in the kink community in New York didn't know.

I didn't know if people that knew me would understand this other side, understand that underneath my calm demeanor was a hunger to conquer. An outlet for my most primitive needs. So, I didn't mix the two—until Sal greeted me, bare pussy glistening under the lights of my living room. Fuck, I pushed myself even harder, finishing the run in record time.

Once back at home, I showered, then busied myself in the kitchen. The clock on the microwave signaled seven when I finished cooking curry goat, white rice, and plantains for Sal and a salad for me. No carbs at night before a show, and I was determined to get on stage in July.

Quiet steps down the stairs made my heart and dick

jump, but this was not the time to show my hand. This was the time to assess if this was a smart move to make for both of us. For this friendship and this marriage that depended on us getting along well. For her safety and my legal status in this country.

"Hey."

She sat on a stool on my kitchen island and stared at me expectantly.

No shyness for Sal.

"Hello." I didn't know where to start with her. She sat there in one of her big t-shirts, biker shorts, and no bra on, frown firmly in place.

"So, what're we gonna do?" she bluntly asked.

"What do you want to do?" I slid a plate in front of her, and she mumbled her thanks, but I didn't miss the crinkle in her eyes and the flush that showed up over the top of her t-shirt.

"I...well, I wanted to reiterate that if you have needs, you should go for it. I mean, as long as you're discreet." She shrugged, and I couldn't believe she was suggesting I fuck someone else *again* when we had that moment just a couple of hours ago.

"No."

"No?" She stared at me as if I'd grown two heads and then shifted on her stool. She took a bite of the food and closed her eyes in ecstasy. It was my turn to shift on my feet.

"No. I don't want to fuck someone else."

"Oh."

We stared at each other, the silence as the tension consolidated around us as thick as the humid air during my run. She bit her lip and then took another bite of the curry, her eyes fluttering as she ran her tongue over her lip. I wanted to bite that lip until it reddened and she moaned, pleading with me to stop, or maybe I wanted her to ask for more. I hadn't planned on opening up to Sal, but here I was about to show her a side people in my life seldom got to see. And I was excited to tell her all about my predilections. I'll be damned.

"Yeah. So, let's talk boundaries."

Twelve

Sal

THE MORNING FOUND me with my hands between my legs, slick and hot, a shuddering orgasm rocking through me as I remembered my negotiation with Devon last night.

"So you like primal play?" he'd asked.

"Yes." He waited me out, and I just stared back.

"That's not gonna cut it; we're gonna discuss this."

Devon's easy charm had disappeared, and a demanding, intense version had emerged instead. As he guided us through each negotiation step, I kept shifting in my seat. My hand sped up again as a second orgasm threatened to flood through me.

"What drives you wild?" His voice was a rumble, the smooth molasses gone, the rough quality all the stimulation I needed. Butterflies erupted in my belly with such foreign sensations I hadn't felt in years.

"I...I love to be uninhibited in my play. I want to be stripped of any artifice. I crave being hunted, but I don't surrender easily," I explained. I took another bite of the delicious curry goat, the spices awakening my palate; maybe if I focused on the food, it would calm the disturbance in my stomach. I needed the butterflies to cease—death by curry.

"I like hunting." Devon nodded, the danger in his gaze wanting me to run to prove his statement.

We negotiated, ensuring we discussed what was explicitly accepted in our future play, each of us sharing soft and hard limits. We reviewed safety, exchanged sexual health statuses, and discussed protection.

The entire conversation was so stimulating that when I stood up from the stool, there was moisture left behind, which I hastily wiped away with a napkin. This man had me puddling—*embarrassing*.

"I need a clear sign from you when you want to play. I don't mess around with assuming you're always game. I need to know."

I searched for a way to tell him, ideas running through my head. I wanted to give him a sign to take me wherever he was. I wanted him to feel the need to chase me, a way to summon him with my desire.

"I'll send you a gif—of a candle. When I'm feeling playful, you'll know."

"A candle... I like that. I can't wait to subdue you and make you mine," he'd whispered in my ear before I went back to my room.

My legs shook so hard I rattled the bed as I came one more time to the thought of Devon's powerful body over me, finally making me his.

———

Two COLD SHOWERS, and I was ready to face the morning. Devon had already left for the day. What I wasn't prepared to face was that yesterday and every day with Devon made me want to know more about him, the things he hid behind that pleasant grin and good-guy charm.

Something else lay behind his eyes. I'd noticed it the day we met, but I didn't want to wade into deep waters with him. Getting to know him as deeply as I wanted felt reckless, making my palms damp and my mouth dry. But I clearly had some masochism in me because I still wanted to prod him for more. The sexual connection was all good—ok, not good; *good* didn't encompass the extraordinary sexual chemistry I felt for him—but that wasn't what intrigued me. Something kept tugging at me...his kink, his past, what he wanted for his future. Who he truly was when the lights were off and his soul was stripped bare.

For fuck's sake, I was over here soliloquizing over this dude.

Someone save me.

As I descended the last set of steps, my phone vibrated in my pocket.

I stared at the name and the picture for a long time until it stopped ringing. *Lilith.* Then it started ringing again. The urge to roll my eyes was intense, but I restrained myself.

"Hello, mother."

"Salome, if I don't call, you don't call."

Here we go.

"Mother, I called for your birthday."

"A month ago!"

"I know." I loved my mom and my sisters. Still, we weren't compatible, no matter how much Lilith tried to make it so.

"When are you gonna drive up to visit us?"

"Maybe I'll drive to Jacksonville for Thanksgiving. We'll see." Or maybe I could spend Thanksgiving with

Devon. I always attempted to keep my behind at home, and every time, either Mila or Aisha made me feel bad until I went to one of their celebrations.

Mom tried to convince me every year, and every year I reminded her we were better off in separate counties during the holidays. The last time we did Thanksgiving together, Magdalene tried to stab me after I reminded her that her second baby father had stolen money from her on the first date, and she'd still been ignorant enough to spread her legs for him.

But somehow, that *doodoo wipe* wasn't the bad guy; no, it was me. So, I stayed my ass in South Florida. And even though I loved spending the day with Mila and her rowdy bunch or Aisha with her grandparents, I wanted a space where I could be as quiet as I wanted to be and not have people wanting me to be more than that.

"You lyin', you not finna come nowhere," Lilith scoffed.

I stayed quiet. She wasn't lying. In the meanwhile, I prepared two travelers' cups, one with hot tea and honey and another with the coffee and sweet condensed milk Devon loved. I hadn't been able to prepare his coffee this morning due to being otherwise occupied. Damn, were my fingers wrinkly? Ugh.

"Listen, little girl, I brought you to this world, and I...."

"Can we skip the threats of death and dismemberment and get to the reason for your call?" Because just as I loved Lilith, she loved me, but she sure as hell couldn't compute how I'd come out of her. She always complained about how God had given me the cutest face of her daughters and the biggest ass, and I didn't want to put either to good use. And that's why I loved Lilith, but I didn't like her. And she didn't like me in turn because I wasn't with the bullshit.

"Someone been lookin' for you. Some Mr. Souza,

talking 'bout he's your brother. I...wanted to... Listen here, remember what I told you about your daddy. He's a hard man, baby girl. You don't want to mess with him."

I froze at the mention of Souza; he'd somehow reached my mom. Souza had no online connection to Juniper. Was he truly my brother, or was this a trap? An ache solidified in my head as I tried to wrap my mind around all that was happening. The lack of control disoriented me and made me hollow with anger and despair.

"What did this Mr. Souza want?"

"Wanted to tell you that he has been trying to reach you; apparently, you have three brothers. And they want to meet you. He figured if he called me, maybe you'd want to talk to 'em, but he don't know you don't listen to me one bit. It seems they don't have a relationship with your dad, which is good. So, you decide what you want to do. In the end, you always do."

"Did you know, Lilith?"

Silence.

"I don't have time for this right now. Bye."

———

I quickly called Mila, and she dutifully picked me up at Devon's apartment. I didn't want to be alone, and I didn't even want to start dissecting what that meant.

"What happened?" she immediately asked as I sank into her passenger seat.

"Nothing. I just needed a change of pace."

"I'm gonna let that be, but I'm here when you're ready to talk."

I nodded, swallowing the lump in my throat, glad for my friends and how well they knew me. I couldn't wrap my mind around Mr. Souza and the life-altering message he'd left with Lilith.

I had three brothers. *I had more siblings.*

My hopes were tempered as I thought of my sisters and the frail relationships I had with them. And Lilith's non-answer... I wanted to scream.

I knew I wasn't easy to love, and they'd tried hard over the years to establish a relationship separate from mine and my mom's. But they did the same things, putting their kids through hell just to get the next dude to pay their rent and car notes. I couldn't sit idly by and watch them destroy their lives just as Lilith did, so I kept them at arm's length, no matter how much it hurt.

"So, you left your million screens to hang out with us at the studio? Might this have something to do with Devon teaching class today?" Mila prodded, trying to get me out of my mood.

"I didn't even know he had class today."

Mila's incredulity nudged me in the arm; her skepticism was so strong it was palpable. I really forgot she'd known me since I was five.

"Girl, you've been gladly fulfilling Aisha's need for help, and once she found a receptionist, you still magically appear at the studio on Tuesdays and Wednesdays. But you go ahead and hold onto the delusion. You know I'll cheer-lead you all the way to the Nile."

I rolled my eyes, holding back my laugh. "Why are you so corny?" I asked instead.

"Why are you lying to yourself? We all have our flaws. Let's own them."

I secretly grinned when Mila focused on the road, glad to have my true sister of the heart with me.

———

Mila was correct; I was lying to myself. I loved coming to see Devon in action. He rarely did full demonstrations for the dancers, but today he was inspired. The fluid grace of his movements enthralled me as he taught the advanced ballet dancers a quick passage of one of his old ballets. The worries about Juniper and my potential three brothers didn't disappear, but the pounding urgency lessened as I sank into the trance of Devon's artistry.

"He's breathtaking, isn't he?" Aisha asked as she leaned against the reception counter, avidly watching the monitors that showed the parents the classes inside. It was her way of letting them see but not interrupt.

"And he's not even putting all his effort because of his tendon," I said and cursed myself when the words left my mouth.

"But how would you know how he looks when he dances without the tendon problem? He's fucking amazing now; I can only imagine how he was before," Mila argued.

Aisha's searching glance prodded me, and even though I felt like ignoring her, I took the difficult path because when don't I? I stared back at her in defiance.

"You've watched some of his performances, haven't you?" Aisha pointed her finger at me.

"And if I did, so what? You introduced a new person to our lives. You know how that goes." I shrugged.

"So when you looked into Knox...did you spend hours looking at his many work accomplishments?" Mila teased.

Maybe today wasn't the day to brazen this out. I pulled up my laptop, trying to remain calm. Heat spread through my chest, and I knew the red was starting to creep up my neck.

"Oh, damn, a full-body blush?" Mila gasped.

"Oh, honey, we haven't seen one of those in a long while since...since that bandit," Aisha said gently, knowing what this could mean. But she was wrong. This wasn't the first time I'd blushed like this. Devon had made me blush several times now. I cleared my throat and punched in my encryption.

"You like him, don't you?" Mila accused. Like I'd done her wrong. I kept typing, my cheeks hot to the touch. I didn't need a mirror to know I could pass for a tomato.

"You should tell him. I think he—" Aisha paused.

Room A's door swung open, and Devon emerged, the slight sheen on his face making me wonder about the flavor of his skin.

What the fuck was happening to me!

His eyes shone brightly in excitement as his students departed, a disjointed chorus of byes in their wake.

Mila and Aisha's attention snapped away from me and to Devon, who grinned at me.

"You came." His sweet smile spread even wider; his contentment was contagious. My usual aplomb left me because I smiled back. The sight of him felt like those old comfy socks that you tried to throw away but kept returning to your sock drawer.

"Oh shit! Did y'all fuck?" Mila fake-whispered, and Devon coughed, then covered his mouth with his fist, hiding a laugh. I couldn't believe Mila. Best friend, yeah, right.

"You should have told me you wanted to die today. I would have worn all black." I shook my head, walking away from the desk. I ignored the giddiness that rushed through me. I hadn't seen him this morning, and I just...I wanted to be close to him. That was all.

He was my friend, just like Mila and Aisha. And I also

wanted to see them today, especially after the call with my mother. There wasn't anything else but the need for support. I pushed the traveler's cup I'd packed toward him, and he took it. The grin that illuminated his face was so beautiful that it made my chest tight.

"Thanks, Sal."

"Mhm." No need to simp for this man more than I had today.

"Are you good?" he asked, concern creeping into his voice.

"Yup, y'all fucking." Mila nodded, forgoing the whisper.

"Mila!" Aisha chided.

"What? *I'm* not the one fucking! He's clearly into her; she brings him coffee. Did she bring you and me coffee? Nah. He noticed she's not good, just like you and I did, just by looking at her face. Like he speaks Sal. I'm telling you, something is going on," Mila said sagely.

"Yeah, I'm alright. I'm gonna answer some O requests in your office, Aisha," I announced. If Mila was gonna talk about me like I wasn't here, then I would make it easier. I smacked her head as I passed her by, and she yelped. When Devon stepped behind me, my heart hiccupped and then kept beating. I guess I could simp a bit more.

When we entered the office, he closed the door softly and stared at me for a second. His eyes made me squirm, but I couldn't let him see that, so I set the laptop on the desk and started typing as he waited me out.

"My mom called me."

"Oh...are you ok? Did you tell her about us?"

Oh, shit. That would have been the perfect opportunity, but the news about my brothers threw me off.

"No." I shook my head.

"Mmm."

Was that disappointment in his voice? It couldn't be. I knew he'd told his parents—not the truth, just that he'd met me a few months ago and we had fallen in love—and of course, Delroy knew the whole truth, but I had yet to say anything to my moms and sisters. I didn't realize this was so important to him. I pressed the base of my palm to my tight chest and rubbed, trying to calm the anxious feeling that emerged from knowing I had the power to disappoint him.

"It's alright, I get it. I know it's hard for you to talk to her, you know?" He gentled and approached the desk, resting himself against it.

"She said a Mr. Souza called her, and...he said he's my brother. And I have two more brothers."

"He called your moms?" All gentleness dissipated, and dangerous Devon, that trait he kept deep down hidden from people, emerged. And why did my pussy purr her approval?

"Yeah, I don't know what to think anymore. A lot is going on." I sighed, and this morning's worries clambered on top of me, pressing my chest down. I gasped for air, wondering when I would get a break.

"I don't want you talking to him. We don't know what's happening, but I can tell you the man looking for Juniper is —" He shook his head. "Delroy is fearless and asked me to treat this with the utmost respect and caution."

Nodding, I wished I could rest my worries on Devon, but that wasn't smart to do. And why did his telling me not to talk to someone made me feel...protected? I didn't need protection, no matter what he thought he'd married me for. I'd agreed because marrying helped him out, and I always helped my friends. And because it gave me space and cover to do what I needed to do to shake Juniper's boyfriend's tail until I could nail him with something to get him off my back.

I would wallow in my feelings today, and tomorrow I'd be back on the hunt; I needed to dig into the dark web to see if I could find anything about that man. I needed something big enough to threaten his livelihood to protect me, my friends, and Juniper.

Devon's nearness tempted me to rest my head on his lap, let him run his fingers over my scalp, let him soothe my worries. But I'd never been able to count on a man that way, and today wasn't the day. I stood up, trying to shake off the cold shiver running through my arms and legs, and his warmth immediately chased it away. His proximity made me want to press against him, but I kept my cool. Two more steps, and he could embrace me and tell me things would be alright with that lilting accent of his, which I suddenly found incredibly sexy.

"Ok, we'll be careful. I need to search deeper into Souza and Juniper's boyfriend, find a connection."

Devon's gaze x-rayed me; for a second, he saw all my fears and how scared I was. I stood still, letting him run his diagnosis, allowing the warmth of his concern and the heat of his stare to consume me. I let him make me believe, just for a second, that I wasn't alone in this.

But I was. I didn't let people in. Only Aisha and Mila got close, and even then—

I spun on my feet, severing the connection. I felt the cold splash of reality soaking me as I stepped away from him.

"I want to go work at your apartment. Do you have more classes?"

"No, and even if I did, I'd take you to my place. Anything you need, Sal. You know that, right?"

"Yeah." I nodded, conceding just for a second. Giving him that.

"I took a picture of that dude that kept showing up. I'll send it to you. See what you can do with it," he told me.

He sighed and followed me back out.

Raised voices filtered into the hallway as we approached the main area. I strained to understand what was happening, but before I could rush into the hallway, Devon's arm whipped around me, pressing me against his hard body. All the air rushed from my lungs as our bodies familiarized themselves. The hard planes of his stomach converged against the curve of my back, his heat touching my soft ass, the lushness of my thighs against his harder ones. My head could easily fit on his shoulder if I only relaxed into him, but I was on high alert. Knox's deep voice commanded someone else's reedy one to leave. A slight scuffle, then a door slammed shut, and Knox cursed loudly.

I tried to pull away from Devon, but I might as well be pushing against steel.

"Let me go!"

"Wait," he commanded, and he should have known better.

"No." I stomped on his good foot, cautious to startle him, not hurt him. He jerked in surprise, and I disentangled myself from him. After less than fifteen minutes, my mind and body protested against any decision that meant I moved away from Devon; what the hell was going on with me?

I rushed to the reception to find Mila's worried face, Aisha's scared one, and Knox's angry snarl.

"What the fuck happened?"

"I told that man not to come back. It seems he intimidated Athena to inform them about you and how you'd just gotten married and moved. Of course, Athena doesn't know where you live, but it's a matter of time before he puts two and two together. I told him he can't come back without the police. No more. We won't help this "search" he has for his cousin's girl. Enough is enough. I got a gun and a—"

"We don't need guns!" Aisha protested, and her anguish punched me in the gut. God, this was creating so much strife for my friends. Mila sat behind the reception desk, her mask in place. She hated confrontation, and I could feel her closing off in concern and protection. I wasn't good like Aisha at getting her out of her shell when she got like this, but I rushed to her side anyway. I stared back at Devon, hoping he understood my desperation. His eyes followed and stayed with me as Aisha and Knox kept arguing, and I nodded back, acknowledging his message of support.

"We need protection. That man is dangerous, Aisha; you heard what he said. He wasn't giving up and threatened retaliation. I can't have you in danger here! Maybe Sal should stay at Devon's until this blows away. Maybe— maybe you should stay away," Knox finished, staring at me intently.

"Knox! How dare you? Sal needs our help right now, not for us to alienate her."

"I don't want to alienate her. I think she needs more protection than the studio can give her," he insisted.

I was about to tell Knox to fuck off and let me worry about my safety, but a growl startled me.

"You don't need to worry about my wife. She has all the protection she needs. If we're not welcome here, then Aisha, you'll need to find someone else to do my classes because I don't intend to let any harm come to Sal. And that promise means no harm comes to any of us."

My wife? *We?*

I stole a glance at Mila, and her eyes were wide saucers. She mouthed, *"His wife?"* at me, and I tore my eyes away from her, lest I cracked and laughed hysterically. It was that or cry. Devon's quiet assurance sent a thrill down my spine, and I cursed my weakness. I didn't need a man to protect me, but here I was, plotting my next dash away from him, just to be captured.

"Fuck, man, I'm sorry. I know I'm wildin', but this is Aisha. She's—"

"Your everything. I get it." And for the first time today, Devon avoided my gaze. And I had no idea what that meant, but it was a good reminder I was in this on my own. Because he and I weren't truly man and wife, we weren't boyfriend and girlfriend; hell, we weren't even lovers yet. Just a baby friendship that hadn't been tested once. Not nearly enough to let me lower my guard, no matter how much my instincts told me I could finally trust a man.

Thirteen

DEVON

THE SILENCE during the car ride home heightened my sense of unease, which had started when that man walked out of Aisha's studio. The afternoon reminded me of the stakes for Sal, of the danger she could be in. The man searching for her wouldn't hesitate to use force by any means necessary if Delroy was right. And Delroy was always right.

Sal sat quietly, her body shifted toward the door, her gaze lost in the window as cars flew by as we approached my building. I wanted to reach across the console and hold her hand, offering her the comfort she needed. No matter what front she presented, she'd have to be scared after this last visit.

There wasn't a place on earth where she was safer than by my side, but she didn't believe that. Not yet. Fuck it, I reached across the cup holders, my hand up, my stomach clenching as I waited for her to reach for me too. She must have sensed my movement because she didn't even turn toward me, but her arm shifted. Softness pressed against my hand, and our fingers intertwined. My heart leaped in triumph. I was done analyzing my emerging feelings for Sal; tonight, I would just let them run their course. Listen to my instincts.

"Your hands are cold."

"Yeah, well, your car is cold."

I hazarded a glance and found a blank mask as she processed today's situation. I turned the AC controls to warm Sal up a bit and ghosted my thumb back and forth on the soft skin of her hand.

"There. Now it's not that cold."

"Maybe not in here..." She shrugged, and her hand shook inside of mine. Fuck, I wanted to fuck that man up for putting her in this state. This quiet, concerned persona instead of the defiant, cantankerous woman I was starting to...care about as a close friend. Yeah, just that.

"Sal, I gotcha, you know? You know you'll be good as long as you're with me?"

She pursed her lips, then pierced me with her inquisitive gaze. She was fucking gorgeous. Her intelligence shone through as she figured out what to say. She bit her mouth while deep in thought, and my stomach went from knotted up to swooping up and down as if in a swing. My physical reactions to her increased daily, and she was oblivious. The sexual tension, yes, but the rest? She was oblivious.

"I know you want to keep me safe, but rationally, there's not much you can do if this man is as dangerous as you've described him."

The thought that she doubted me fucked with me; I couldn't front. But I could understand her hesitation. She didn't understand that even though I didn't work for my brother *anymore*, I knew how to handle business.

"You underestimate what I can and cannot do."

She squinted as we drove into the enclosed garage. Silence reigned as I navigated the turns until we reached the floor for my space. Once I parked, I sat still for a minute, letting her search for whatever reassurance she needed to find.

"So you *did* work with your brother?"

"He couldn't do what he did and have a brother that couldn't look after himself," I deflected.

"Alright. That's good to know. Still, we have no idea what happens next. He just came to fuck with my mind, and I can't do much about it. We can only wait. I'll run that pic and hope Juniper's boyfriend shows his hand soon. And hope she is safe and far away from here."

"I wonder why he's so pressed to have her back?" I had my theories but didn't know if it even mattered to mention them to her. From the little I knew, she was protective of her work and, by extension, protective of the women she helped.

"You think she stole more than money?"

"Or destroyed it, not necessarily took it with her."

"Yeah, I've been thinking the same. What she took was insignificant to what he probably makes while dealing," she reasoned.

"So you're not tight that she might have put you in a precarious situation?"

"I knew what I was getting myself into when I started this work." She shrugged, and I wanted to rail at her for her lack of care for her well-being, but then she stared at me, and the thread of fear in her eyes called to something in me.

"Doesn't mean you get to be careless with your safety because I—we all care." Shit, I almost slipped.

"Ok...ok," she begrudgingly agreed and squeezed my

hand. The gesture was innocent, but I was primed after everything that had transpired between us the night before. The threat of danger concerned me but at the same time... I couldn't deny that having the opportunity to step beside Sal and block any threat made my blood sing in anticipation. If only in my mind, I got to call her mine to protect, mine to keep safe.

Then she tried to let go. I pulled her hand, a grunt escaping her, making my dick respond. I could sense her, her pheromones calling to me. How had I missed that she smelled like licorice, one of my favorite sweets? How her tongue flicked to moisten her top lip when she was nervous? And how had I missed how fucking alluring my name sounded from her mouth?

"Devon..." Was that a warning or an invitation?

I stayed quiet, her hand shaking inside of mine. Without breaking eye contact with me, she pulled out her cell phone. Her thumb moved impressively fast; then, a vibration went off in my pocket. My entire focus was on Sal, on how her nose flared when she heard the vibration, on the crimson creeping up above her 'Eat, Sleep, Anime, Repeat' tee, but her eyes urged me to look at my cell phone. I pulled it out and stared impatiently at my screen.

The gif of an ivory candle flickered at me. For a second, everything in me froze.

Before I could react, Sal stormed out of the car, and the loud slam of the door spurred me to action.

I calculated how long it would take me to get to her and gave her a few seconds of headway. She couldn't run fast enough, and we both knew it. My laughter rang in the car as my lower limbs tingled, my primal instinct activating at Sal's invitation.

I stepped out of the car, and my heart raced as Sal sped

through the parking lot. Blood rushed to my ears, my eyesight sharpened, and I pounded the asphalt lot, eating up the headway I'd gifted her.

"You can run, but we both know what's gonna happen," I taunted her.

She pushed the door open with a blast. For an instant, I worried we should have kept our chase to my apartment, but then her husky laugh greeted me as the door shut closed, and my brain short-circuited. My target sped away, and I needed to capture her. My thoughts disintegrated into primitive instincts.

My steps echoed in the hallway as I charged through the door. Sal's laugh trailed behind her as she raced toward the elevator. My apartment was on the second-highest floor, and the adjacent garage lot didn't go as high. I bolted behind her, attempting to get her before the elevator arrived. The elevator chimed its arrival, and Sal's heavy sigh of relief followed. I was gaining ground behind her.

"You might as well stop now," I warned, my veins full of volcanic desire for her.

"Fuck off." She laughed, and that husky sound would be the background music of all my future jerk-off sessions.

Sal made the mistake of checking on my approach; her beautiful brown eyes dilated in excitement. She took my breath away. She almost tripped in her haste to get in the elevator, and I was so close I could smell her sweet licorice scent and her mouthwatering arousal. Stunned at the power of the need coursing through me, my muscles moved too slowly, my fingers grazing her just a second before she slithered away from me into the elevator. The last thing I saw was her smirk as the elevator doors closed on me.

Impatience coursed through me, leaving me raw in its wake. The next elevator chimed five seconds after Sal had ascended, and I hurried, hoping it would be empty. Luck was on my side, and the elevator went straight to my floor, the smooth doors sliding open as Sal raced toward my apartment.

The thumping of my heart was so hard it made my ears vibrate with the beat. Charging after Sal, my mind rejoiced, and my dick hardened, relishing the chase.

If I truly wanted to catch her, I could, but she was enjoying herself too much. I was enjoying myself too much. The worries that threatened to overwhelm us, overwhelm her, simmered down in the thrill of the chase.

That husky laugh lured me again as Sal punched the code to the door, then attempted to slam it closed in my face. I anticipated her move, jamming my arm against the wooden door, preventing her from locking me out. Her eyes flashed in defiance, and she probably calculated if it was worth making her stance here but quickly realized it would leave us too exposed and backed herself into the apartment.

I prowled behind her, the taste of victory so fucking close it was delightful.

"You don't scare me," she boasted, looking behind her as she scrambled backward toward the staircase, avoiding the big sectional and the coffee table next to it. I'd already decided it ended here. My dick had turned to steel in my pants, and there was no way I'd make it up the stairs with this erection.

I yearned for Sal, for every moment I'd had to pretend polite interest around her, for every benign conversation I'd tried to start with her just to get her to lower her guard.

"Really, so why are you breathing so hard?" The rise and fall of her chest was mesmerizing, and the ragged breaths out of her lush lips enthralled me. Sal thought she was going to get to the stairs. Cute.

The moment she made her move, I pounced. She turned her back to me to go up the steps, and I pulled her into me, one arm across her soft belly, the other tugging her short curls, the pull just enough to sting.

"You're mine. I tell you when to go and when to stand still," I breathed into her ear. My blood sang triumphantly as I held her in my arms, my skin burning to feel her suppleness. I tightened my grip on her belly and rolled my hips into her soft, abundant ass, and she gasped. Then she tortured me with a slow grind.

"Fuck, Sal, I— *Woof.*" All the air in my lungs fled as a sharp elbow connected with my stomach. A dull ache spread quickly, but I couldn't even feel it; Sal had managed to slip away from me and bolted toward the living room.

"There's...nowhere to go," I gasped and darted behind her. She whooped as she navigated the area, turning to the kitchen as if I'd fall for that. Reversing my direction, I pivoted and stretched an arm out to grab her elbow just as she tried to go up the stairs again.

Sal was hot to the touch, and she glowed with a light sheen of sweat. I could feel my own trickling down my back. I yanked her toward me, her softness crashing into me, and we tumbled down to the floor. I shifted to protect her, and we missed the coffee table, landing on the area rug.

We both breathed together, the cold air of the AC searing through my lungs, calming the inferno inside of me.

Brown eyes were wide in excitement; her lips parted, and freckles danced all over her cheeks and nose. How fucking mind-blowing it was to have Sal like this; beautiful, hot, and sweaty, smelling like licorice, with her scrumptious pussy ready for me.

"You alright?" I asked her.

"Fuck, I usually hate check-ins during this type of play,

but when you do it... Yeah, I'm good." Her eyes crinkled even though she'd attempted to frown.

"How should I check in with you next time?" I understood that in this, breaking the primitive rawness of it all could be jarring, but this was our first time, and I wasn't about to fuck it up with Sal thinking I was reading all her signs correctly. I was dying to rip her biker shorts off and discover what lay beneath, but I wasn't making that move without checking in with her first.

"A quick two taps on my wrist. If I respond with two taps back, good. One tap back, bad." Then with that quick check, she tried to buck me, and she almost achieved it.

"Fucking stay still," I growled at her, but she refused.

We fought for dominance, our arms entangling. She suddenly became Ursula, all limbs as I attempted to subdue her. Sal's ragged breath increased in tempo and volume as she fought me for dominance, trying to buck me again.

I yanked one arm above her head, trapping it in one hand. She clawed at me with her free hand, wiggling her trapped one until I gripped hold of one of her breasts and squeezed it hard.

"Mmmm, oh god, Devon," she moaned, and I almost came right there. This was too much for our first time, too much to take, savor, and encompass. My dick wanted to strain out of my dance pants and sink into Sal's invitation.

I squeezed her tit harder until her nipple poked my palm, and she yelped in pleasure-pain.

"Stay fucking still," I reminded her, and her gaze was full of aroused defiance. Before she could formulate her next move, I forcefully grabbed her other arm above her head and locked both wrists under my hold.

"Next time, I'm gonna need cuffs, Ursula."

"Next time you won't catch me, Mufasa, with all your growling." I guffawed at her snipe.

My hand itched to sink into her softness again, but this time I needed to touch her bare skin. I tugged her tee up, and her ample tits emerged, her sandy brown skin covered in freckles here too.

"Oh, I'm gonna love licking each one of these," I promised, pressure building in my spine, but for now, I palmed her breast, then switched to the other as Sal moaned her approval.

"Yes, baby, I just want to make you feel good." I bent closer to her, then sharp teeth sank into my shoulder, and I felt my skin break. I didn't let her go, but the bite startled me enough that she wiggled her way out from under me and unlocked her arms. A surge of pure hunger drove me, and I tackled her as she attempted to crawl away from me. Her startled, husky giggle made my dick twitch in desperation. Enough.

With her soft body under me again, I wasted no time.

"You play too much." I ripped her shorts and underwear down as she shimmied, still fucking trying to escape. Her determination was such a turn-on.

Sal's pussy smelled so good I wondered if she'd stay still enough for me to taste her, but then she tried to buck me yet again, making my heart skip a beat.

Pressing all my weight on her, I pulled my pants off. She tangled her hands with mine to aid my efforts. At this point, we were both working on the same goal. I rejoiced at the melodic sounds of her moans and groans.

"Fuck, you're so wet, Sal," I groaned when my fingers greeted the silky wetness between her legs, and still she locked her thighs around my hand, preventing further movement. Then in a surprising twist, she started humping my hand in undulating moves, with my dick trapped against her soft belly, and I was afraid I would come. This shit was too good; it had never been this raw with anyone else. And I hadn't even been inside her yet. Thank God we'd discussed our statuses because I'd be tempted to fuck her bare even without knowing we had each other's results and she took the pill.

"I need to be...I need inside." I'd lost all sense of poise; only instinct carried me now.

Sal thrashed under me, eyes closed, but whatever she heard in my voice made her stare up at me. Her eyes softened for a second, then she opened below me. I raised up, trusting she wouldn't try to run anymore, and lined up my aching dick with her entrance.

We stared at each other, her brown eyes and their black speckles mesmerizing me. A triumphant growl escaped me as Sal's heat enveloped my dick. Everything stopped. The stillness of the room became palpable. There was no noise; we both had stopped breathing. Her tongue snaked over her bottom lip, and we continued to stare at each other.

"Kiss me," Sal whispered, and a warm shiver ran through me. The hair on my arms rose as I lowered myself to meet her lips.

The kiss was the opposite of everything that had just happened between us. There was a soft vulnerability and sweetness in the swipe of her tongue, then she sucked mine into her mouth, and I groaned in appreciation. My chest tightened with emotions that were better left unnamed, and our bodies naturally connected with each other in every way they could. Sinking into Sal as she kissed me senseless was the most sensual experience I'd ever had. She was hot and snug, and I knew right there and then that she'd be my undoing.

Pussy shouldn't feel this good. This was criminal.

My strokes were erratic from the get-go as our tongues continued to tangle. I'd been so amped up during our play that my legs already felt heavy, almost numb with pleasure. My spine tightened, and my balls contracted as I savored Sal in deep, hard strokes that made her quiver every time I bottomed out. She let my lips go.

"Yes, please, fuck me hard. It's been so long," she confessed, and that shit just made me thrust harder inside her. The knowledge that I had the privilege to be inside her when she hadn't done this in a while was intoxicating. That she had let me in, even if just in this, was humbling.

"It's been long for me too." I owed her that confession back. The slickness of our lower bodies made movement so easy. Her shirt was still tugged up, and I nipped her nipple, then laved it with loving care as I surged inside of her. Sal didn't stay still under me. That was no surprise; she met every thrust, and her quivering pussy had me in a grip that would stay with me for days.

Hooking one leg over my hips, Sal opened to me, and I immediately increased the speed of my strokes, my dick growing impossibly hard. Every nook of her pussy surrounded my length, and her quivers began to intensify.

"I'm about to come," she said.

"Yes, fucking come for me; make me come with you," I ordered. She didn't disappoint. Again, our gazes collided, and she ground her pussy against me.

I'd made sure to position myself in a way that hit her clit every time I stroked her, and she took advantage of the angle to stimulate herself even more. I crushed her into me, pressing all my weight down on her, unable to keep eye contact any longer.

I had no control over my expression. No control over my

words, no control over my body. Our first time and I was afraid to strip myself bare to her. I bit her neck, and she shuddered, then she gripped my dick in a vice, her orgasm fluttering around me, her moans a constant song in my ear.

"Fuuuuck," she groaned in my ear, and fuck if that wasn't the best thing I'd ever heard.

Her orgasm triggered mine, and I emptied myself into her. My dick felt like a new entity surrounded by her throbbing pussy, and I kept coming and coming.

"Oh, Sal, ohhh fuck!" I cried out and collapsed on top of her, sure she had just ruined me for all others.

Fourteen

"My dick is ruined. No other pussy will ever do."

Devon sighed as he lay staring up at the ceiling. I snorted in response.

My muscles stopped working the moment I came. I sprawled next to him, the scent of our sex mingling in the air. I didn't even have the energy to fix my t-shirt. Tits out, my pants ripped, letting my pussy breathe after its stellar performance. I should give her a pat.

"You gonna move?" Devon asked.

"Yeah," I responded, but the channel from brain to muscles short-circuited, and instead of standing, I burrowed into Devon. The heat of his body felt wonderful as my skin started to cool under the cold air.

"Do you want to talk about today?"

"About us fucking? I guess it was inevitable." I shrugged, but inside, I was freaking out. I couldn't let him see, though. I didn't think fucking him would be this damn good. How was I supposed to pretend he annoyed me when I wanted another go on his ride?

"Not about us fucking, even though I don't mind that topic."

"Alright," I answered and stretched, rubbing my side against him.

"Ever."

"Ok." I closed my eyes and rested my head on his chest, enjoying where his scent of salty sea and citrus was stronger. I wanted to lick him, figure out the taste of his skin.

"Just to make it clear," he continued, and I realized I had lost track of our conversation.

"Wait a minute, what are you babbling on about?" I tried to rise to look at him, but it was a failed attempt. The rumble of his laughter felt like the crash of waves on the shore, and for a second, I imagined having this with him for more than the occasional fun I planned to extract from him during these next few months we lived together.

"I don't even fucking know. But my original question wasn't about us having sex."

"That wasn't sex," I interrupted him. "That was hard-core fucking. And I loved it."

"I knew you'd be a freak. I just knew it."

"I'll take that as a compliment." I rolled off his chest, sad to lose his heat, but I needed a flat surface under me. I lay on my side, propping my head up on my fist.

"As you should."

I definitely wanted to ride him again. He lay with his arms crossed behind his head, his eyes closed in contentment. I took the time to study him now that he was devoid of that sweet, easygoing mask he put on with everyone else. He did it with me too, but I'd seen more lately. I'd noticed glimpses of the real him.

"So, what was the question about?" I asked him.

"About that dude, coming to the studio trying to fuck with you."

"Can I be honest?"

"Are you never not honest?"

"True. Well, I'll deal with what's coming."

"*We*. We will deal," he interrupted, and warmth spread through my chest at his words. I didn't plan on depending on him for much, but the fact that he felt so strongly about his support was comforting.

"Yeah, well, I don't want to talk about it tonight. Not 'cause I'm a punk but because...well, this is nice. Just talking to you for tonight. Getting to know you a little." I said the last bit quickly, afraid to lose my sense of closeness with him. I wouldn't spill all my guts to him, but telling him a little...was tempting.

I cupped his cheek, turning his head to stare in my direction, his soulful brown eyes studying me for a while, then he nodded once as if he'd come to a conclusion and went back to staring at the ceiling.

"What you wanna know?"

"How come even though you and Aisha were in the same circle, she had no idea about your kink? From what she's told me, there was a group of dancers who all hung out with each other in that sex club she was part of in New York?"

Devon sighed and shifted his legs, getting comfortable on the floor.

"Because I don't share my kink with people that know me. I...I have this persona in my dance world that I've cultivated for years. My kink is mine and private and shows a side of me that might make me intimidating."

"I...I don't get it."

"When I first moved to the States, to Florida, the first company I joined was not diverse." Devon shifted to face me, mirroring my pose.

"Some dancers, especially the white women, were suspicious of me at first. Always tentative around me. I was a tall Black dude with dreads in that sea of white, and they didn't know what to do about me. I kept to myself and realized how they perceived me. See, I'd lived my whole life in Jamaica. Of course, there were white people there, but *we* are the majority. Delroy had warned me about what I would encounter once I moved, but I hadn't been ready, y'know? So here I am, this tall Black dude—back then, I was a bit bulkier, so even more intimidating—and I was quiet." He paused.

"Because you're shy." I nodded.

"Yeah, so of course, that translated to scary, intimidating dude. And from Jamaica? Even more. So, I kept to myself, and I worked hard. I've always been a good-humored man. Always. I also knew how to show people what they wanted to see. At home with my parents in Jamaica, I was manly. Never making them doubt my sexuality, even though my orientation was my business. With these people, I was extra polite and nice to everyone, always smiling because I realized how people reacted around me when I was serious. I learned to present myself in a way that seemed less...less threatening to my fellow dancers. And it worked. But then...then the invitations started." Devon broke eye contact, his eyes glazing as he stared into the distance, some memories returning to him.

"The invitations?"

"The sexual invitations. They wanted to fuck the big Black dude. I mean, I'm not even that big. Just taller than some of the other dancers. One dancer said she wanted to hop on my Big Black Cock."

"What the fuck?" What was wrong with people? I was outraged on his behalf while Devon just lay next to me, head propped up, face relaxed as if this was any ol' conversation.

"Yeah, so I decided then and there I wasn't gonna shit where I worked, y'know?" he said, his accent deepening as he settled into his story. "By the time I left, wanting to work in a more diverse company, I found the Harlem troupe. It sucked moving away from Delroy, but at the time...it was the right move." He paused, and there was something in that pause, a different quality to his tone of voice, that stayed with me.

Why had it been right to move away from his brother? I refocused as he continued.

"By then, I'd been in Florida for a...while, and my instinct to show only what people wanted to see continued. Of course, I was now with people like me; many immigrants came with the company via work visas, so we had similar stories. I didn't hide from my colleagues, but I didn't show them everything. So that group that all did kink together wasn't my vibe. I heard of the parties they did and the stuff they explored. They invited me a few times but got tired once they realized I wouldn't attend. Anything I did was away from my job and my colleagues. They didn't need to know about my private life." Devon stayed quiet, his beautiful brown eyes trained on me, the silence between us the type that made your muscles relax and your mind wander, content in the knowledge no effort needed to be done to entertain anyone.

"I get it. I...people say they want to know the whole of you, but rarely are they genuine about that. I know some are, and for those that really are, I always give them a chance. But I'm not out here holding my breath for people to want to know me." It was my turn to lie on my back, searching the ceiling for whatever, wondering if Devon had found words of truth and comfort above us.

"So what did it for you? What made you hide?" he whispered.

Again, the similarities between both of us were uncanny. We both felt it, even though I did my level best to ignore it. Our cheeriness and moodiness were opposite sides of the same damn coin, and Devon prodded to reveal that other side.

I didn't know if this was a good idea, if talking about these things, opening up our pasts would entangle us more in the present. We needed to be allies and friends; nothing messy to threaten his status here, or my safety. Nothing to complicate things. But I was so drawn to Devon. There was a pull I couldn't ignore when I was around him, no matter how much I wanted to pretend I was unaffected.

So here I lay, thinking of letting Devon see under my shell to what lay beneath.

"Well, I've told you about my mom."

"Yeah."

Devon shifted closer to me and ran his palm down my exposed belly, letting it linger close to my fupa. His warm palm cupped underneath my belly button, where my stomach was the softest, and I sighed, wanting to feel that heat everywhere.

"So, it probably started there. My mom used to tell my grandpa I was a duppy, planted with her daughters to confound her life."

"Is your moms from the Caribbean?"

"Her mom was half-Jamaican, half-American. Mom

knew her American side more than anything, but yeah, I have some Jamaican in me."

"You have a whole lot now through injection," Devon deadpanned, and I held back the laughter that wanted to fizz out. I couldn't believe he had just said that, and I wondered why it felt like someone had thrown confetti inside my belly.

"I'mma ignore that."

"There is no ignoring it. But you try to do that," he said with a satisfied smirk.

"Anyway...I fell in love. Tale as old as time. It wasn't what my mom had envisioned for me. I'd fallen in love with the boy next door, who went to my school and loved anime the same as I did and hadn't a lick in the bank. I was a senior in high school and wanted to move out of my mom's, tired of her weird obsession with our appearance and us catching older boyfriends. It was all ick as fuck."

Devon's face clouded as his eyes grew murderous, his anger palpable.

"Nothing like that, no, no. She would push for us to be ready for when we were *older*, but older was just eighteen and above. She never did anything anyone could miscon-strue as illegal. But the messaging was clear. We needed to present ourselves in a certain way to attract a certain type of man. And my little school boyfriend wasn't that.

"It was great because I was sticking it to my mom, and at the same time, I was spending time with the love of my life. Or so I thought. So, to show him I loved him, I made a video game. I'm romantic like that," I deadpanned. "Only the video game blew up online, and I started making bread. I ignorantly opened a joint bank account with him because we were planning to move in together."

Devon frowned, and I reached out and gently ran my

palm down his face, hoping the gesture would relax his expression. He tightened his grip on my belly, then pulled me closer to him, our bodies now touching. Every nerve ending that connected to his skin crackled and vibrated under his touch. I sighed. The attraction was one thing, but this? This ran deeper than attraction; this was something on the molecular level, and I didn't want to even think what that meant.

"Mhm?" He urged me to continue.

"Yeah, sorry, I got distracted."

His amusement was evident, the reverberation of his silent laughter shaking me as well. Fuck, I could imagine nights just like this, just laughing together.

No, this wasn't that type of story. I needed to stop daydreaming. We'd married for convenience, and I'd best remember we had an expiration date. This was how it started with men, and it was how it had started with my ex: all deep connections and new and exciting emotions. I knew better now.

I knew better.

"Funny. Listen, I gotta go to bed." I stretched, pretending to be unaffected, then sat up, detangling myself from his tempting heat and comforting laughs.

"What?" He scowled, then sat up as I stood, fixing my shirt to cover my lower half. I was gonna have to Winnie the Pooh my way out of this one.

"Don't do that." He shook his head, still sitting on the floor with his strong legs bent and his arms crossed resting over his knees, watching me as I gathered my pants and underwear.

"Don't do what?" I felt a different type of heat emerging from within. The kind of heat that gathered when I was frustrated, and I didn't want to be frustrated with Devon. I didn't need him to push for more than I had to give. I was already giving him a lot.

"Don't shut down."

"Mhm..." I stared at him for a minute, deciding to tell him the rest of my story.

"When I started making money, I placed it all in our joint account. My video game sold 10,000 units on the first day. I charged $10 a head. I'd made more money than my mom had ever tried to swindle out of any dude on any given day. And like a dumbass, I saved it in the account. We had put down a deposit for our little studio apartment. I thought I was grown, about to move out of my Momma's house. No such luck."

Devon frowned, probably guessing what was coming next.

"In the days leading up to our move, he started acting weird. His dad had been giving him a hard time about us moving in together, and he started to distance himself from me. I should've known. I arrived at the apartment to find out he'd withdrawn the deposit. I went to the bank, and he had depleted the account. I didn't have a leg to stand on. I quickly diverted my earnings to a new account he had no access to, but he had vanished. Come to realize he'd taken the money and moved out of town with his pops. I'll never know what happened, but Calvin was gone."

Devon's jaw clenched, and finally, he stood up, my eyes following him. I refused to look away.

"So yuh think I like yuh likkle ex-boyfren? Mi a grown man, don't get it twisted, Sal." He stood, feet wide, stance menacing, his sculpted chest gleaming in the living room light. His accent—he'd let go of the more Americanized cadence he usually spoke with and gave me his unvarnished self. And my pussy caved and became his biggest stan. I inhaled the scent of sea and sex surrounding him, letting the air calm my racing pulse.

"I know. I know you're a man. But I don't make the same mistakes over and over, and you best remember that." And with that warning, I left him behind, his eyes following me all the way up the stairs.

Fifteen

Devon

Sweat beaded down my back as I limped my way across the parking lot. The sweltering heat signaled the early arrival of the summer. Not that South Florida had any semblance of four seasons—it could be December and still be hot like today. I craved Jamaica on days like this, where the oppressive heat couldn't compare with the island's warmth tempered by the sea breeze.

The potential threat loomed over us but couldn't cloud over the two weeks Sal and I'd had. During breakfast after the night we first fucked, we'd discussed what we knew of the situation and concluded the man still hadn't singled Sal out for anything concrete, which meant they were still trying to figure out who Oriole was and how to get to her.

I put my phone away after making an order for dinner as I hobbled to the elevator, thinking of Oriole, Sal's Robin Hoodesque identity.

In the past few days, she'd taken the time to explain Oriole's persona more in detail, how she actually had social media presence and communicated with women in need through private encrypted chats.

Every minute I spent with her, lust and growing interest simmered in the pit of my stomach, ready to be aired whenever I was ready. I couldn't give proper space to the infatuation I had with my fake wife. To how I ran home to hang out with her. To how my thoughts trailed off and morphed into memories of our night together. Of the touch of her skin and the cadence of her moans, the tightness of her pussy, and the glimpse of the girl she once was. She'd let me in, if only for an hour, and I was hungry for more.

More Sal.

I'd kept to my promise of letting her call the shots in our casual sexual arrangement, and she hadn't sent me another gif, so we danced around each other day and night, the decadent tension tempting me to change the rules of engagement. But something told me I had to let Sal keep the pace. She'd been the one to set our speed from day one, from tentative friendship to growing trust to her bringing me into her circle and then accepting my proposal. It all had been set by her, and damn if I wasn't content to follow that lead for now.

I rotated my heels before opening my door, wanting to avoid Sal noticing the limp. She had enough concerns with everything happening to her to have to carry one more worry. I swung the door open and felt the mask go over me, ill-fitting in my home, around her.

"Wa gwaan, wifey?" I'd taken to calling her that in the past few days because it made her eyebrows twitch. She was sitting on the kitchen island on her laptop, and she didn't look up, but her sculpted right eyebrow raised, and I stifled a laugh.

"I told you to stop calling me that."

"But you're my wife." I grinned when she closed her laptop and crossed her arms. No bra today, the fucking tease. There was no way she wasn't aware of how her nipples poked out in greeting anytime I was around. And a sleeveless tee, the side cleavage utterly distracting. I refused to let my eyes roam...at least not too much.

"Stop calling me wifey, or I'll call you hubby."

My mask slipped for a minute, and I cringed.

"Mhm." She raised her eyebrow, smug at catching my reaction.

"I can deal with *hubby* if it means I get to call you wifey."

The eye roll she gave me was impressive. I strolled to the fridge, reaching for a bottle of water.

"Why you limping?" Sal asked in the same tone one would say, "Why did you kill all my puppies?"

I kept moving around the kitchen, attempting to minimize the hobble as I cut a mango.

"Hubby, dear," Sal said in a sticky sweet tone that I never wanted to hear again.

"What's up, pretty wifey?" I pivoted to face her, and she was scowling at me.

"You worked too hard today," she accused.

"I didn't."

Nah, I did. Even my trainer said I'd done too much. I needed to be back on stage, though. The pull was growing stronger as I grew more confident in my abilities. I'd been dancing since I was twelve and on stage since sixteen. Every muscle in my body knew to dance. It was as necessary as eating, sleeping, and taking a shit. It was what saved my soul from darkness. It just was. It was an essential daily function in my life.

"So, you're just gonna answer in the negative?"

"I gon' eat mi mango salad." I put the mango slices in a bowl and seasoned them with salt, pepper, and vinegar.

The scrape of wood against wood told me Sal had hopped off the stool. I didn't look up; I just kept savoring my mango salad, the pleasant mask in place, hoping she'd leave her concerns alone. Stomps up the steps told me she was annoyed, so I'd probably be eating dinner by myself. Fuck. I'd wanted to hang out with her tonight.

I was about to cave and tell her she was right when she stomped back down the stairs, a foot-soaking tub in her hands.

"Sit down on the sofa," she commanded, not even bothering to see if I would move. She was that bossy. I fucking loved it. Knowing she was like this but liked her kink the way she wanted it... Her complexities were fascinating.

"What you waiting for?" She tapped her foot at me, her plump thigh jiggling below her shorts.

She must have washed her hair today because her light brown curls were slick, and a soft cloud surrounded her face. The downy hair framed her cherub features so well. She'd look so innocent if it weren't for her jaded brown gaze, with her short, pretty lashes, wide button nose, and the scattered freckles across her light brown cheeks. The contrast that was Sal captivated me. I forgot my resolve to keep things uncomplicated with her. I didn't know what I wanted, but I sure as hell didn't want to pretend I was unaffected anymore.

"What's that?" I asked.

"I put some Epsom salts and lavender oil to help with any swelling that might form. Well, the lavender oil is to soothe you. And it's one of those that has the fancy massage and jets. If you're gonna go this hard, you gotta take care of your foot," she said, and it almost sounded like she cared.

My legs tingled, the motion traveling a mix of warmth and cold all up my spine and down my arms at the possibility that Sal might feel the same. I wasn't gonna tell her I had a whole warm pad, compression socks, and ice packs upstairs. These were all things my trainer had suggested I have on hand to treat my tendon on days like this. Her reluctant concern and fussiness made my heart ache, my mind hope, and my dick twitch, even the reactions she elicited from me were layered. It made me yearn for things that were not possible. Sal wasn't meant to be my endgame.

I made my way to the sofa, my smile never wavering as I sat down and sank my feet into the warm water.

"Shiiit, that feels good," I hissed.

"I know. Now sit there for twenty minutes, then I'll bring you some ice to apply. Ok?" said Bossy Sal, crossing her arms under her ample breasts, making the side cleavage more prominent. I searched her face and saw resolve and, dare I hope, concern. But Sal *would* feel concerned for me. I was part of her circle. This was who she was—she might appear detached and aloof, but she was all the way dialed in with her friends. I'd seen it so many times these past months. I'd best keep things light between us like these last two weeks.

"What you gon' do in the meanwhile, wifey?"

She padded back to the kitchen island, retrieved her laptop, and then plopped herself on the opposite end of the sectional.

"I'm gonna chat with my friends."

"The two mysterious online whizzes?" She'd told me about the two other women she collaborated with online.

"Yes," she deadpanned, and her fingers flew over her keypad, the speed impressive.

I flexed my foot in the hot water, the scent of the lavender calming.

"So, what are y'all talking about today?"

"One of my friends, Cora, the one in Seychelles, is the contact for the ladies we help after they leave. They never contact me because if the worst happens, it doesn't make sense that the one person that lives in the US knows their whereabouts. My friend knows and keeps that information encrypted away from the rest of us. If we were to need to help someone, then my friend would disseminate the info as needed."

"So y'all talking about Juniper?"

"Yeah, checking to see if she's good. She'll confirm all is well, with no other details. It'll help me sleep better at night. Then I'll see if I can take other Oriole cases, straightforward ones."

I loved how Sal had slowly opened up more as the days progressed. She didn't mince words and was economical in her communication, but she no longer hoarded her thoughts; it was addictive.

"You're amazing, y'know that? You're in potential danger but more worried about Juniper and planning to take on more cases?"

"She's the one truly in danger if her ex finds her, not me. I'm just the person in the middle, and they don't even know it's really me." She shrugged and kept typing.

I settled into my seat, the click-clack of Sal's typing lulling me for a minute. My eyes were shutting down when I jumped, water sloshing out of the tub as a growling sound reverberated in the room.

"What's that?" I swiveled back and forth, searching for whatever animal had somehow infiltrated my fortress.

Sal mumbled something as I pushed to get up, and I stared at her as she gestured for me to sit back down.

"What was that?" I couldn't have heard right. It sounded like a lion had trekked from the savannas into my spot.

"You don't have to exaggerate; my stomach wasn't that bad."

"That Mufasa growl was your stomach?"

"You're supposed to be Mufasa," she grumbled.

"Clearly not. I mean that shit...damn, Ursula, you hangry?" I beamed at her.

She shook her head, her eyebrows knitting together. She rubbed her belly, the tee shifting over her, and for a second, I forgot she was hungry and that I'd already ordered dinner from her favorite Chinese spot and followed the places the fabric bunched and straightened. The most mundane gestures turned me on.

Damn, her pussy really had ruined my dick.

"I can't even focus on this latest animation Cora just sent me for my video game, I'm that hungry. Let me go figure out what we can have for dinner."

Now it was my turn to motion her to stay.

"Nah, you good. I already ordered."

My phone rang as if the driver had been waiting for those words.

"What's up, Chris?" I greeted one of the security guards downstairs.

"You ordered some Chinese?"

"Yeah, can you bring it up?"

"You know I'm good for that. I need to do my rounds anyway."

"Thanks. I owe you, man; you know I got you."

I hung up and grinned at Sal.

"So you'd already ordered from Mr. Chen?"

I nodded, satisfied to see red creep up over her tee. She rubbed her hand between her breasts. Was she as confused as I was by these feelings? It was as if she tried to calm herself with that soft caress in such a vulnerable place. Next time she sent me a gif, I planned to kiss her there, soothe away whatever anxiety gathered that she kept hidden away from everyone.

"Why are you staring at me? You're weird." She scoffed, but I saw the slight upturn of her lips and the crinkles at her eyes as she jumped up to answer the door.

I stayed sitting, the myriad of emotions overwhelming.

"Thanks, Chris— What are you doin' here?" I turned to see Mila with the food.

"I was just checking in with security when Chris said he was going upstairs, so he let me in. You know I'm on the official super-secret list." Mila strolled into my apartment and placed the bags on the counter, immediately opening them and pulling plates from the cabinet.

Any other day, I'd be glad to see Mila, but right now? I wanted alone time with Sal. We lived together, but I was jealous of every second that didn't translate to quality time with Sal.

"Wa gwaan, Mila?" I stood up, politeness too ingrained in me to stay sitting, soaking my feet.

"Sit down," Sal grunted from the kitchen as she helped Mila serve dinner. We stared at each other for a second, her gaze implacable, mine amused. I sat down again, conceding for now. I needed her to send that text ASAP.

"I thought you both probably needed some company," Mila chatted as she finished serving. I watched as Mila went to get my plate, but Sal had already grabbed it with a glass of ginger ale and marched toward me. She placed the plate in my hands and the drink on the coffee table before me. Then she went back to get her own, and Mila followed behind, her head swiveling between both of us.

Sal reclaimed her seat on the opposite end of the sectional, and Mila sat on the armchair across from us.

"So, what's new?" Mila asked as Sal and I ate. I now understood why Sal did what she sometimes did. I really didn't want to speak much; maybe if we were quiet enough, Mila would take the hint and leave after dinner. I felt awful for putting that energy out there, but not enough to stop.

"Nothing," Sal answered for the two of us.

Mila paused mid-chew and studied us both.

"Right... I also came for something else. That dude, he was checking out your apartment again."

I froze at the news.

"Which one?" Sal asked.

Which one? This was our life right now. This was Sal's life. It was such a sobering reminder.

"Oh, I didn't think to ask, now that you mention. It might have been Souza, but I'll check. I emptied your fridge and put some baking soda in there just to keep it fresh."

"Thanks, Mila," Sal said, then kept eating, unbothered.

"So that's it?" Mila asked.

"Well, we don't know who it is, but I meant to tell both of you I made some headway with that picture you gave me." Sal smiled at me, and that shit hit me like a ray of sun on Hellshire Beach.

"What did you find?" Mila asked as I had lost the ability to speak.

"Nothing much at first...but then once I went into the dark web, I found an odd match. This dude used to be a cop like fifteen years ago, then all his records were removed from the local database. Like he does not exist. I looked him up under his government name, James Perez, and same shit. He had a house, was married, paying bills, then nada. It shows a divorce around the same time his record was removed. Then James Perez doesn't exist for fifteen years until that pic you took of him."

"Wow, you really walked into some shady shit, didn't you?" Mila said, slowly chewing her food, her fear evident. Sal scoffed, which meant she was probably spooked too. Before I could say anything, Mila rearranged her features, and Sal relaxed.

What the heck did this all mean about James Perez? I had to share some of this with Delroy, see what he thought. This web tangled around Sal made no sense.

"Are you gonna try to reach Souza and your brothers?" Mila asked, posing the other question we had danced around for days.

"Well, I want to," Sal answered, and my stomach knotted. It wasn't a good idea; what if this was a ploy to bring her out? What if Souza and Perez knew each other?

"If it's true, it's exciting news, isn't it?" Mila said gently, and I understood; she came from an overall tight family. Sal's experience was alien to her, so, for Mila, this revelation was exciting. But I had my doubts.

"It is." Sal agreed and took a bite, then stared at me. I shook my head, unable to agree with the idea of her meeting this brother but also acutely aware it wasn't my place to say.

But then, Sal surprised me; she made a non-committal head bob, then nodded. I felt lighter at her silent message. Elated, I grinned at her. The entire moment was mere seconds but momentous.

"Oh my God! I told Aisha the two of you were fucking, but she didn't want to believe me. And don't deny it! I know Sal, even when she thinks she is masking her thoughts. I'm gonna leave because, clearly, I'm the third wheel here. Let me call Aisha and Knox to see if Trin is away. Being the third wheel with them is way more satisfying." Mila got up. "But I'mma take all the leftovers, ok? I don't feel like cooking tomorrow."

Sal stared at her, then rolled her eyes and kept eating.

I wanted to laugh but followed wifey's example.

She might be onto something here.

Sixteen

The morning light filtered through my bedroom, and I stretched in bed, wondering why it had woken me up. I wasn't an early riser, and having to lay low at Devon's meant I could indulge and sleep in. A knock sounded on the door, and I scrambled to pull the sheets up to cover my bare breasts.

"Can I come in?" His muffled voice resonated in my room.

"Eh, sure."

Devon had already seen me practically naked that night. We'd fucked each other's brains out, but I still preferred to cover up.

He strolled in, then stopped in his tracks when he realized the state of undress I was in, the blanket covering my chest.

"Morning," he said in that deep, rich voice of his. I stretched my legs under the covers, then crossed them.

"Morning," I nodded, waiting expectantly. Since I'd

moved in, he'd never come to my room, giving me privacy once I stepped through this door. Staying with him had put us in close quarters since day one but having him in the one space I dared to think of as mine made things seem more real between us. The spacious room suddenly felt warmer, homier with him inside. But innocent thoughts were far from my mind.

He looked scrumptious wearing a muscle tee, his lean muscles smooth—I now knew that for a fact. He had on his pleasant smile, his full lips surrounded by that beard of his that had me dreaming of seats and thrones last night. I uncrossed and recrossed my legs and cursed the fact I didn't have my laptop to escape the intensity of my reaction to him.

"I left you some ackee and saltfish downstairs; not sure if your grandma ever cooked that fah yuh, but it's some good food. Oh, I got the confirmation that my request for status change is in. I'll keep you updated. I'm gonna see Delroy today, so I moved my therapy early. See you later?" He stared at me expectantly, waiting for something from me. I wasn't sure what, but I felt his gaze morph from friendly to heated. My hands itched to move the covers and invite him into my bed instead of allowing him to abuse his feet again.

"I...thank you," I answered, teasing my upper lip with my tongue, the caress a poor substitution for what I really wanted to feel right now.

"Alright then, see you later. Be good, ya hear?" he said, and I wondered at this comfort of relaxing his accent around me. I'd been around him enough to know he only softened it when he spoke to family and friends or about his brother. I couldn't deny the shiver that ran through me; his eyes seemed to be burning through the sheets to see what lay beneath. Fuck, this man made me hungry.

"I'm never good." I shook my head, wanting to break the tension. He'd just been about to leave the room but stood stock still. Then, before I could react, he was braced over me, his arms stretched, trapping me between them. His heat and scent surrounded me. I stared up at him defiantly because I am who I am and I never back down, and he watched me back with such earnest regard I had to look away.

"You're good. Such a good person. You're not nice, but you're good, and that is why I can't seem to let this be what it was supposed to be."

I admired his lips, the urge to kiss him making me shake until I pulled him into me, sighing in triumph as I tasted him. He took his time exploring my mouth, licking, biting, then sucking my tongue until I moaned in absolute pleasure.

I'd let go of the sheets when I grabbed him, and I loved the feel of his tee against my bare chest. Things were getting real interesting when he pulled back.

"Listen, I have to go, but make sure you send me that text later, ok?" He stared at me, our ragged breaths loud in my room.

"Ok, I will."

He gazed a little longer, then nodded once, pushing away from me.

My body tingled as he swaggered out, and I knew I'd be keyed up the whole day, but Devon's sweet smile at my promise would stay with me the most. I was grown enough and woman enough to admit I wanted to trust him entirely. It was scary to think what things could be if we both opened up fully to each other.

After eating the breakfast Devon left for me, I took a long shower and washed my hair. Two hours later, I stood in the spacious bathroom following my hair routine, massaging my scalp and moisturizing my coils. As I finished, my phone vibrated, and I saw it was a video call.

"Mila, we aren't the Jetsons."

"Says the software engineering hacker and video game developer," Mila replied with her usual sass.

"What do you want?" I asked and saw her roll her eyes at my lovely greeting.

"Wait, wait, I'm gon' connect Aisha."

"What's going on, ladies?" Aisha answered from her office at the studio.

"Aisha, when I get there, you need to pay up: Sal and Devon are fucking."

"I don't have time for this." I attempted to hang up, but Aisha's shout was so loud I froze before pressing the end button.

"Is it true?!" Aisha stared at me, and I felt that same flutter I'd first thought was indigestion but soon realized was my body's annoying reaction to all things Devon.

"Why do we have to tell each other everything? What happened to privacy?"

"Girl, please, you know you signed that shit away when you accepted Aisha's friendship invitation letter in the third grade."

"A decision I've regretted ever since," I deadpanned, and Aisha giggled.

"See, you got Aisha giggling. Poised, centered Aisha!" Mila said.

"This is a pointless call. I'm not telling you anything."

"Oh, man! I always wondered about Devon's skills. I mean, the man can dance, and those rock-sculpted thighs, I... Yeah, is everything as advertised?" Aisha whispered.

"Is Knox around? Is that why you're whispering about Devon's penis?" I answered loudly.

"Shhhhhh, you know Knox is irrationally possessive," Aisha admonished, then grinned like that shit was cute. Fucking love, it ruined the best of us.

"Listen, can one of you come get me?"

"Why, do you want to come see the old ball and chain at work?" Mila smirked.

"I swear I truly don't understand how this friendship has lasted so long," I lamented.

"Oh please, you love us. Listen, I can't, but I can send Knox over if you like?"

"Oh, that's good 'cause I can't either. I'm rushing from the burlesque club to the studio. We have a staff meeting right before Jazz 1, ugh," said Mila.

I hesitated. I wondered what Knox really thought about everything but figured he'd say something if he wasn't thrilled. I liked him because he wasn't one to hold his peace. He was a straight shooter.

"Ok, tell him to text me when he's downstairs."

"Alright, Salome, don't think I didn't notice you didn't deny you two are fucking."

I hung up the call.

SEVENTEEN

DEVON

THE OFFICIAL LETTER with the country's government stamp sat next to me in my car as I parked outside the prison. I'd read it before driving out to my therapy, and the simple message had danced loops around my brain as I worked my tendon out. I'd already received notice that they had my application.

Now, it was an appointment for my biometrics. I knew what came next after this notice—the interview. Sal and I needed to be a unit by then, comfortable with any questions and able to answer quickly without stress. I felt I knew her; I knew what she liked for dinner and how her face scrunched up when she was annoyed, I knew why she disliked her name and what motivated her, but the rest...

We hadn't put any bank accounts together, and the moment she explained what had happened with her ex, I knew she'd be leery of doing a joint account. We hadn't had any taxes filed together yet, and no bills had been transferred to her name. We needed paperwork to prove a union beyond just pictures and words; the website recommendations were joint accounts, utility bills in the same address— financial ties. Sal and I still led entirely separate lives on paper, regardless of her current address.

Any conversation about making some of these arrangements meant we needed to trust each other, and I wasn't sure we were there yet. For all that Sal was decisive in her life, she took her time warming up to people, and with good reason.

I didn't want to rush her, but I was running out of time. I wanted to share my fears about never dancing and the nights I woke up sweating, visited by my past actions, but I didn't know how she would take it. Could I be that vulnerable with her?

I made my way without much thought, navigating the hallways I'd learned after four years of visiting. I went through the motions at the checkpoint, emptying all my belongings and following the instructions stated as if I'd never seen them before. But it all was for the best reasons, so I didn't stress the process too much. I looked at the state of the prison, always worried about the mold and poor conditions I knew my brother had to endure, and I couldn't do shit about it. And just like every other time, I mapped out the way I would get him out of here. Help him escape. I loved and hated visiting him.

"Wa gwaan, baby bro?" Delroy greeted me as I sat at his table. I did my usual scan and sensed immediately that something was off.

"Wa gwaan?"

"Nah, you first. You got something on your mind." He sat back down and stretched his legs before him, eyeing me. He should know better, but I couldn't stay for long this visit, so I wasn't planning to beat around the bush.

"I got my biometrics appointment."

"Why you vex then?" He straightened, not missing a thing as I stared back.

"I'm not vexed, but I gotta ensure Sal and I have more documents to show in our interview. We had very minimal to send in with the application knowing we had time to build more as we got closer to the interview, but if the biometrics app is already in..."

"Then the interview will soon follow, I hear ya. Just talk to her then." Delroy stated the obvious, and I grinned. His urge to try to fix all my problems would never go away, even though I'd stopped needing that support a long time ago.

"I will, I just... I want her to take her time. To figure out things between us." I sighed, running my fingers through my locs. I never struggled explaining things to Delroy but couldn't explain something I didn't fully understand myself.

"Listen...she agreed to dis. She knew what was at stake; just have the conversation."

"Yeah," I replied, uncomfortable with the ask.

"Also, Carpenter stopped by on Tuesday."

Carpenter was Delroy's top enforcer of a few years. Delroy's operation rarely required a big show of force, but Carpenter did it when necessary. He was the most unassuming, gentle giant you could imagine, but you never wanted to get a visit from Carpenter ordered by Delroy. Doing that job stayed with you. I would know. I had shared with both him and Delroy the news about Perez. Carpenter knew all the chatter on the streets better than me now, so I sat up straight, eager to learn if we had a breakthrough.

"We still can't figure out who Perez is or how he went from being squeaky clean to a dealer. Word is, di gyal robbed his boss. Big time. The dude's actually put outta bolo, hopin' to smoke the gyal out. It ain't good. I won't be surprised if he done the same for Sal, even if he can't fully pinpoint who's she. But me nah buy that. Perez kept going to di ballet studio. Best believe he probably knows who she is and is playin'ndi long game. Be careful; protect her. Do what you gotta do but move strategically. Give Carpenter a call if yuh need backup."

Nothing Delroy said was much of a surprise to me; I had been doing the math myself. And I'd been wondering if I should make a move and neutralize the threat to Sal, but that could cause ripples to Delroy's status in the game and on the streets, and I might not be ready to withstand it. If D was free, it would be a different story.

"Mi nah know enough of that man." I fought the urge to bang my fist on the table. Delroy understood; this wasn't how I moved. I didn't rush in without intel.

"Well, yuh betta handle yuh business. Yuh were there before Carpenter. Yuh know what it takes."

———

DELROY'S WORDS haunted me as I navigated the South Florida traffic to Aisha's studio. I needed to tell Sal what my brother had said, though I loathed worrying her. But we'd promised to keep it 100% with each other, so I needed to figure out how to tell her asap. She and I were getting better, but she still had a way of shutting me down when she didn't want to talk, and I needed this to be a frank conversation.

"Wa gwaan," I greeted Athena and Mila as I strolled into the studio. My class didn't start for an hour, but I'd gotten a text from Sal that she'd caught a ride with Knox, and I wanted to see her. I always wanted to see her.

"Hey, Devon!" the ladies said in unison. Mila was deep

in her iPad screen, probably programming the playlist for her next class.

Sal wasn't at the reception desk, and my bubble of anticipation burst as I scanned the rest of the area. Maybe she hadn't come with Knox after all. Maybe she'd decided to stay at the apartment and work on her video game. It made sense, but I'd felt hopeful knowing she wanted to come to the studio and hang out.

I shook the disappointment and smiled my way through the usual chit-chat with the ladies. If Sal wasn't here, I might as well rehearse the pas de deux the Ballet had asked me to perform in our summer showcase, a subtle way for them to test my strength. The showcase was a collaboration from our best choreographers, each preparing a routine to Afro diaspora contemporary music. They wanted me to perform to "Satisfy My Soul" by Bob Marley, and Jacqueline, the choreographer, had shown me the first part a few days ago.

"I'm gonna rehearse until my class," I told the ladies and made my way to the empty classroom.

I walked in, and my breath caught. Sal stood in front of the barre, her lush leg fully extended and propped up on the poplar wood. The graceful arch of her body draped over her legs. "Come to See Me" by Jill Scott played in the background, and the words slid into my subconscious, hopeful.

The ring I gave her shined under the studio lights, and my heart soared, a roar building inside, pride at the sign that she was, if only for now, mine.

The sight of Sal stretching unfolded like the fabric of a long-ago wish materializing in flesh and blood. A sense of pure hunger and yearning captured me as she dropped her leg gracefully and made the same movement with the other. All this time, I knew she had some dance experience; after all, the previous Mrs. Brown's dance school had catalyzed Sal, Aisha, and Mila's friendship. But she was the only one that hadn't pursued that passion past her formative years, or so I thought.

She dropped her other leg and, with nimble dexterity, moved to do a rond de jambe, then turned around at the barre to face me, an eyebrow raised as she continued moving.

"I wouldn't have added 'creep' to your good guy personality."

"Sorry, I thought the room was empty." I stepped inside fully and shut the door. Sal's mouth quirked up, and I pushed forward.

"You don't sound very sorry to interrupt."

" I'm not," I said, unwilling to look away. "I didn't realize you still dance to this..." I paused, searching for more words as Sal stepped away from the barre and slid down into a front split.

"Nothing to say?" she challenged.

"I... Why haven't you used my dance studio?" For some reason, that was what was nagging me the most. She had the opportunity to do this at home with me. She could have been doing this with me.

"I do; I exercise when you're out. I left earlier than planned, which is why I did my routine here. I'm just finishing now." She raised herself slowly, and I approached, standing behind her.

"I was going to rehearse some of the combinations for the choreography, the ones I dance on my own, but with you here..." The change of songs coincided with the pause in my chest.

"Are you asking me to practice your pas de deux? Aren't you supposed to be focusing on your therapy and listening to your body?" A tinge of concern colored her question as she stood in fifth position in front of the barre again. The mirror reflected Sal in her leotard, a black crop top over it, dance tights, and pointe shoes, and I memorized how beautiful she looked in dance attire. How beautiful she was every day.

"I'm supposed to be getting back on stage," I said calmly. This wasn't something up for debate. If she even got me a little...maybe she'd understand.

"How are your tours en l'air?" she asked with deceptive calm.

Damn. How did she know the one question to ask to completely put me on guard? How did she know that one of my most iconic moves, the reason why choreographers loved working with me, my expertise with intricate turns and jumps, had become a mental block as I continued to strengthen my tendon?

Our gazes connected through the mirror, and a century passed as a connection was created and forged through our eyes. I felt her aura mold, the edges always so sharp around her rounding a bit, just enough for mine to fit closer. Still dangerous, but reachable. I was tempted to open up and tell her all about my worries, but if I did that, I wouldn't be able to teach later.

Instead, I instructed her on the first combination. I wasn't ready to speak about my double and triple tours en l'air, and my other jumps were barely up to my exacting standards. All indications of a bigger problem, but I knew it was all in my mind. It had to be. My body had never failed me before. And without dance... I couldn't think of that.

I asked her to change the music, and she shifted the playlist to "Satisfy My Soul." The first notes started, and it was instant. Our bodies synced up for the first sixteen counts as I walked up to stand behind her. She followed the instructions; her pirouettes, although not perfect, were perfectly functional, her spotting impeccable. She held herself with confidence while she did the arabesque combos as I seized her waist, the warmth of her body making my hand itch to hold on tighter. Her sweet-bitter scent and her perspiration lured me to stand closer than I needed, not giving her the proper space to continue.

"Mufasa..." she warned, but she had that smirk from earlier.

"Ursula..."

"Why are you pushing yourself so much?"

Damn her for asking when no one else does.

"Sal, I... I need to."

"No, you don't. You have other options. You could teach, or you could open a professional company of your own. You could work with your brother... I just don't want you to think you have no other options."

Options. She wasn't incorrect. My tendon still twinged from therapy, but I'd grown adept at ignoring the constant pain. I didn't need to be 100% back; if I could get to ninety-five, I would be good. What Sal suggested wasn't new; many of my old fellow dancers, now friends, had reminded me that with the prestige I'd gained in the dance world, I could take other routes if my foot never recovered to my expectations. And working with my brother...if she only knew. But none of those were options for me. None of those would be like oxygen, which was exactly what performing was for me.

I grunted noncommittally, not wanting to lose this closeness I felt with Sal right now. Her walls weren't completely down, but I felt a mellowing, progressive yield that spoke to trust earned.

"Devon, I see you coming to the apartment limping, exhausted. You do your therapy, practice at home, dictate classes, rehearse with your choreographer. I don't know if you're listening to your body or your foot enough."

She raised her leg gracefully, her arabesque a clean, elegant line, and I held onto her lushness, held onto this open and caring Sal. This Sal who worried about me. That called me nicknames.

We were moving her and me to new territory, and it all felt fragile. I didn't want to upset anything between us, so I nodded through the mirror, unwilling to lie, but accepted that she wasn't wrong about me pushing too hard. But I wasn't any ordinary dancer, and I knew my limits well. Her concern, though, was a warm embrace that I'd accept any day.

We repeated the sixteen counts over and over until we both moved in unison. Regardless of her level of expertise, Sal's style spoke to me and made me want to be dancing this choreography with her. Made me wish for things that suddenly seemed possible.

"I'm willing to help you even though I think you're doing too much. But I see the hunger in your eyes, don't think I don't see it. It's the same hunger I'm feeling right now to run home and design the next scene. That hunger to never stop, always keep moving. It's a compulsion. For me, it's essential." She turned in my arms and pressed herself against me as the music stopped, and the cacophony of children seeped in from outside the door, my students arriving for their class.

I didn't want this space of truth and trust to end. I studied her, her freckles scattered under the lights of the studio, her brown eyes shining with an emotion I couldn't quite place. Once I opened the door, Sal would revert to aloof mode, and I'd switch back to protective mode. And that was alright, but just for now, I'd enjoy us seeing each other without any embellishments. Fitting that it would be while dancing.

"That we can agree upon. That compulsion, that feeling like it's oxygen and you ain't gon' be right if you don't do it... That's it. Right there." I gave her that, at least. I owed her that truth. All the other things I needed to say to her lingered in my mind, but this moment? It had been necessary. It was the stepping stone for everything else to follow. I'd find the time to speak to her later today.

Sal nodded, then raised up to her pointes and whispered in my ear.

"The gif...consider it permanently sent from now on. I'm going home to create myself. I'm inspired."

And just like that, images of Sal naked under me solidified in my mind so strongly I knew they'd been in the periphery the entire time we'd danced. And now all I could think of was getting back home to her.

Eighteen

Devon

The intermediate ballet class stretched never-ending after Sal's departure. She'd caught a ride with Knox, not waiting for my class to start. I never lost patience when instructing, but today as I guided the dancers through a petit allegro, I found myself tapping my foot edgily as my dancers continuously seemed to mess up, the same sissonne tripping them repeatedly. I'd been so excited to teach them the combination as it was for more advanced students, but I knew they could handle it. But my famed calmness had run dry the moment Sal strolled out of the studio with an air of inspired confidence, her tight leggings molding her wide, lush ass. Mila had guffawed at my gawking, turned to Aisha, and loudly whispered, "Told you so."

Now they both were pestering me with questions as I packed up to go home. I had no patience left in me as my fingers tingled in remembrance of Sal's waist as she prome-naded in arabesque or when a little smile emerged as I amped her up after a series of pirouettes that had given her problems the first couple of tries.

"So, are you going home to your wiiiiiife?" Mila sing-songed just to annoy me. I smiled at her and kept putting my iPad and computer in my backpack, then put away my performance shoes.

"He seems awfully in a rush, so he better be," Aisha chimed in.

I shook my head at their persistence and zipped up my backpack. Letting them talk, I walked toward the door, and just when I was about to open it, I glanced back at them both standing by the reception counter.

"I'm going home to my wife, and I plan to stay in…the whole night."

The gasps that erupted as I marched out were worth it.

After breaking every speed limit from the studio to my apartment, I rushed up to find Sal sitting on the couch, mesmerized by the scene she was playing. It looked different than the last one she'd been masturbating to but couldn't be what she had just created as the graphics wouldn't look this crisp if that was the case.

I'd learned a little about Alix and Jax from what I'd pulled out of Sal. I knew how much she thought Alix was a badass and how she sometimes used her as inspiration in her own decision-making. And I knew every single time she'd told me she was going to work on a new scene, it came after a moment when she'd felt strongly about something. I didn't know if she'd put two and two together, but this video game was her pressure-release valve. Funny what weeks of living together had uncovered. The layers of her unveiled themselves to me, little by little, all by process of patience and observation, letting her reveal herself at her own pace.

I stood there for a minute, willing her to turn back to

look at me, but she refused, playing through a scene where Alix was fighting against a sex demon, and Jax was fucking another one in a corner, succumbing to their allure. I wondered what that meant.

At this point, I'd let my primitive need take over, and I didn't have time to play games with her. I didn't even feel like chasing her, but I knew with Sal, I was gonna need to earn this fuck. And I would.

"Sal, I'm home."

She turned and stared back, sitting crisscrossed on the large sectional. She still had her dance tights on but had taken off the leotard and was just wearing the black crop top she had earlier. Her eyebrow raised in challenge, then she turned back to the video game. The entire movement happened in less than seconds, but it felt like long hours to me.

There was a roar building in the pit of my stomach. A hunger so acute I felt a chasm open up; nothing would fill it but the touch of Sal's warm skin against mine. Nothing would appease me but her pliant and soft under me.

I needed this; I needed her the way she let me lead her earlier through the combinations of "Satisfy My Soul." I needed her trust, how she gave me the little snippets of herself interspersed with her sharp tongue and acid remarks. I wanted it all, and I didn't know how to ask because I'd kept myself hidden for so long; I couldn't pull all the truths that needed to be said for her to fully trust me.

She hadn't seen the whole of me. Glimpses, yes. She understood something about me others chose to look past in their focus on the kind, smiling man.

"Sal, if you don't want to be fucked raw right now, I suggest you go upstairs and finish playing there, ya hear?"

A raspy, melodic sound tickled my ears, and it took me a

second to realize it was Sal's giggle. She was fucking chuckling at me, and any other time, I would have stopped and enjoyed the notes of her laughter, but right now? I was going to fuck her just like I promised.

The sex demon in the video game slashed at Alix, and she retaliated with her weapon. The combo of her movements was so fast and lyrical I should have known Sal had incorporated ballet into this as well.

I took my shirt off and stayed in my dance tights, approaching her at the sectional. Sal's gaze flickered to mine as her concentration faltered, and the scent of her arousal was another piece to the puzzle of her game tonight.

Whatever Sal did in the game caused Alix to stumble back, then turn to Jax. Jax had extricated himself from under the sex demon, but now Alix fell on him while the sex fiend cackled. She hesitated when the game asked if she wanted:

1. For Alix to succumb to the potent venom of the sex demons and fuck Jax,
2. Square off and fight the sex demons, or
3. Run and fight again.

She pressed A and put the game into manual player mode. She stayed dialed in, pretending I wasn't standing next to her.

My heart was hammering in my chest, and the need to conquer, to gain her trust, the need for connection ran through me and left me breathless. Sal pretended to be unaffected, but her breathing grew shallow as she guided Alix through the fight/sex scene. Alix swiped a leg under Jax, who tumbled back, avoiding hitting Alix, who roared at him and pounced.

Just as Alix attacked, I caressed Sal's head, the soft, wispy coils yielding under my palm, then as she relaxed into the touch, I tugged hard enough to get her full fucking attention.

"So this is how you want to play it?" I asked, searching her gaze for full consent. Her lashes fluttered, then she opened her eyes again.

"Do your worst," she taunted, then cackled.

I swallowed her laughter, my tongue ramming into her mouth. There was no finesse to this kiss, raw need meeting boldness, and we clashed, our moans louder than the TV speakers. She flicked her tongue against mine, and I buckled, but I wouldn't go down like that. As my feet faltered, I sat on the sectional, and she scrambled into my lap, thick legs surrounding me as she nipped, bit, and scratched. Running a hand over her hair again, I pulled her away from me even as my hips flexed up to meet the sweet heat between her lushness.

Sal's eyes were dazed, and she panted, confused at my move.

"Nah, you wanted to play your game, little Ursula, so play your game."

I picked her up and turned her, so she was still on my lap but facing the TV. I bent over, holding her to me, and picked up the controller that had slipped to the floor to hand it to her.

"Go ahead," I prompted.

She turned her head back to stare at me as I made myself comfortable underneath her, her fucking luscious ass making me want to play this differently, but she'd pushed a button I didn't know she had access to, and I wanted to show her she wasn't the only one calling the shots.

"Don't threaten me with a good time, Devon."

"Go ahead. If you can finish this scene victorious, you get to call the shots every time we fuck, but if I get to distract you..."

"What...what will you do?"

"Then we split this shit 50-50, and you relinquish some control."

NINETEEN

SAL

ALERT! Alert! All systems, there is a threat to the interface.

Relinquish control? What on earth was this man talking about? Just the fact that I was primal meant I believed in relinquishing control. What did he mean by that? And why did I feel like he'd just stripped me bare, leaving me wondering if I was showing him more than I'd intended?

I didn't like the smug tone he'd used and how he just reclined back on the seat, his muscular legs spread open below me while mine draped over his. No matter how lean he was compared to me, an air of sturdiness emanated from him that didn't make me worry. This man could handle all of me. If anything, I felt like he could do some hurting from below.

And the way he'd been looking at me while we danced together had me shaken. So, I'd come home and worked on the next scene, and then Patrice sent me the art for this one. Knowing he would be coming home ready to do some destruction, I needed to remind him I wasn't one to take anything he had to give lying down.

But now, with him under me, as I continued to play the game feeling heated and reckless, I could admit I had just wanted him to take over. Fuck me until I had no voice left.

Something happened in that dance room, and I wasn't ready to deal with it. He'd felt it too, and he was pushing, unwilling to be passive about it. That dangerous trace to him lingered in the air as Jax and Alix danced their sexy fight scene, kissing, biting, body parts against body parts as they rolled back and forth on the earth.

Playing in manual, I dictated what Alix did, counteracting Jax's attempts to stop things. And then, just as I had designed, his eyes flashed with need, and he said, "Alright, Alix, I will fuck you because that's the only way to get you back clear-minded. And we agreed to do this for each other if a sex demon poisoned us, even though it feels wrong without full mental clarity." I needed consent to be clear from the beginning, and I reiterated here in the game that agreement was always present, if somewhat dubious at times.

Could Devon be right about the control thing? I'd wanted to be with him since the first time we fucked. Who was I kidding? Even before that, I had wielded my approval like a hammer, and for *us*, it made more sense for it to be a scalpel.

There was nothing wrong with how I practiced my consent. Black and white was what usually worked best for me. With Devon, though, I could dare allow my primal play to be colored with a bit of gray, but I refused to do so, and he'd called me out on it.

I had been holding back.

Devon never crossed the line.

Never had he initiated without my say-so.

And in doing so, I removed all the potential to initiate he could ever have. Today I had dropped that line, but he still wanted more, and I didn't know what that all meant.

"I can hear you thinking so hard right now. It's ok, this is new for me too." His words whispered against my ear as he sat up a bit straighter, his breath tickling me, making things wetter than they were before.

His tongue flicked over my helix, and I quivered. He bit my lobe, then proceeded to suck on my neck. I squirmed on his lap, but I was determined to focus on the game. His hands ghosted over my belly, the hair of my arms raising as his fingers dragged against the soft skin of my abdomen. The tips of his thumbs were high enough that they slipped under my crop top and teased the underside of my breasts.

Air. I needed air; why couldn't I breathe? Damn, I was holding it all in; that's why. I let it go with a sigh and taunted Devon with my ass, making myself comfortable on his hardness.

"Sal..." he cautioned. But I ignored the warning; Alix was on top of Jax as he thrust into her, the visual alternating from her bouncing, everything jiggling hentai-style, her little breathy moans coming out as she closed her eyes, to the wetness slipping in and out of her as Jax's dick slid between her folds. My brain was a nasty, nasty place when I'd come up with those precise instructions to the illustrators. *Wow.*

I should be blushing, but fuck it, I wanted something hot, and that was a heroine kicking ass and taking names, so I'd created her. And if it was horny as fuck in the meanwhile, so what? Women were sexual beings. They also could have base needs and want to fulfill them. And right now, I wanted to be fulfilled by Devon all night.

I took a leaf from Alix's page and started bouncing on top of Devon's lap. If he thought I was gonna just fold like a green girl and come the instant he started biting me and licking me, he was sadly mistaken.

This moment seemed to mean more to him...who was I kidding? It meant more to me too. I couldn't articulate precisely what it meant, not when his hot breath touched my shoulder, his fingers digging into my hip, and then he whined his dick into me, the friction of his leggings and my tights making me desperate for skin-to-skin.

I tried to stay in the game, pushing through the next commands. Alix was now on all fours, Jax behind her with a tortured face but drilling into her with enthusiasm as I pressed buttons, trying to remember what came next. I needed to win, which meant I needed to take Alix and Jax through this scene, get Alix unstuck, and have them beat the sex demons. But I kept lingering on the sex scene as Devon bit my shoulder through my crop top, then, with a growl, the sound of tearing fabric reverberated in the living area. He ripped the seam at my shoulder, and the delicious pain of his teeth sinking into my skin, then grazing made my movements falter.

"Oh, fuck, you don't play fair," I grumbled. The words escaped me before I could say anything else.

He chuckled, then groaned when I jiggled against him again.

Devon's retaliation? His hand snaked its way between my breasts before he ran his fingers softly between them, and I froze. I...that felt a little more intimate than I was ready for, and I gasped when his fingers trailed up again, then his other hand gripped my neck, the large hand locking onto me and making my head lay on his shoulder.

I didn't let go of the controller, but it took all of me to

have the presence of mind not to. Devon licked into my mouth, and everything in me melted, a whimper of surrender escaping me. Fuck, I couldn't lose it so quickly, but *fuck*, he made me want it so bad.

He kissed me, a diabolically soft kiss that made me reach out for him the moment he stopped. I whined again, waiting for more of his lips on me, his tongue meshing with mine.

"The sex demons are coming for Alix and Jax." Warm breath tickled against my open mouth.

The sex demons? *What sex demons...*

"Oh fuck!" I tightened my grip on the controller and focused on the next combos. Jax and Alix were done fucking, and the sex demons were on them. The fight began again, and I pulled out Alix's staff and kicked some ass.

One by one, the demons were pulverized in a puff of fire and smoke. Yes! Now I just needed to finish the other one off, and then I could surrender to the need that threatened to crawl out of me.

Devon's hands moved, and he palmed my tits. He served as my own personal bra, and if bras felt so fucking good and warm, I'd wear them every day. I tried to concentrate as he started telling me all the things he wanted to do to me. How he wanted to fuck me, how he wanted to be outside with me, take me to Jamaica and run in the bush, the both of us naked, until he found me and took me hard against a tree. It was the most delicious information overload, and I didn't want it to stop. His hands caressed up and down my belly, breasts, and hips, searing every atom in my body. This man was turning me inside out with his words, and his touch, and his...

A loud tear went through the room as Devon's hands met at the juncture between my legs, and with an ease that impressed me and left me breathless, he ripped the tights open, cold air seeping in through the hole he left.

Then he truly made me wild.

His finger teased my nub for a few seconds, the sensation so light I thought I'd be able to keep my concentration, but just as he lulled me into a false sense of confidence, three fingers slid into my soaking channel, and he started fingering me while rubbing my clit with his other hand.

I kept playing, pretending for a minute that I was unaffected, but who was I kidding? All the teasing and taunting had borne fruit for him, and I was ripe to his touch. My legs shook at the pleasure that built so quickly inside of me that it threatened to spill all over his hands.

"Give it to me, Ursula, soak my hand. Wet it up," he growled.

How decadent to be sitting on his lap, spread wide open, pliant and his to play with. Everything felt swollen between my clit and the spot that Devon kept pressing. Pressure built inside, and the urge to release overwhelmed me and...

Liquid shot out of me, wetting his hand just as he asked. The release was exquisite. While I had played my game, Devon played me with an expertise that made me squirt all over his lap, fluid splashing to the floor.

"Fuck me, Sal, that was..." He jostled under me, and hot flesh met my wet pussy.

Then before I had time to process, to take a breath, he bent me over, ass up, face on the coffee table in front of me, and the cold controller kissed the top of my cheeks. Somehow, he'd managed to grab the controller and started playing the game, making quick work of the last attacking sex demon as his dick glided into my waiting entrance, stretching me wide, making me whimper.

I couldn't believe he had me propped up like his human lap desk after I squirted like a shaken soda can. I had never done that before, and I was loving every minute of it.

"There, you won the level. I wouldn't have ever let you lose, Sal. Remember that." He growled as he finished the demon off. "So now you know not to play with me. I might be nice, but I'm not good. Not when it comes to this." He chucked the controller to the floor, then proceeded to fuck me with life-changing, bad gyal-taming strokes.

I had to close my eyes because I couldn't take anything more than what he gave me, the warning and the promise. I let him penetrate me just as the want and wish to trust him had conquered me from the second I opened my eyes today. And when he came, warm and inevitable inside of me, I let myself yield, if only for today.

Twenty

A MENTAL INVENTORY told me all was well with my body. I felt sore in places that didn't ever see the light of day, but the comforting weight lying on my chest and wrapping around me made it all worth it. Damn, if I told Aisha or Mila that, they'd never let me hear the end of it. Which meant I was taking this to the grave.

Devon slept on, a puff of his soft locs pillowed on my chest, his hand nestled between my thighs. After fucking last night, we bathed together, and I gave him a rundown of the scene I'd created and the overall story arc. He listened intently, giving feedback when I was open to hearing it and exchanging ideas about the direction I was planning to take. For a while, I forgot all the adversities stacked up against me, against us.

Devon somehow managed to insinuate himself past defenses I'd carefully built for long years with his patience, his attentiveness, and his hidden corners. He'd warned me we needed to talk about real life this morning, but I had asked him for a reprieve. I didn't want to talk about Perez or his USCIS case, not even Oriole—nothing but us for a moment.

The feeling persisted this morning, and I was so tempted to caress his hair and just burrow deeper into bed with him. I seldom woke up feeling so good, so cherished, and for a second, I wanted more. Succumbing to the instinct, I ran my hand over his soft locs, the glint of my gold ring distracting me. I couldn't believe how quickly I had gotten used to the piece of jewelry. I stretched my hand, staring at the gold band, so perfect for me. I would never tell Devon that, lest he get smug, but this was another sign of how well he got me.

He stirred, and his breathing changed as sleep slipped away and he woke up.

"Morning, gorgeous," he said, raising his head and staring at me. Fuck, he looked good in the morning, his scruffy beard and plump lips curving in a sexy smile and tender eyes that made me yearn for this to be how I woke up every day. What the heck was this man doing to me?

"What's up?" I nodded, and he chuckled.

"So, we are back to that?"

Watching those animal and nature shows Mila likes, I learned one day that Queen Alexandra's birdwings were the largest butterflies in the world. Apparently, they had moved into my stomach and were currently throwing a party in there as Devon studied me with quiet amusement.

"I mean, I am who I am? But...no, we're not going 'back to that.' Let's...let's go with the flow." My mouth went dry at the words.

He nodded, then shifted to lie next to me, facing me.

"So yuh gonna let me sleep in yuh bed? I've never slept

so well in my life," he whispered, making wings flap danger-
ously close to my rib cage.

"Sure, that could be arranged," I shrugged, unwilling to
waver against his intense, amused gaze.

"Good, because if not, I'd be sleeping in mine with you.
But it seems this bed is better. I don't wanna be away from
you at night anymore."

One of the birdwings fully infiltrated my chest as
Devon stared at me tenderly. It was too much.

"Don't you have therapy today? You're gonna be late." I
broke eye contact and busied myself with the covers.

"I do have it, but I couldn't resist sleeping in. My pillow
was mad warm, and my hands..."

"Yeah, yeah. Get up; we'll be back in bed before you
know it." I wiggled myself out of bed, glad I'd thought of
wearing underwear and a tank top to sleep. I had a feeling if
I'd been naked, I wouldn't have escaped the bed so easily.

"Where yuh going, woman?" Devon grumbled.

"To take a shower—"

"Good idea. My shower is big, we can both—"

"—here in my room, on my own. Because I won't be
blamed for you being late. See you downstairs."

"Tonight, I'll make sure I give it to you so good you don't
wake up first. Then that way, I can wake *you* up," he
promised, and I walked to my bathroom with a hidden smile
on my face.

———

"Are you really gonna keep me in suspense? Look at you!
You're glowing!" Mila whined as she opened the studio. I'd
asked for a ride with her. The habit of not being on my own

grew old, especially since things had simmered down after the Perez dude stopped coming to the studio.

From my calls to my neighbor, no one had been back to check on my apartment, at least to her knowledge. Maybe, just maybe, things were starting to settle down, and I could relax my vigilance.

The marriage with Devon still made sense, no matter my situation. Of the three of us, I was the one the least invested in a happily ever after, and nothing material would change in my life outside of the additional protection I'd gained from my association with Devon. I hadn't told him, but I'd made an app that tracked similar USCIS cases to his so that I would have a good idea of our time together. Once he got his green card approved in the next couple of months, moving out would be plausible, but I didn't want to dwell on that much.

So yeah, I had no regrets in that department, and now that things were taking an interesting turn between us, even less. We would figure out what would happen after the three years of marriage.

"I got hit up by another woman needing help. This one is more straightforward. She and her husband owned a car wash together; he managed all the finances. She found out he has two other secret families. She wants money to dip and leave him behind," I said to Mila as we settled ourselves behind the reception desk.

"I ask you about your sex life, and you answer back with the reckless idea of putting yourself in danger again?" Mila crossed her arms, annoyed at me. I brushed off her concern and opened my laptop.

"Things have settled down here, so maybe." I shrugged.

"Nah, you really think things have settled down? Do you think that man Perez and his boss aren't biding their time? Everything we know about Perez tells us he's dangerous, sweetcakes, come on!"

Murmurs interrupted our conversation, and we both looked up to realize the camera for Room A, the feed that allowed parents to see their kids in class, was on. And the audio too. Aisha and Devon stood by the back of the room by the barre, discussing something intently.

"You'd think Aisha learned her lesson after her drama." Mila shook her head, turning to the computer controlling the camera feeds.

Mila was about to shut down the camera, but something made me stop her—some deep-seated pull. I trusted Devon —I mean, as much as I could. But this was a rare opportunity to see him in action without him knowing. I knew it wasn't right to eavesdrop, but...as things got heavy between us, why not make sure he was as solid as he presented himself to be?

"What? They don't know we're here yet," Mila protested.

"Shhh."

I was tempted to bring up the volume, but that would make the invasion of privacy even worse. I listened intently while a very uncomfortable Mila stood next to me.

"So, you need advice?" Aisha asked.

"Yeah. I need to talk to Sal, but...she keeps asking me to wait. And I need to figure out ways to communicate with her so that she is receptive to what I have to say. D told me all about it yesterday, and I tried to bring it up, but we got caught up, and... I don't know how to bring up the subject with her. That man is out here trying to smoke out Juniper and probably Sal. And I want to talk to her about opening some accounts together...the interview is approaching, and I — Shit, I don't know. Sometimes I feel is better not to say anything with her, yuh know? Like she wants to keep things surface-level?"

My stomach plummeted to hear Devon discussing these things with Aisha instead of with me, his fake wife. I mean, I get it. I can be unapproachable, but I thought... For a second, I thought things were different between us.

"Mhm, do you know Sal?" I heard Aisha ask, but I signaled to Mila to shut it off.

"Salome..."

"Nah, I'm good. I'm gonna take an Uber to my apartment. There are some things I've been needing, and Devon and I haven't had the time to swing by. I promise I'll be safe. I'll have the Uber wait for me outside and knock on Mrs. Marshall's door."

"No, that's not what we agreed to do. That man could be waiting for you at the apartment."

"I doubt it, didn't you hear Devon? They're trying to smoke out Juniper. *Juniper.* Which he should have told me the moment he found out so I could use my network to warn her, but...apparently, I'm inaccessible."

"Can we talk a minute and acknowledge that lately, you've been *very* communicative and almost verbose?" Mila said earnestly.

I rolled my eyes at her attempt at humor and put my laptop back in its bag.

"I'll be fine."

"Fucking drama, there's never a dull moment in this place!" Mila threw her hands up in exasperation as I exited the studio. I debated turning around and calming her down, but I couldn't handle both her and my emotions right now.

The Uber was a quick drive to the apartment with my mind full of recriminations and hurt. I knew better than to expect things with Devon to be different.

We'd promised each other truth and communication, and here I was, finding out things because I had to eavesdrop on his conversation. I wasn't even the kind of person to do that shit—alright, sometimes I was—but he'd relegated me to snooping on him, and that didn't sit well.

I didn't want to examine how upset I felt about it all or how much I was blowing things out of proportion, so I needed to distance myself from him until I could think things through. The entrance to my apartment looked the same, and I made sure to see if there was any suspicious activity around before letting the Uber go. I'd changed my mind about them staying—I needed some time in my apartment. Not Devon's, not the studio; my own space.

I grabbed a bag and found some clothes I had forgotten in the rush to pack. I pulled out some of my games and other controllers, wondering if Devon would want to play with me, then immediately got upset that I was even thinking of what he would like while simultaneously being mad at him. I wasn't cut out for this drama.

My stomach decided to remind me in that moment that I hadn't had lunch. Just as I was going to check my kitchen and order something, someone knocked on my door. Lost in thought, I moved automatically without registering my actions.

I shouldn't have opened it. I should have known better, but my mind was all over the place as I worked out why I was so upset about Devon's words, so I opened the door.

"Salome? I'm Xavier Souza. Your brother."

TWENTY-ONE

DEVON

WHERE IN THE bomboclat was that woman?

I arrived home after class to find Sal was gone; all calls to her cell phone went straight to voicemail. No communication, no text.

No explanation.

I'd gone to her apartment and banged on the door; she wasn't there. The neighbor wasn't in either, so I left the complex with no answers.

According to Mila, who had looked distinctively uncomfortable under my stare, Sal had promised to be careful, but she wouldn't say more than that, not even after Aisha begged her to share more with me.

Aisha and Mila exchanged looks, and somehow, Aisha blanched.

What did that even fucking mean? How could she put herself in jeopardy like this? Hadn't I explained? But I hadn't; I hadn't told her the latest. I hadn't warned her to be careful that people could be after her right now. I felt sick to my stomach that I'd prioritized my feelings over her safety last night. That I'd carved out a space for us to connect physically instead of us talking. Fuck.

It had been hours since I left the studio, and it was already dark outside; I'd ordered Mr. Chen with the ridiculous hope she'd show up safe and acidic, all Sal. But I wasn't a man to sit idle, so while I prepared for the best, I'd also made calls, preparing for the worst.

"Carpenter, let's meet at her spot and take it from there. Alright, man, mi hit yuh up there." A sense of pure determination and focus rolled through me.

My heart slowed to a steady, reliable pace that allowed me to be fully in tune with every single detail around me, the feeling similar to the rush right before performing on stage. I wished the sensations weren't alike. Nothing that came after holding a gun in my hand had good memories. But I was as good, if not better, at this as I was a dancer.

Today, though, I was willing to do anything and more to ensure Sal's safety. None of my past, my nightmares, or my doubts clouded me as I pushed the clip into my Glock and holstered the piece on my belt. Just as I approached the door, it clicked open, and Sal waltzed in with a bag on her shoulder.

I straightened up, unsure if she'd seen what I was doing but truly not giving a fuck right now.

"Sal."

She raised a hand and closed the door softly behind her, then locked it for good measure. She turned around, and my eyes frantically studied her. She was ok. She was safe. Her expression, though... Sal braced herself as if she was Alix about to battle some demons, as if she was the one wronged.

It took everything in me to keep my stance relaxed, my voice modulated. Years of smiling and gentleness and making myself less scary paid off. I was able to keep it together.

"Hey. I'm sorry I didn't answer. I didn't feel like talking."

Rass, this gyal.

I ran my hand over my lips and stayed quiet. Better than saying something unwise.

"I heard you and Aisha today," she continued.

Damn, and even after that, she didn't care to take care of herself? I felt awful, she shouldn't have heard that, but at the same time, I'd always had the intention of speaking with her, so she could spare me the indignation.

"Ok, so you heard us, and still you ghosted me?" I asked.

"Oh, you think you're in the right, my guy?"

"I think we're both wrong right now, but one is more wrong than the other."

She chuckled without any humor behind it, nothing like her melodic giggles. She walked toward the stairs, never breaking away from my gaze.

"Well, you think that. I'm gonna take a shower."

"Nah, I'm not the one, Sal. You better talk to me, or I'm gonna think we're not a team."

"Oh, now you want to be a team? Not earlier when you were telling Aisha all our business?"

"Don't act like you don't understand me going to a friend to get some advice. There's nothing wrong with that." I couldn't help the volcanic anger that bubbled up at her words. I knew deep down she had a point. I knew that in this fragile balance of trust we were building, this could be a betrayal for her. But that didn't mean my intentions were wrong. It hurt that she would paint my mistakes with that brush.

"I haven't told them anything. Everything that has

happened between us has been sacred to me, and until we figured out what was happening, I wasn't planning on saying anything. Because this shit is between us, not everyone else. How can I trust we are on the same page when you go around talking to other people about our business? Then we're synced!" She shook her head. "Listen. I didn't come here to fight. I planned to stay at my apartment tonight, but I realized that would be reckless. So here I am."

She padded silently up the stairs, and I stood there stunned.

We. She'd used the word "we" several times; maybe she meant "team" in a different manner. But that "we" shit carried weight in her words. Not her and Aisha, not her and Mila. Her and I. *We.*

I'd fucked up.

I called Carpenter and called off the opps. Someone would contact Delroy, who'd probably already been informed inside as well. I needed to go see him tomorrow to ease his mind, but tonight? Tonight, I needed to fix shit with Sal. We needed to be on the same page.

Twenty-Two

Devon strapping up to search for me would stay embedded in my brain for a long time. His face had transformed from lethal to determined to worried, then the heat of his eyes studied me everywhere, ensuring I was good. For a second, I forgot my confusion and anger, the feeling of betrayal—not only from him but my mother and everything she'd kept away from me. A brother. Three brothers, to be exact.

To then return to Devon's and encounter the intensity of his authentic self had been too much. I knew I wasn't wrong being mad because it was how I felt, and my feelings were valid, but he wasn't wrong when he said I shouldn't have ghosted him. But I'd never expected to meet my flesh and blood today.

Thoughts swirled in my head as I walked out of the shower and threw on a pair of underwear and a tank top. I heard a dull thud hit the door and paused.

"I can hear you in there." Devon's muffled voice came through.

"What are you doing?"

"Sitting here until you let me in. I told you I'm not sleeping without you. I'm sorry I hurt you, sweets."

The way my heart had chosen to react to this man's words was very inconvenient and, quite frankly, the biggest betrayal of them all. Why did I feel like opening the door and hugging him until we were good again? This marriage was fake; we were just friends, right? But we had crossed so many lines. Lately, I didn't even know what to call him anymore. My heart protested and insisted I should call him mine. Fuck, I was in trouble.

"Go to bed. We can talk tomorrow. I'm exhausted." I wasn't lying. I couldn't take any more emoting tonight. It was too much.

"Then I'm sleeping here." I heard him shuffle behind the door; I imagined him getting comfortable. Why was this man doing this? Why did he make me want to lower my guard so quickly? I didn't like it. I didn't like it one bit.

Attempting to ignore the person outside the door, I moisturized, taking my sweet time, covering every part of my skin. When I finished and still felt the urge to open the door, I batted the thought away and instead went to the bathroom and did my long face routine.

The one with six steps.

When that didn't help, I noticed my curls needed brushing, so I took my time with them until the coils were lustrous under the bathroom light.

Unable to take it anymore, I stomped over to the door and yanked it open. I moved so quickly that Devon plopped right onto my feet, his warm back cradled by my slippers. His pout was the first thing I saw when I looked down, his sad upside-down face, bare chest, and sweatpants greeting my eyes.

"Rass, Ursula, I wasn't expecting you to soften up so quickly. I was just getting comfortable."

"Get off." I moved my feet, trying to dislodge him, but he shifted, and somehow, I found myself on my ass, sprawled on the floor. Thank God for all the extra cushion on me because I was getting tackled on the daily now.

"Let's talk," he said, placing himself next to me, and I glared at him from my vantage point on the floor.

"That shit hurt; my ass is bruised."

"Oh, I'm sorry. Here, turn around." He manhandled me, making me lie on my belly, then laid his big palms on my fabric-covered ass, patting and massaging the globes while making "there, there" noises. I felt an inconvenient tingle blossom between my legs, and I pushed myself up and away from him.

"Nah, if we are going to talk, let's talk. You hurt me today."

"I'm sorry... And you did too." Devon sat up slowly, stared at me, and then got up and sat on my bed. I knew if I sat next to him, this would be over way before we actually had a constructive conversation, so I made my way to my gaming chair across the room. The more distance, the better. Devon smiled kindly at my move like he thought I was cute or something. I wasn't cute. I had bite.

When did I lose my edge over him?

If I thought he would make this easier, he didn't. I explained, attempting to describe how I felt when I heard him and Aisha, how the lance of betrayal penetrated me swiftly and unexpectedly. How I thought after yesterday... we had something. His eyes went from determined to a soft tenderness I wasn't ready to see.

"I hear you, Sal, I do. You were upset I didn't think I could come to you that easy."

Fuck me. I had expected him to be obtuse. To push back, to argue. Not to understand my point of view. But no, he had to go and get it in one.

Well, fuck...I had to get used to being seen now, didn't I? Not only by my friends, my found family, but this man I'd unwittingly allowed into my heart.

I could keep pretending all I wanted that this was a convenient arrangement with him, but I wanted more. And it scared me, which was why it was so easy to feel betrayed today. To put him in a box.

"Yeah, and I think I was scared after yesterday."

"After you realized we can be something more?"

"At least for these few months before the green card..."

His face clouded, then he smiled that gentle smile again.

"Yeah, at least for this time. I'm sorry. I should have talked to you. I should have come to you. I should have trusted our partnership more than that. I'm so sorry I made you feel betrayed. I tried...never mind; it doesn't matter. I want us to be able to come to each other. Open up to each other without fear." He pressed his hand to his chest, and I felt a little faint. I...damn. I was softening like butter under the sun, and I couldn't help the melting process.

I wasn't ever butter before him! But along came Devon with his kind smiles and his gentle way of getting to know me, and I couldn't keep him at bay. I didn't want to keep him at bay. Not anymore.

"My brother found me at the apartment. That's why it took me so long to come back. I was shocked by his revelation."

"What?" Devon jumped up from the bed and powered

over to where I was sitting. He plucked me from the gaming chair like I was a size 2 instead of a 22 and walked me over to the bed. Then he sat me down between his legs and crossed his arms around my belly.

"There. Better. So WHAT?"

Oh. This felt lovely.

"Damn, you just yelled in my ear." I smiled, but then I explained to him what had happened.

How Xavier Souza, a debonair brother a little darker than me with the same lips, slightly slanted brown eyes, and curly hair more evident in his beard since he was bald, had approached me at my apartment.

He had a sense of familiarity to me, of blood calling blood that made me believe him the moment I saw him. Then he'd shown me a little mark on the inside of his arm close to his armpit. It had been uncomfortable when he asked if it was ok to divest himself of his jacket and shirt to do so, but he had been quiet, controlled, almost imposing in my house. I was explaining how he and his brothers just wanted the opportunity to know me.

"Just like this one here." I showed Devon the same little spot that looked like a watermarked kiss on the inside of my arm. Lilith used to tell me it was an angel's kiss, but I'd found out today it was a common trait on my father's side. "He asked me to meet my other two brothers. They are all open to doing DNA tests to confirm our affinity. But, honestly, Devon, the dude looks just like me, just darker and skinnier. He said his baby brother has hair just like mine but darker. I...I want to meet them."

Silence.

"So, what do you think?" I asked tentatively. Devon inhaled, his chest pushing me in the effort, then he released the air with a sigh, taking his time. Whatever he had to say, he thought I wouldn't like it. I tensed up, and he pinched my hip to calm me down.

"Listen, if we are a team—" He paused.

"I thought we just decided we are, if only for now."

"Then I have to say, teammate, that this shit makes me uncomfortable. What if these dudes, your brothers, try to use this to smoke you out for Juniper's boyfriend? You know nothing of them. I visited Delroy as you heard, and Juniper's man and his enforcer are looking for her, and probably for you."

"I..." I paused before resorting to combativeness. *Trying to find it...* I didn't want to argue with him.

"I'll consider your concern. Maybe we can find a way where I meet them with you around?"

Devon let out an "mhmm" that sounded so Jamaican, I felt like I was standing on the beach of Montego Bay, and I'd never been there.

"Ok, then. That's that," I said and shifted until we were face to face with my legs around his waist.

"So you're not fighting me anymore?" he asked, a thread of concern still marring his beautiful face. I shook my head, tired of talking. I hadn't realized how gorgeous he was. Empirically, I saw his attraction, but it didn't used to have a physical effect on me. Now, though...I couldn't get enough of his face with the hooded eyes, broad nose, eyebrows so sculpted it looked like he waxed, and the beard covering his structured jaw, so many favorite features. I could look at him every day and never grow tired. I now understood all the noise the ladies made when he came to class. The difference was they only saw the outside; I saw the inside.

"If you keep looking at me like that, we won't be going to sleep anytime soon."

"Who said I wanted to sleep?" I asked, grinding on his hardening erection.

"Fuck, Sal. Have I told you how lovely you are? I know you're a badass hacker, and you take shit from no one, but you're so fucking lovely. It just comes from within; you can't even hide it. Not from me. I want to be able to share all of this with you."

God. Why was he so good at words when I just wanted to be fucked?

The feelings were too much right now, so I needed a diversion. I bent over and ran my tongue from the center of his chest, gliding upward, his salty skin yielding under my touch. I finished with a deep suck of his neck and a little twirl of my hips for good measure.

"Oh, so you want to get *fucked* fucked, huh?"

"I—Oh fuck!" Devon flipped me over, and I bounced on the bed. I tried to scramble up on my elbows, but he was faster than I was. The scrape of his beard was the first thing I felt. Then he sank his teeth into the softest part of my left asscheek, and I yipped.

He snickered and bit the other cheek, this time harder, enough for me to know I'd be sitting gingerly tomorrow. Enough to make me dripping wet in seconds. His warm chest ghosted over my back, and his weight on me was delicious. I tried bucking him off me, but he was too strong, and I relished that knowledge.

His warm breath kissed the skin on the back of my neck, and he growled in my ear. Goosebumps rose all over my skin in anticipation of his taking. I needed it.

"You're not gonna try to escape today, Ursula," he warned. I ignored him and shimmied myself down toward the head of the bed. My ass wiggled against his crotch, making him gasp and forget himself for a second, causing him to shift to give me space to get on all fours.

That was all the space I needed, and I braced my left arm against the bed to roll to the right. Before I could move away, Devon clamped a hand on my neck, keeping me in place.

"Nah, you stay right there and take what I have to give."

The pain that radiated through my arms as Devon held them together behind my back was welcomed. I relished the roughness he unleashed on me; I needed him to feel as primal as I felt.

Applying pressure to my back, he straddled me, his face facing my ass and legs. I ended up in a relaxed doggie-style position with Devon sitting on my upper back. His weight calmed the raging inside of me. Then he bent over and bit my ass again so hard I yelped.

I thrashed and bucked, but there was no dislodging him. He spread my cheeks and spit between them, the warm liquid hitting my crack, then, before I could recuperate from Devon's hidden nastiness, he ran his tongue from the top of my crack all the way to my asshole. His tongue circled around my entrance, making me pucker in anticipation. I didn't want him to stop anymore.

I had my entire chest on the bed, my breasts squished and my face pressed down with Devon's delicious weight on me. Trapped under him, I was helpless but to accept the relentless tongue-lashing he gave me. Emptiness took over; I needed him to fill me up.

To erase the feeling of betrayal from this afternoon from my mom too. Erase all the things that weren't going well and all the ones that were growing between us. Without me asking, he shifted off me, his knee dipping the mattress, pressing on the small of my back until I was fully relaxed on the bed.

"Yield," he commanded, and I fought the urge not to comply.

He lined up atop me, resting his warm dick between my ass. His heart galloped so hard I could feel it against my back. His hands trailed down my arms, making me shiver and transforming me to pure liquid hunger. Pressed down, safety lay underneath him. Then he rose up enough to relieve me of some of the weight and dropped a chaste kiss on the crown of my curls. His scent of sea and lemon was so strong here in the little space I'd made for myself.

Devon nipped my ear, and my chest tightened. An open-mouthed kiss on my temple and my stomach did a triple tour en l'air. He licked my cheek, and I shook in surrender. He nuzzled my neck, and I grew desperate for him.

Then I begged.

And here lies Salome Blackwell. She perished of unresolved sexual need and emotional atrophy.

"Please, please, Devon, please, I *need*—" My voice grew ragged.

"I know what you need, Sal, I know." He pressed a kiss on my ear and licked my earlobe one more time, and everything inside contracted.

"Then give it to me, you asshole, and stop tormenting me!"

He chuckled. He had the audacity to laugh, a belly laugh full of joy, wonder, and wickedness.

With one hand, he plumped my ass, making me push it out just enough for him to line up with my apex. The need for him suffocated me; my mouth dried in anticipation.

"You just had to ask, sweets," he murmured, and he

glided inside my pussy with such languid grace my eyes started burning. Unshed tears shook in the corner of my eye.

"Oh, sweets, that's ok. Let it out," he commanded, and I didn't know what was happening, but I did let it out. I cried in ecstasy as Devon rocked into me, my orgasm making him hold onto me lest I buck him for real. The headboard bounced against the wall, the ruckus so loud someone would think I was being killed. And maybe I was, to be reborn into this soft-ass, corny, believes-in-love, dickmatized woman.

Maybe.

Twenty-Three

Devon

Every morning with Sal was an adventure. Sometimes I woke up to find her already glued to the computer, investigating, working on a project, occupied with her video game, or communicating with some of the women she helped as Oriole. Those mornings I always conspired on ways to get her back to bed, at least until I could have her screaming my name just the way I liked it.

Other mornings I woke up, and she was playful, making me work for it, running around the apartment naked, taunting me as I followed her until she let herself be caught. We had already christened every corner of the apartment in our endeavors.

Then there were the mornings like today when I woke up before her, and she was still asleep. My sleep at night had been the best since before I moved to the States because of her. I cherished these mornings the most because they allowed me to appreciate her while she lay sprawled in bed.

For the most part, we slept entangled in each other,

usually with my head on her chest, my hand between her legs. But some nights, it was as if her dreams couldn't be contained, and she shifted all around the bed, pushing me with her lush ass until I was in one corner, and took possession of the rest of the king-size bed. She would wake up sprawled, usually one breast out of her tank top as if her tits wanted to escape, just as restless as their owner.

Fancifully, I thought these were the nights she created in her sleep, and usually, she woke up full of ideas and thoughts, either to find her enemies or create a new scene. She hadn't worked on a new scene since she learned about her brothers a few days ago, and I wondered what would dislodge her creative mode. Her moods were intrinsically tied to her creative disposition, and for now, she focused on programming all the art she had received from her friend online.

I trailed my hand over her shoulder and plump arm, then I gripped the soft skin over her elbow and played with it until she huffed.

"I hate when you do that," Sal grumbled.

"Nah, you like it."

She stayed quiet and pushed herself closer to me, proving me right. I growled in satisfaction and nuzzled her neck, my animal ready to play if she was too. I was always ready around her. It was instinctual. For all I was primal, that instinct didn't activate with just anyone, and it was never as strong as it had been with Sal. The moment I allowed myself to think of her as more than a friend, that was it for me. Every single cell in me needed to be close to hers. Learning her. Exploring her, making her wild.

"It's one of the fattest parts of my body."

"I don't think you've seen your ass. Nor your freckle-covered cheeks, nor your inner thighs closest to your puna—"

"Fucking pervert."

"I'm just describing my favorite physical parts of yours, and you're over here acting like they are minuses instead of a big triple-plus."

"I'll give you triple-plus, alright," she mumbled, and I smiled. I buried my nose in her hair; it smelled like grapefruit. She'd just washed it yesterday. I had fallen in love with the shampoo and started using it too until she complained, so I bought us a new bottle.

"Are you nervous?" I asked, and she shook her head. She had her 'Sal unbothered' mask on, but her pulse was visible at the top of her neck. It had been two and a half weeks since Xavier Souza had approached her, and they were going to open the DNA results together today.

"Teammate..."

"We have too many nicknames between us; this is getting ridiculous," she grumbled, then she snuggled into me even more. I smiled and let her keep that one.

"I gotta go to therapy, then to the company rehearsal, but I will be in the studio for the meeting, ya hear?"

She pursed her lips, letting air escape from them, then nodded; she searched for my hand behind her and made me grab her titty. I gently squeezed and sighed in contentment, knowing she needed a few more minutes. I'd have to whip up breakfast quick-quick, but it would be worth it for these stolen minutes. It would all be worth it for her.

———

Sal

The studio had never felt smaller to me than today.

Both Aisha and Mila had come to pick me up at the apartment, wanting to be there to support me. The ball of nerves in my stomach had prevented me from having the delicious breakfast Devon had prepared. And I couldn't even eat the Mr. Chen leftovers, a true tragedy.

Today I found out if I had three more siblings. Today I found out about my father.

I started pacing again while Mila sat on the reception desk watching me like a hawk, and Aisha sat in the waiting area, feet bouncing up and down as she played with her hair.

Classes were done for the day, and it was just us. Athena had left already. I needed privacy for this meeting. Aisha and Mila could be here; anything I learned, they'd learn too. They were my family of the heart. And Devon—well, of course, he needed to be here. We had agreed to be on the same team, and I wanted to respect his concerns. He was way off base, but oh, well.

Once I'd met Xavier, he shared some more information that allowed me more sleuthing. His younger sibling was half of Z.J. Grousant, and my inner Blerd rejoiced at the news. Xavier was a big-shot lawyer, and I learned more about some high-profile cases he had in his career, but I already knew all of that. I had even accessed some of his bank accounts before he'd found me. But the eldest of the three? Still elusive.

"Ok, so are we just gonna sit here and wait silently?" Mila asked, her voice resonating in the waiting room. I whirled around to her, and just as I was about to speak, Devon entered.

"Hey, sorry, rehearsal was long today. Hey, sweets, yuh good?"

A trickle of relief calmed me as Devon's strong arms

surrounded my waist, his arms around me so yummy I thought of bailing out.

"Maybe we should just go to our apartment?" I whispered in his ear, then bit his earlobe. He groaned into my ear, then he froze.

"Did you say *our* apartment?" he whispered back, and it was my turn to freeze.

"Uh..."

"Did I leave you speechless?" He chuckled as he stepped away from me.

"Ok, so we aren't wondering anymore, are we? Are we?" Mila asked no one in particular.

"No, Milita, I think you're right, and these two have been mingling DNA." Aisha smiled at me and winked; I took the gesture for the blessing it was.

"Nah, that's not just mingling; this is passion, fire, desire," Mila said in a decidedly annoyed tone.

"Why are you so annoyed?" I asked her, concerned. I didn't understand why she was upset.

"Never mind me, just that I'm happy for you both, and you kept it under wraps for so long. Great. Ok. Good, I appreciate not knowing..." Mila grumbled, and Aisha's eyes widened as she shook her head.

"Well, yeah, we're kind of together. There. Now you know," I said, exasperated.

Now Devon stared at me, a frown materializing on his face.

Great. I started pacing again when the doorbell went off. A sharp pang radiated from my chest, and three men strolled into the studio.

Xavier stood in front of me and offered me his hand. I shook it in a daze at seeing the three of them together.

Yeah, it tracked. Xavier was the one that looked the

most like me; we all had the same slanted eyes, but his facial structure resembled mine the most. He was the shortest of the three, though he was taller than me. Not as tall as Devon, so he must be a bit under six feet tall.

Xavier had that reserved air to him that didn't quite allow me to relax. He still made me feel anxious regardless of our parentage.

Next to him was a younger dude with a similar complexion to mine but with an olive undertone to it that made him appear beautifully darker. Zac wore ripped jeans with a Black Goku t-shirt, and I smiled at the drawing. He grinned back, and his gentle eyes made me feel comfortable immediately. Zac was the tallest of the three and had a head full of ink-black curls that shined under the studio lights.

Then the eldest. He stood imposingly; even though he wasn't the tallest man in the room, it felt like he was. The man was solid, wearing a suit, with a face that had such character it made me want to sit up straighter and, at the same time, put all my worries in his capable hands. He looked the least like the other two, with deep mahogany skin and a bald head with features so striking, handsome wasn't enough to describe him.

"Master Q! Guys?" Aisha exclaimed as I let go of Xavier's hand.

"Aisha, you good? How is your Sir?" the eldest said. The other two waved at Aisha, and the youngest one winked at her.

"I... You're... Oh wow." Aisha plopped down on one of the chairs closest to the hallway to the office. Devon's eyebrows rose, and he moved closer to me. I was thankful for the support even though I was ok. I nodded at him, and he read me right, going to Aisha and sitting down next to her.

The eldest of the men tracked the whole situation and watched Devon closely, then settled his gaze on me again.

"Xavier says you have the Souza mark?" Master Q asked. I'd heard enough about him to know *this* was the famous Dom Aisha had talked about. Mila knew of him too, and her sister attended his sex club. Shock was an understatement.

What were the odds?

The Master Q...my brother.

"Sure, yeah. Why don't you sit down and let's open the envelope first? I mean, I don't want to waste anyone's time if we aren't siblings," I reminded everyone.

Zac grinned mischievously and pulled chairs into a circle so we could all face each other. Devon and Aisha stayed in the back, and Mila remained by the desk. I stared at her, and she might as well have a bucket of popcorn in her hands.

I should have done this on my own.

"Ok, little sis, you're a straight shooter. I like that. Xavier?" Master Q asked for the envelope and opened it right there in front of us all. The rip of the envelope made my heart jump, and then he handed me the paper. I appreciated that he didn't monopolize the information and allowed me to read it first. I held my breath as I read the report, which showed that we were all considered very close relatives, probably siblings.

"It's true," I whispered.

"So, I know we're a lot, but let me introduce these two formally," Xavier said after a beat.

"This is Zacarias Joaquim."

Zacarias reached out and grasped both of my hands in his bigger ones. "Olá, irmã."

I stared at Zac Souza, *the* Zac Souza, graphic illustrator

and fantasy author. One part of the writer duo that was Z.J. Grousant. I wasn't about to fangirl over the man, so I played it cool.

"I know who you are. What's up?" That was all I could manage; I had a knot in my throat. I glanced toward Aisha and Devon, and she was beaming while Devon watched everything like the lion he was, studying the situation with rapt attention. I was glad for it; my senses were all haywire, feelings all over the place. I needed someone to pay attention to the details I was missing.

"This is Quentino João, or as your friend called him, Master Q."

Master Q bowed his head at me, and I nodded at him.

"How come I couldn't find you when I searched Xavier?"

"I don't go by Souza. I go by my mother's last name, Santos."

"Mhm." That explained a bit, and I hadn't put too much into the search, to be honest, between Perez and Juniper, and fuck, everything. I was honestly overwhelmed.

"And I am Xavier Jardel. By any chance, do you have a middle name?" Xavier asked me quizzically, hand on his chest.

"I...No. Not on my birth certificate, but once when I was around twelve, I was bothering Lilith—my mom," I explained at their quizzical looks, "with questions about my dad. She said that he would have wanted to name me Julinha. I was too young to understand where the name could come from, and she refused to explain how it was written."

"That tracks; he's nothing if not a narcissist. His name is Julio João; he named us all with J names," Master Q said.

"Master Q, what can you tell me of him?" I wanted to

know; I couldn't believe that I had Lilith, and these men were implying my father was a narcissist as well. How could that be? Just my luck. I needed to know more.

"Could you not call me that? Call me João; it's what these two call me." Master Q grimaced.

"Why? Doesn't everyone call you Master Q?"

"People that go to my sex club, that are part of the lifestyle and my kink family call me that. My blood calls me different," he said, frowning when he saw the stolen glance between Devon and me. He glanced behind his back toward where Devon was sitting, then at me again. I raised an eyebrow in response. This man had just walked into my life; he surely wasn't about to act up around me. Q nodded, and I hoped it was in recognition that he had no say in my life. He was a stranger to me.

"Listen, what these two knuckleheads can't say is that our Pai...he ain't a good dude. The story is long, and we have time to get to know each other first before we tell it all, but what you need to know is that he's done a lot of women wrong, including our mother. After we learned what he did to her, we started finding out about his treatment of other women. He's made a habit of preying on women that have more to lose than he does, and in searching to make things right...we found you," Zacarias said, clearly the level-headed one of the bunch.

"So, this was all a happy coincidence?"

"I don't always believe in coincidences, but in this case, I don't have another explanation yet. It seems your mother was able to escape our dad before things got...bad. He's not too keen on allowing his side pieces to get pregnant. He has a very high-profile wife, and he can't afford slip-ups."

"So, what about you three?" I asked, confused.

"He was with Mai before he got married, committed

bigamy in theory. But we recently found out how he forged his marriage license to Mai," Xavier said, a wave of deep anger radiating from him. Shit, whatever this dude—my father—had done wasn't good. The repercussions of the man's actions shone on each of their faces.

"Listen, this is a lot. We're happy to have found you; it's just the three of us now..." Q's eyes clouded before he continued, "But we understand this can be overwhelming. We have each other, and we know you have your mom and sisters. It's up to you if you want a relationship with us. But at least we wanted you to know."

It's just the three of us now... Did that mean my dad was dead? Was their mom gone too?

I nodded, staring at the three of them. Q with his imposing aura, Zacarias with his handsome, goofy, kind smile, and Xavier with his 'I got no time for this' energy.

"Alright, Q..."

"I thought I asked—" Q started.

"Yeah, I know, João. But we're not that close, no matter the blood. You gotta give me time. I figured Q works?"

Q studied me, then nodded.

"I'm guessing you two call each other by your J names too?"

"You guessed it, irmã." Zacarias grinned.

"So Zacarias and Xavier it is." I nodded, clapping my hands on my thighs and standing up, ending the reunion with one decisive gesture. Q was right; I was suddenly feeling overwhelmed by it all. There was a lot to take in, and I needed space.

Devon stood up and approached me, his calm presence a balm to my racing thoughts. He rested his palm on the small of my back right above my ass, and I shivered at the touch. I never thought I'd like being touched like this, but I kept discovering new likes with Devon.

"Ok, Salome. Call us when you are ready," Q said, and I grunted.

"I don't like being called Salome. Call me Sal."

"Mhm, but you call me Q?"

Touché.

"Fine, call me Salome." I waved my hand in exasperation.

"Are you gonna introduce us to your other friends?" Zacarias asked in curiosity, gazing at Devon, then at Mila.

"Oh, yeah. This is Mila, one of my best friends."

"Ah, hello, handsome brothers of Sal!" Mila waved, mesmerized, and I swear that girl needed to calm down.

"And that is Aisha, who maybe some of you know?"

The three men nodded, and Aisha blushed. Oh god, I didn't want to know.

"And this, this is my...my husband, Devon Reid," I said, gazing up at Devon. There was an intense regard in his eyes I couldn't fully understand. I didn't want to study things too much. We were just getting warmed up, him and I; the marriage was still one of convenience.

Q stared at Devon for a long while, nodded again, then stood up and approached us, dapping him on the shoulder.

"Nice to meet you, man," Q said, and for the first time today, this moment didn't feel surreal. Suddenly, with Devon's support, I imagined a path forward. I could picture getting to know my brothers.

Twenty-Four

Devon

The weeks after Sal's meeting with her brothers were filled with many changes for the two of us.

Sal spent two days hanging out in her room watching some old anime, *Yu Yu Hakusho*. She said she needed a comfort watch, but every time I checked on her, there was some bloody fight on the screen, making me wonder what her definition of comfort was. Just another insight into what made her tick. She only came out to eat or to open the door for me to lay down for the night. By unspoken agreement, her room became ours, and even though she was in a reflective mood, she still let me hold her at night.

On the third day, I woke up to find Sal, wearing one of my Bob Marley t-shirts and nothing below, sitting in front of her laptop, drinking tea and composing an email to her brothers. She'd taken to drinking her tea with sweet condensed milk, the same as my coffee. A cup of coffee waited for me on the nightstand. I sat up, letting the sheet drape over my lap, appreciative of how comfortable she'd grown with the idea of us.

"I want to know more about them." That was all she said.

"And if they are part of this whole mess?" I couldn't shake the feeling that their appearance in her life was no simple coincidence, but I didn't get bad vibes from them. And we knew Aisha knew Q, so there's that. I just had a deep-seated belief their story had more to it than just what they shared with her that evening.

"You don't think it's a coincidence?"

"No."

"Ok, I'll keep your concern in mind. I just...I need to do this." She said it with her usual bravado, but I saw the vulnerability she hid deep down.

I had noticed it at odd times when she thought I wasn't paying attention. When she got really excited about Alix and Jax's adventure or told me about her memories of watching *Bleach*, one of her first animes. Of seeing Yoruichi and her joy at discovering a Black character in her beloved animations. When she opened up and spoke about her past and how her view of self had been shaped and warped by her mother. Or when I asked her about getting a joint account, which I'd done the night before, and she'd gone quiet and asked me for time to think.

"You know you can always talk to me, right?" I held her gaze, and after a few seconds, she gave me a suspicious glare.

"Oh, you want me to be all soft and shit and spill my guts? It's not enough that we're playing house and I let you call me fifty-leven nicknames. All corny, by the way."

I fought the urge to smirk and won.

"You call me nicknames, too." I crossed my arms over

my chest, the top hand holding my cup of coffee. I sipped slowly, then I grinned.

She huffed, a sound that had become one of my top three favorites, rolled her eyes, and gave me her back, but no typing happened. I waited her out. I'd learned that Sal would talk when she was ready. There was no rushing her.

"I used to be boy-hungry. I loved hanging out with the boys at school; I was that girl, the one who was quick and smart and made them laugh. And at the same time, I had Mila and Aisha, so I wasn't a pick me or anything; I just had a good rapport with dudes." She said everything while still facing the laptop. I was dying to see her face but took what she could give me now. And it was plenty.

"I always had a crush or two. I would instigate Mila and Aisha to sneak out and go to parties when we were sixteen. Knew how to do my makeup and theirs, dress all cutesy; I was *that* kid. I mean, the same abrasive personality, but I wasn't averse to hanging out with dudes like now.

"But my mom? Oh, she liked saying I was the pretty one. The one that would get us all out of poverty. She didn't want me to just hang out with boys my age; she wanted me to learn how to finesse.

"By the time I hit sixteen, she was teaching me how to bag dudes that could pay the bills. And I hated it. I hated it so badly. I was convinced mom was wrong, that men weren't just good for only that. I thought that she was jaded and bitter, and I didn't want to be that person. I hated that my father, whoever he was, had done that to her. Then my ex-boyfriend betrayed me, as you already know. And at first, I was so angry." She shook her head and turned around. Her expression was blank, but then her hand went to her chest, and I knew.

Sal didn't open up easily. My instinct was to haul her

into the bed with me so I could hold her while she told me more, but her body language screamed *closed off*. So, I gave her space.

"But then I tried to be rational and convinced myself it was a fluke. I had a few other relationships. All very private, mostly with dudes online. I lived the swirl life for a hot second, but I stopped that real quick when I realized a lot of the anime dudes that weren't Black were high-key racist. But regardless of race, they proved me wrong repeatedly. Some took advantage of my goodness in collaboration while I was still naïve...taking credit for work I did. Or swiping clients looking for software development work." She sighed and continued. "I never even told the girls about that.

"I'm not intransigent. I know that there are men out there that are trustworthy. I just haven't had the best of luck. So now my radar for bullshit is damn near foolproof. All this blabbering is to say that...with my brothers...I have to trust my instinct. Because my instinct also tells me I can trust you. That after a long, long time, I might have found someone I can be more myself with. And I don't want to think my instincts are off..."

Fuck, how could I argue with that?

Trusting my own instinct, I grabbed her arm and pulled her toward the bed. She refused at first but then let herself fall softly next to me. Gathering her into my arms, I kissed the top of her head as she snuggled herself into my chest and side.

"I hear you, and we're gonna trust that instinct. But promise me you'll keep your eyes open."

She nodded into my chest.

"You know, I miss that old me sometimes. The optimistic Sal."

"I think she's in there somewhere. You just don't like letting her out because some of her has things you have equated with your moms and sisters. For the longest time, when Delroy got me into ballet schools and I was honing my craft, I was confused about who I was. I might have hidden myself from colleagues, but outside of the ballet scene...my masculinity...the danger you detect is spot-on," I said as Sal's warm hand skated up and down my back.

"I've done stuff. I've let my need to prove to my family, even sometimes Delroy, that I'm the man they want me to be obscure the person I truly am. I'm soft and dangerous, quiet and primal, chill and passionate about my art; all of that is me. And when I'm behind these walls, I let it all out. You should try that sometimes, Sal." My chest tightened, and I closed my eyes as her warm breath skated over my skin and she listened. "You can try, if you want, with me. And...I would like to be able to talk to you too... There are things that weigh on my mind, things that—"

Sal stopped me with a soft kiss against my chest, making me moan.

"Shhh," she murmured, and I wanted to believe it was because she understood. Because she saw me past all the bullshit we had to contend with every day outside these walls.

Seconds became minutes as we lay on the bed, silent with the promise of protection and trust, the promise of space for a vulnerability like neither of us had ever experienced.

"Fuck, you *really* want us to just spill all our guts, don't you?" Sal finally said into my chest, then pressed the softest of kisses to my nipple, causing a ripple effect everywhere.

"And you want me to fuck you, don't you?" I replied,

sliding my hands beneath my T-shirt, finding her soaking wet.

"Yes. Always."

Maybe another day we would continue this promise of vulnerability. There was always tomorrow.

Twenty-Five

"GIRL! Where did you get that Aoba Johsai merch? And it's so sexy; you trying for that husband of yours to catch you slipping or what?" Cora's curious gaze met mine through the video.

Even though it was the weekend, we were having a working meeting. I pursed my lips but couldn't help the red flush of my neck. I couldn't front; I did think the cute crop top jersey in white and light blue from *Haikyu!!* was adorable. And if the shorts were a little shorter than my usual biker shorts...well, there was nothing wrong with that. I hadn't cosplayed in ages; the merch I got was always utili-tarian, t-shirts and hoodies. But the conversation with Devon a few days ago had stuck in my mind, and I'd ordered this little ensemble the next day in a rush, treating myself to the gift.

"Girl, I need you to focus. Have you heard from Juniper?"

"No, she has cut off all communication, even with me."

Fuck, I was worried. Patrice, Cora, and I had been searching for information about Juniper's connection with her boyfriend, trying to link Perez as well.

I'd had a win when I discovered that Perez used to own the apartment Juniper's boyfriend had gifted her. The rest all led to dead ends, and my confidence was dwindling. I kept convincing myself all was good through bravado and avoidance, but it wasn't working that well anymore.

"Listen, girly, why don't you let us continue the search? Things over there are getting complicated for you, aren't they? And if you're trying things out with the husband?" Patrice paused.

"Wifey, where you at?" Devon hollered from upstairs, and I rolled my eyes, then grinned. I really shouldn't have let him see me smiling the other day when he used one of his many nicknames for me. He probably thought I was putty in his hands now.

"Aww shit, did you just smile??" Patrice asked.

"Shhh, Patrice, please." I shook my head, but it was too late; he was bounding down the stairs, two steps at a time, wearing nothing but short dance tights and dance shoes.

"Nah, Patrice, tell me more. Was wifey blushing too?" Devon approached me and planted a kiss on my head.

Tough-as-nails Patrice, who didn't take bullshit from anyone, giggled at Devon's teasing, and I couldn't help but melt at that. Patrice was even more complex than I was, and here she was, sprung.

"Hey, Devon! Yeah, she was. You have our girl changing, we love to see it," Patrice answered, and I stared at her in amazement.

"Wao." That was all that I could say.

"Damn," Cora replied.

"You needed me?" I asked him, attempting to regain some type of control.

"Oh, Sal, we sent you a wedding present. Now I think it will be for both of you. It should arrive soon! Enjoy!"

They both logged off with goofy expressions on their faces, and that left the two of us.

"What do you think it could be?" he asked as if he hadn't just disturbed my meeting and gotten my girls all riled up with his smiles and shirtless state and... Damn, it was supposed to get better, this hunger. Now that we were fucking and talking and opening up, it was supposed to calm down. But here I was, thirsty.

"Lord knows, but you didn't come down to check on that," I said and then reran how my words sounded. Damn, I was getting better about sounding snappy with him, but sometimes it escaped.

I looked up, and he was grinning like he understood and knew me, and I couldn't help but feel like a little kid in a candy shop, just ecstatic to be here. Even with all the shit weighing us down, I was happy to be with him. Despite all the mess that led to us marrying and all that was to come, I was glad to be with him today.

The app I'd created to track the USCIS cases told me similar cases to ours were taking less time than usual. That meant time was running out for us. I didn't know what would come tomorrow, but I planned to enjoy myself for now.

"I needed your help with the choreography." Devon extended his hand to me, and I took it, following him up the stairs with a goofy smile. Damn, this man.

"Have I told you what 'senpai' means?" I asked him when we walked into the dance room.

"Yeah, you explained it to me...why? You wanna make

me your Senpai?" He smirked, standing in the middle of the dance room, hands on his hips, and I wondered if I could entice him to play a little. I did want him to be my Senpai for a little role-playing... Cosplaying would be a fantasy come true with him. I would have never thought this would be a possibility, but I was now wishing and hoping. His smile transformed into a suspicious glare, and he shook his head.

"No, I brought you up to dance, not to play." He crossed his sinewy arms over his chest. Well, that wasn't helping his cause. My left eyebrow became its own entity, reaching new heights.

"Nah, stop tempting me; come here." He pointed next to him, and the timbre in his voice, so serious, so...

"Stop biting your lips, Sal, or I'll make you pay tonight. I really need this."

That did it; that hint of worry in his voice teleported me to his side.

"Ok, these are the last sixty-four counts of the choreo, and I need your assistance."

He showed me the ballerina's part, and I marveled at his talent.

Watching Devon felt like witnessing tangible joy, art personified. Once he showed me twice, he played the song, and I was able to give a utilitarian version of the dance, enough for him to dance behind me, mimicking the moves with much more grace.

When I thought this was just for him to get to touch me, he danced away from me, going to the corner of the room, his regal stance mesmerizing.

With his feet in fifth and arms in third, he paused, and his hesitation permeated the room, removing all ease and wonder.

"You gotta jump there?" I paused as well and turned toward him, sensing his unease.

"Yeah, I...I have been doing sautés and several movements en l'air, but they ain't clean and not to my standards. And..." He shook his head, and his legs sprang into action.

Now any dancer would have killed to do a triple turn like that; I sure as hell couldn't even touch his jump. But I'd seen some of his performances online, videos of his celebrated talent, and I knew this wasn't Devon at his peak. He landed and finished the dance, but his whole stance was off, and once done, a slight limp emerged.

I wasn't a person prone to worry; I was a doer. And if I couldn't do it, then I didn't bother with it until I could fix whatever it was. There was no fixing Devon's tendon, I understood that, but nausea rolled in my stomach at the thought of him constantly pushing past what his body could currently do and swept me away, leaving me breathless.

"You should stop for the day."

Devon froze, probably interpreting my worry for something else.

"Nah, we can do it a few more times. I need to run through these last counts until they sink in. Let's start from the top of this section."

He stood again in the middle of the room, facing the mirror. Why was he being so stubborn? I knew from seeing him instruct and interact with students that he was a born leader and teacher. I'd also seen him do a few of the choreographies for the recital. He didn't need to push himself to these limits to prove that damn company anything.

"I married you so you wouldn't have to go through this pressure."

Devon slowly turned toward me, the perplexed look on his face surprising.

"No, *you* married me so I wouldn't have to depend on a job for my status here."

I paused; he wasn't wrong. That was the overall result, but I also hated the fact that the ballet company was pressuring him to perform when he didn't feel 100% yet.

"That was part of it, yes, but you're still going to therapy every day. That means you're still in recovery." I gestured to his bandaged foot and back at him.

Frustration roiled inside me in waves. I didn't know why I felt so strongly about this, but somehow, I did.

I hated seeing him push past his limits every day, leaving in the morning for therapy to then rehearse for hours and go teach. He came home beat half of the time and still with this smile on his face like he was trying to hide what I could see clear as day. He was running himself ragged, and I'd married him, so he had options. But somehow, he refused to explore any of them.

"No, I ain't in recovery; I'm conditioning and—" He frowned when I crossed my arms over my chest. "I ain't wanna vex you."

I scoffed. "I'm not vexed, I'm worried."

Men. *Oblivious.*

Wonderment flashed on his face at my words, at my worry; then he stalked toward me. A flash of danger detonated inside of me at his determination. His eyes darkened, and he bared his teeth. Goosebumps erupted on my skin, and before he could reach me, I whirled around, yanked the door open, and sped away from him.

The imminent peril of his pounding steps told me I wasn't running fast enough, and the searing feel of his arm clasping around my waist confirmed the fact.

Damn, I hadn't reached my room. He left me breathless as he carried me with one arm by the waist. The steel of his body behind me, exhilaration and security, mingled with the need to escape. How dare he distract me like this? I didn't miss the fact he'd used the chase to pump my adrenaline, and it was working.

"Let me go, Mufasa."

"Nah, use all your arms, little witch; I got you." He tightened his grip on me, dragging me back to the dance room while I made myself as heavy as I could. In the meanwhile, my veins were the perfect conduit for my molten desire, my shorts already soaking wet, and we hadn't even done much. Once we crossed the threshold, he manhandled me into the room, making me moan as I stumbled back, and he locked the door. Then he turned around again.

"You wanted to play. Let's play."

"Oh, please bring it—"

Devon sprang toward me so quickly that I wasn't ready.

He tackled me to the ground, and I landed on my ass. His heavy weight was comforting on top of me, his chest against my chest, our breathing mirroring each other. Time slowed down as I lost myself in his warm brown eyes. I hadn't realized there were specks of gold in them, making the leonine references even more real.

His locs cascaded around his face, tickling my skin. I caressed his cheek, the springy hair of his beard prickling my fingers as I traversed his angles. My hand continued its journey over his ear, behind his head, to tangle in his soft hair. His gaze shuttered, and his breathing deepened at my caresses. Oh, this man... I was liquid napalm under him.

"Sal," he whispered, his plump lips inviting me to kiss. I pushed up to do just that and felt his sigh of relief.

Gotcha.

"Bomboclat!"

I pulled his hair hard enough to get him off me but not

tug any essentials out of the scalp. The second he realized the play wasn't over, he leaped, crouching low, hands splayed as if ready to tussle.

I scrambled, crab-like, away from him, trying to stand before shit got real, then I folded, spread my legs in a split, and let him take me until I couldn't walk. But he didn't even let me breathe; in some wrestling move, he swiped his legs in a graceful circle under him capoeira-style.

I was faster, though, and hopped to miss his feet. He grinned a feral smile that made me wonder what I'd missed, then with his feline speed, he lunged, locking my legs in a hug, and I toppled like a bowling pin.

I didn't land on the floor. With impressive control, Devon kept his forward momentum, cushioning my fall. I landed half on him, the wind completely out of me, my crop top all in disarray, my heart smitten, my pussy throbbing.

"You gonna stop playing?" he growled.

"Neverrrr," I taunted. I couldn't. If I stopped, if I let myself investigate why I was so worried about him, why I cared about his concerns... How Devon's advice had become integral to my decision-making process, and how I'd started to wish for things I had never imagined for myself in a long time. I couldn't go there, or I would freak myself out.

He groaned, and I felt his hardness behind my thigh, ready for me. He accommodated himself under me, his arms embracing me, Devon becoming my floor pillow. He slid his hands under my crop top, pushing all the way to expose my breasts, my nipples hard as diamonds. The cold that hit me in the front was blunted by the radiating heat of my back against his chest.

Devon massaged my belly, then his hand skidded over my skin, weighing my breasts. He avoided the nipples, driving me wild with want. He ghosted his fingers on the soft undercleavage, then tickled the sides of my breasts.

All of my focus converged on Devon as he hovered over my nipples and swirled his tongue around my earlobe. I quivered, his strength so obvious as he cradled me over him. With a pounding heart, I thrust my chest against his palms, but he was ready, shifting his hands away to land them on my hips, and he ground me against him. His hardness was evident against my ass, and I couldn't help but search for him. I needed him inside me like I needed to code every day.

"Stop playing!"

"Nah, you wanted to play, so let's play."

I pushed my ass against him again, and sweet pain lanced through as his sharp teeth dug into my shoulder. Desperate for more, I flipped over and then straddled him, taking control. He chuckled as I hovered over him, undulating myself on him. The delicious friction was intoxicating until—

"Oop!"

In a whirl, Devon rolled us over, his weight back on top of me, with a devilish smile on his face. I shivered at the intensity of his gaze as he pushed down his shorts, springing free in a glorious display. Without breaking eye contact, he slid the gusset of my panties to the side, and his heaviness penetrated me in one decisive thrust.

A silent scream caught in my throat. I gasped for air as Devon relentlessly took me to new heights. His strokes punctuated all the sweet things he growled to me as he surged into me repeatedly. It was too much; he saw too much and gave too much. Overstimulation took hold of me by the feel of his skin, the tenderness of his gaze, and the rightness of his dick.

"Ahh, I need you to fuck me harder," I begged, needing it rough so the tenderness didn't catch me.

Leaving me empty, Devon flipped me, positioning me on all fours. I arched my back to receive him, and he didn't disappoint. From this angle, he felt more present, more demanding.

"Just because you can't deal with how real this is don't mean it's not," Devon whispered in my ear as his strokes filled me with untold delight.

The scent of us mingled in this room where he created art, and we made something new, raw, and primitive. We designed visual art together, the image of Devon pounding behind me in the mirror breathtaking. We created music with our bodies, the smack of skin against skin keeping the tempo.

I gasped when his large hand went to my neck, holding me in place for his backshots. I arched completely and surrendered to the feel of our bodies in perfect synchronization, the rhythm so unyielding and naked, the orgasm we created snuck up on me.

My arms faltered, and Devon kept going. My screams filled the room and even then, Devon kept me together. And when I sobbed with feelings for him bursting out of me, Devon came with a shout and my name on his tongue.

———

So my limbs were now Jell-O. I sat crisscrossed on my gamer chair in the dance room, in the little corner Devon had created for me to work. Devon sat on the floor, his soft hair caressing my legs as he played the guitar. He'd taken it out of the room's closet, surprising me yet again with a hidden talent. His clear tenor voice rang in the room as he serenaded me with...

"Are you really singing 'Hold You' to me?"

"Gyptian was onto something when he made this song," Devon said, then continued singing the song with the double entendre in the chorus.

"Are you trying to tell me something?" I chuckled as he sang the chorus again to me, this time with extra soul, going in on the part where he told his lady she gave him the tightest hold he had ever experienced.

"I'm just inspired after the way you distracted me from my rehearsal," he said and looked up at me, winking.

"Oh, please, you knew the moment you brought me here what was up." I snorted as he sang, the lyrics making me smile. "You have a beautiful voice, yet another thing you can do."

He finished singing the song, the strings of the guitar resonating in the room.

"You should hear Delroy; he's the real singer. I just do it to relax," Devon said, putting down the guitar.

"Am I stressing you out?"

"You know that's a no. But once, a long time ago...I used to do things that required me to clear my head." He stood up, and I marveled at how easily he moved when I could lie down in bed right now and fall asleep in seconds. I didn't miss his implication and stored the comment in my Devon file. I wasn't ready for all of Devon. Once I received the entirety of him, I would never want to leave.

"Mhm," I murmured.

"I gotta sing to you; maybe that way, you'll hear me better..." he crooned back. My heart halted, then resumed again, the rush of panic swift and gone before it could poison the moment.

"We don't have a lot of time left. I...I made an algorithm to tell me the times for cases like yours. They will probably mail you soon; I know that interview is coming."

"So we keep pretending this isn't real... I got time to wait you out, Sal. Trust me."

I was no coward, but I knew when to keep my mouth shut. Devon shook his head and grinned, but the smile didn't have all the sweetness of usual.

"You gonna stay here working, or do you want me to make you some dinner?" He offered me his hand. I took it and stood up, feeling the evidence of our play saturating my shorts. I followed behind him, my hand secure in his as he guided us down the stairs.

"I can still feel you." I paused, wanting a shower before anything else. I needed a minute; maybe that way, I could gather my thoughts. Articulating the ideas Devon put in my head scared me. To trust him...to trust like that again... What if he hurt me?

He stayed quiet for a second, then nodded, turning me toward my bedroom.

"Let's shower, then we eat."

Even with all my thoughts, I wanted this moment with him to linger, so putting my concerns aside, I followed him.

"Ok. So you're not gonna rehearse anymore?" I asked him as we walked into the room, and he went straight into the bathroom to turn on the hot water.

"Nah, I just want to spend time with my wifey tonight. I don't know if I'll always have that privilege."

I stood there watching him get into the shower, frozen at the spark of hope and fear his words ignited.

"Woman, you coming or what?" Devon beckoned from the shower, and damn if I didn't follow right along.

Twenty-Six

Change is the only constant in life. I seldom bothered fighting against the inevitable waves caused by the many changes I'd lived through in my thirty-three years. But the ominous cloud that threatened Sal's and my idyllic situation worried me about what was to come.

Sal and I walked into the dance studio. In the past few days, we had meshed our routines to allow her to have time out of the apartment but still in my company. She was starting to get restless, and I understood her need to reclaim her independence. Somehow, we both sensed that a turn in the corner was imminent.

"Oh, look, it's the newlyweds," Mila announced.

"Are you still annoyed at me?" Sal asked bluntly. Damn, but she really didn't mince words, and that shit was so enticing to me.

"You know, I...never mind." Mila shook her head, storming away to the back office.

Aisha started at Mila as she walked past her, and then at Sal.

"What you do now?" Aisha accused.

"I didn't do anything. I just asked her if she was still mad at me." Sal shrugged, and Aisha rolled her eyes. Tension was affecting us all, and as the clock ticked away, I wondered if I should make some decisions about how to move forward and keep Sal safe.

"This is how they both get when they're stressed out. Sal because, well, we know why, and Mila... Well, she's hurt about Sal not telling her things, but at this point, I don't know why she gets upset. Sal has always been like this," Aisha explained, exasperated with her two friends.

"I'm right here."

"I know, babe, and you know Mila is hurt, but you acting like it's nothing. Like always." Aisha walked toward the desk and gave Sal a hug. Sal sighed and leaned into Aisha's embrace, the tension clear in her shoulders, and a wave of deep-seated anger settled in my belly at the impotence of this situation. I wanted to fix all this for Sal, and soon, I'd have to act and let the chips fall.

I knew she was actively searching for Juniper's man. With not many leads to follow and Juniper not answering, she grew increasingly frustrated each day that went by. In her investigations, she'd found out that Perez was slated to go into the FBI before he disappeared.

The news freaked her out, and Sal stopped hacking into government databases after that. Seeing Sal freak out...my tough Sal... I thought I knew anguish, but that was before I saw my woman fretting about something we couldn't fix together.

The discovery of her brothers and father was another recurring topic, setting off disagreements that left us in opposite corners of the apartment until one or the other would yield.

I was distrustful of the coincidence of their arrival in her life. They'd showed up right after we found out Perez had a bolo on Juniper, and although she agreed with the odd timing, Sal was adamant about trusting her gut with them. The impasse was a loud roommate in our home.

Our home.

Somewhere along the line, I'd started thinking of the apartment as ours. We slept in the same bed every night, and I'd moved my things to her room. My room became a mausoleum for the things that I didn't require daily.

Sal said we were playing house, but for me, it was more than that. I wanted to make this a reality, but I didn't know how to persuade her that we had a future past this marriage of convenience I'd trapped myself in with her.

If I hadn't proposed the arrangement, maybe if I'd waited and gathered the courage to approach her with nothing but my sincere regard and attraction, we would have had a chance. But life had dictated how we came together, and now I was tangled in a web of confusing expectations.

"This is all so messed up. That girl put your whole life on hold and now threats are looming over you? I'm sorry, babes. You're out here trying to be Robin Hood, but things didn't work out," Aisha said.

"Nah, it's all good. I mean, she's probably safe, and that counts for something. But this shit is deeper than I realized, and it has been a lesson. Finding out that Perez guy was going into the FBI... Something's not adding up here, but I know I'm going to figure it out." Sal's spine straightened, and the vulnerability dissipated. Aisha nodded and attempted to let her concerns go, even though we all felt the same sense of unease. Leaving us in the waiting room, Aisha went into Room A to prepare for her class.

"You a'ight, my likkle lady?" I approached Sal and gathered her in my arms. She felt like hope, potential, and a whole lot of trouble against me. Damn, she had me gone.

"Here you go." She snuggled into me, sighing, the line of her shoulder sagging again. Knowing she could be vulnerable with me, the same as Aisha, soothed some of the frustrations away.

"I know you've been wanting to reach out to your brothers. Call them tonight. Let's arrange something."

She stared at me and nodded slowly.

"I was giving you one more day, and then I was gonna do that anyway." She shrugged, and I wanted to tumble her to the ground and laugh at the same time. She'd never let me fully take care of her how I wanted, but she'd yield enough for me how I needed her to. It was an odd distinction I hadn't understood of myself until Sal. I thought I wanted someone to take care of, but what I needed was someone that could take care of themselves and allow me the privilege of carrying the load with them.

———

Sal

This time we met at Q's. He gave us directions to access a side of his club that was only for him and his family.

"I live in the building, but you'd never know my home was connected to the club," Q said as we followed him into his two-story home. He lived in a small neighborhood, just three houses in a cul-de-sac.

"Where is the sex club?" Devon asked.

"Behind the house." Q pointed toward the opposite side of the entrance as we walked in. The living room smelled of cigars, some lovely wood scent, and greenery. If I were to guess who Q was by his space, I'd say he was meticulous, a creature of comfort, close to his culture, and well-read. We were surrounded by leather furniture and wood, dark gray and black, and surprisingly a lot of green. Two fiddle-leaf fig trees stood at opposite ends by a wall-encompassing rustic bookcase so large it required one of these library ladders. Devon surveyed the room, then found an armchair and sat down.

"Want something to drink?" Q approached a wet bar that had a plethora of whiskies.

"Nah, I'm driving." Devon shook his head with a nod, but I gladly accepted the offer.

"What's your poison, Salome?" he asked, and I pursed my lips.

"What do you have?" I asked, giddy, walking over to the wet bar. I spied so many wonderful bottles, but then my eyes found a Balvenie, and I pointed to it.

"Good choice, lil' sis. On the rocks?" I nodded, and the musical clink of ice fell into the tumblers. Amber liquid trickled into the glasses, and he handed me mine.

"Too soon." I accepted the glass but not the moniker.

The front door opened, and both Devon and I turned toward the sound. Q strode over to the leather sofa and reclined on it.

"It's Jardel and Joaquim," Q said more to Devon than to me, and I was surprised Q had also noticed his tension. I was working on getting used to being so attuned to him; every movement of Devon's, every gesture I picked up on immediately—which was why I knew there was more on his mind than he was letting on.

Zacarias strode into the room, sharing hellos, followed by a silent Xavier.

"Irmã." Zacarias reached out a hand and then asked for permission for a hug. Despite my dislike of public affection, I accepted his, secretly smiling at his tightening arms around me. The fact we had so much in common made me want to geek out and just shoot the shit with him, but it was too soon.

Xavier nodded my way and gave me a sweet smile that surprised me.

"Hey, Sal, you good? I thought you were gonna decide not to reach out to us." Xavier shrugged, his gaze softening, startling me. I nodded, a smile slipping away from me. Then I peeked at Devon, who was intently watching the whole exchange. The tension from before had eased, and a soft grin shined through.

My brothers' presence reassured me that I could trust myself. It was inexplicable; somehow, these very distinctively different men made me feel comfortable. There was comfort here I couldn't find around my sisters and Lilith.

"I want to know more."

The ride home was quiet. The Js, as I'd started calling them in my head, had given me a lot to think about.

"You feel better?" Devon asked as we entered our apartment.

"I feel more enlightened, which is a better feeling than this morning. I've been in the dark for so many weeks, searching and hacking in vain. Looking for a phantom in the dark. This might not be related, but at least it's some answers."

Devon stayed quiet, nodding along as I approached the fridge and pulled out some passionfruit juice.

"You still think this is connected?"

I sighed, knowing he needed this. Independence was second nature to me, but somehow that glitched at the edges around Devon. Our personalities integrated so that my freedom didn't disappear, but it yielded slightly to his distinct need to protect. From day one, when we married, I knew what he considered he brought to the table.

Protection.

We'd both pretended it was something else, but the layers of that pretense continued to peel back as time progressed.

"Your brothers just explained to you that your father is a narcissistic emotional abuser that goes through women, starting with their mom, who he got deported to marry his current wife. He's a habitual cheater, including your mother and many others." Devon washed his hands and then wandered to the living room.

"Yes, that is a good summary. You missed that he is a DEA agent and, on top of that, rich as fuck." I turned on the kettle, knowing he'd probably want some tea before bed.

"Mhm, that wasn't my full impression." His loud sigh was an audible reminder of where we stood regarding my brothers. I was trying so hard not to be annoyed at the fact that he felt so reluctant to trust them. Shit, I was usually the untrusting one.

"Yes, I know there are holes in their story."

"Not holes. They specifically told you there were things they wouldn't share with you."

"Which is why I trust them more now than I did when I walked into that house. They might not be telling me everything, but they're honest about it."

Devon kissed his teeth.

Oh, hell no he didn't. You know what...let me count right now. One, two, three, four... I poured tea into the cup I had prepared, then stomped to the sitting area and shoved the scalding mug at him.

"Here." The liquid splashed a little on his hand, and Devon jumped to avoid it landing on his lap. Damn, I hadn't meant to do that. I dabbed his hand with my T-shirt. Yes, a little forcefully, but still, I wasn't looking to burn him. He watched me with a mellow face as I plopped myself on the opposite side of the sofa.

"I think we're gonna have to agree to disagree here," Devon said, and I studied his face. He didn't have the smiley mask he could sometimes put on, which calmed me a bit. Instead, there was caution and observance.

I paused, knowing that no matter what I had to say, I would antagonize him. But I didn't want to set the wrong expectation.

"We can agree to disagree, but in the end, they are *my* brothers." I sipped on my juice unperturbed.

"Yeah, that's right. They are *your* brothers. But regardless of your feelings, I don't want you getting hurt. I know this marriage might be convenient, but when I stood in that backyard, I meant those vows, even if they are only for a few years." And with that, Devon stood up, cup in hand, and left me in turmoil to deal with the aftermath of his words.

Twenty-Seven

Devon

The USCIS letter sat on the kitchen counter. There were so many things in flux right now that the looming deadline was one more complication Sal didn't need in her life.

Last night things had remained tense, Sal slipping into the bed in silence, her frustration palpable and permeating the calm in the room. I couldn't deny her when she reached out in anger, her scratches and bites spurring me on until I flipped us over and thrust into her, her warm grip surrounding me, her desperation mine. We never broke eye contact, her beautiful brown irises darkening as she shivered in pleasure underneath me.

This was no way to live. The tension of our situation flowed over every aspect of our life together, not allowing us to be at ease. Not allowing her to rest easy until she figured out what was happening. Not allowing us to grow into any possibilities on the horizon.

I let Sal soothe me with her wet snugness, and I

comforted her with the security of my endless need for her. My strokes communicated what I couldn't say. Not yet, when there was so much in the air between us, so much to secure.

She urged me on with taunts and pleas, and the vehemence in her need compelled me. With forceful thrusts, I drove into her until my everything was Sal. Her fragrant scent of sex and licorice and her lush softness enticed me to lose myself. My spine tingled as my orgasm flared to life, unstoppable in its magnitude. I grunted in her ear as I emptied myself in her, and Sal shuddered in ecstasy under me.

Now in the early morning light, I wondered how to let Sal know. Her decisive steps resonated in the apartment over the tune of "Too Experienced" by Barrington Levy.

"Morning." I greeted her, waiting for her move. She approached me with a determined look in her eyes, and then the impact of her soft body hit me.

"I don't want us to argue. There's enough shit going on," Sal whispered into my ear, and everything in me roared in satisfaction.

"I don't like it when you're cross with me, Empress. I never want to hurt you."

"Oh, that's a new one." She chuckled into my chest.

"You like it? Is it the one?"

"I mean, it's not too bad." She shrugged in my arms, then slowly reached back, giving me a sweet smile as her eyes wandered to the letter.

"Is that..."

"Yes, it's...my interview letter." I nodded and went to the fridge.

"Oh, you mean *our*?" The tone of her voice was light, and I whirled around to find her smirking at me.

"Yes, wifey."

"Yeah, we can retire that one now." She waved me away and came into the kitchen, and we prepared breakfast together. The harmony that reigned in the apartment was held by the weight of our silent agreement to tackle things as they came. Our frustrations from last night had not ceased, but the lens on how we saw them changed when we agreed to be a unit again.

"What are you gonna do today? Want me to take you to the studio on my way to therapy?"

"I feel like I've only seen the inside of the studio and this apartment these past weeks," Sal complained as we ate our eggs and bacon.

"Yeah, well, I was thinking of having a fish fry at my brother's house. So you can meet some of our close friends, change of environment. Maybe we stay at his place for the night?"

Sal paused mid-chew and stared at me.

"You want me to meet your friends?" She sounded nervous, but that couldn't be, not my Sal.

"For sure, why wouldn't I?"

"I...ok, sure. That's fine." She waved a hand and then kept chewing, but her hand ran in between her breasts. A wave of protectiveness ran over me.

When she put her hand on the counter next to her plate, I slid mine on top of hers.

"What I told you about the vows last night? I don't know what comes next, but what I do know is I want more than an agreement of convenience between us. The marriage, that's just a piece of paper, I get it, but you and me...we could be more." We were more, at least for me. But I didn't want to spook her right now, so I kept my touch light on her hand even though I wanted to interlace my fingers with hers and squeeze with the depth of my feelings.

"We could, yeah, but we kind of are, aren't we? I've never been afraid of doing scary things, and I won't punk out now. While we live here, being together makes sense, but I'm not going to pretend this isn't scary. After you get your green card and I can move out...we can reassess."

Somehow Sal kept surprising me and, at the same time, doing exactly what I hoped she'd do—keeping herself protected. I had no energy to push her, and I knew that wasn't what she needed right now.

"Come here." I pulled her hand toward me. She paused, then raised a finger, took one more forkful of eggs, and pinched two slabs of bacon. I held back my chuckle, loving the way she ate my cooking. Then with the familiarity of a thousand mornings together, she settled her warm weight on my lap, sitting with her chest against mine. She nibbled the bacon in her hand and gave me the other piece.

"So, we are doing this for now, huh? Girlfriend and boyfriend shit?" she asked with a bit of red creeping up her neck.

"As you said, we've been doing that." I bit her plump bottom lip, beautifully pink.

"Yeah, but now we both know..." She winked and chased my lips as I sat back, my fingers digging into where her hips curved to her ass. What I knew was I wanted more than *for now*, but I'd take what she was giving.

"Mmm, sweets, have I told you I love it when you wear these shorts?"

"Why you think I keep wearing them?"

Damn, this woman. I knew what the gesture meant, what those words meant. It was my turn to press my mouth to hers, sucking her tongue until she moaned and squirmed on my lap.

"Usually, I wear a tee and panties at home, but I've been wearing the shorts for you," she teased, and I clapped her cheeks, making her yelp.

"Come on, I'll take you to the studio."

———

Sal

Mila had been quiet since I arrived earlier. We both were hanging out, awaiting the arrival of her first class of the day.

I had been working on a new job creating an app for a client, and while running the codes for it, I'd been searching Juniper's old bank account, hoping I saw some activity to give an idea of where she was. I ran a search on her known associates and found an encrypted WhatsApp message I was able to hack where she didn't share a location but said she was safe.

I was still worried about Juniper, but her safety set me slightly at ease. Mila next to me worried me more. I rarely argued with her, and when I did, I knew exactly why. She was pissed, and I superficially understood why, but not the undercurrents.

"Ok, you're mad, and I don't know why. And you're acting shitty, and that is rare of you, and I—well, I don't like it."

She kept swiping her tablet, working on her class schedule for the next couple of weeks, but I could feel the annoyance radiating from her.

"Try that again, Salome," Mila deadpanned.

Fuck, she was *mad* mad. I knew I was in the wrong, I

didn't want to hurt her and wanted to make things right, but I still didn't understand what was happening.

"I have feelings for Devon," I tried again.

"Yes, you have feelings for Devon, but that's not why I am mad."

"Right, well, I... I know I've been a bit distant, but I'm just scared. I'm scared of what's happening and these people possibly after me to find Juniper and how all of this is affecting you in the process. I'm scared of the marriage I've gotten myself into with Devon, and I'm afraid that I've found someone that makes me want to change my stance on relationships, and I—" I let out a shuddering breath, hating feeling this vulnerable.

"Oh, sweetcakes, that's why I was mad. Because I felt you just bottling everything up, and I know that shit is no good for you." Mila turned around, finally making eye contact with me. "This is a lot you're going through, and I want to make sure you're good. But how can I when you're shutting me out?"

My heart seized at her words, knowing I was in over my head. I kept blustering my way through the days. I'd never been this out of control in my life. This was such an odd feeling, to have to trust my gut that things would work out.

"So, we're good?" I asked, and Mila shook her head as if I was a lost cause.

"Of course. We're always good." She approached and gave me a hug, and I let myself feel everything I couldn't process.

"Are you ok?" she whispered once we separated, and the words tripped over each other in my throat, unable to come out. I nodded, looking away just as the bell rang. It was time for her students to start arriving; there was no more time for commiserations and discussions. No more conversation about how concerned I was about not only everything with Juniper but my brothers' story about my father and, most importantly, Devon, who just now was probably rehearsing himself to death. He was performing way more confidently so it probably was working, but I just wished he could let his body heal.

The door opened, and Trinity, Aisha's boyfriend's daughter, walked in with her mom—what was her name again, Chantal? Chantal had become a more active parent to Trinity in the past few months, but this was the first time she'd actually dropped her off for class instead of Knox.

"Hey, Ms. Torres, hey, Ms. Sal, how are you?" Trinity's sweet greeting floated from the waiting area.

"Hi, ladies, how are you?" Chantal's husky voice reached us, and I responded in kind, saying hello to both. I had mixed feelings about Chantal and her tumultuous road to recovery, from what we knew of what Knox had shared with Aisha, but Aisha and her noble heart had nothing but kind things to say about her boyfriend's baby mother, so I fell in line. I didn't need another friend mad at me.

I turned to Mila, who was oddly quiet, face blank.

Chantal stared at Mila for a second with a peculiar expression, then shrugged, going to sit down next to her daughter in the reception area.

"You not gonna say hello?" I asked Mila, who was still staring at Chantal and Trinity. I couldn't decipher her expression; it morphed between awe, concern, loathing, and then thirst. But I knew she wasn't with me at the moment.

"Earth to Mila." I tugged her arm, and she startled, then visibly shook herself.

"Hi, Chantal, and hi, sweetie. Are you ready for class?" And Mila walked away, holding Trin's hand, her effervescent self again.

Well, that was strange. Just as I tried to piece together what had just happened, Chantal walked out, and I got a text message from Devon.

Devon: I'mma pick you up at 7 pm. I have rehearsal the whole day. Did you bring a change of clothes for the fish fry?

Sal: No, we need to go home first.

Devon: Alright, wifey. I can't wait to lime with you and have you meet my people.

The ever-existing kaleidoscope in my stomach fluttered, so present I pressed my hand on my belly. I texted Aisha and Mila and told them I needed virtual assistance tonight. Before I could put my phone down, Mila burst out of Room B, her cell in her hand and an incredulous look on her face.

"We haven't had a dress-up summit for you in years. Actually, not since college?" She stared at me in amazement.

"I know. Take this as me opening up."

"Alright, bitch, we not doing this virtually then. This has to be in person!"

And she rushed back to the classroom, leaving me with a secret smile. I was glad to be back in her good graces; no matter what was happening, I needed to be good with my girls.

Twenty-Eight

Sal

"Wow, that's the one. You look amazing!" Aisha grinned, clapping as she gazed at me from the gamer chair in the corner.

"What, are you saying I don't always look amazing?" I planted my hand on my hip, and I saw her eyes widen in comical alarm. She tried to make eye contact with Mila, but Mila vehemently shook her head and avoided the interaction.

"Y'all some fools," I chuckled.

"You always look great, Sal, and you know this. Skin always smooth and soft, eyebrows sculpted, cute little gamer t-shirts... But you also know you rarely dress up." Mila shrugged, taking one for the team.

"Yeah, that's what I meant, like this, dressed *up*." Aisha nodded.

"For you..." Mila said under her breath, and I grabbed a pillow from my bed and launched it at her. She ducked, then flashed me an amused look. "That makeup is flawless, and you look just like the teenage Sal that was about to conquer the world." Her smile warmed my heart. Really, between them and Devon, they were softening me up too much.

I was wearing a cute, colorful skort with wide leg openings that flared out, giving the illusion of a flowy short skirt. I needed comfort, so I had on cute flat strappy gold sandals and on top, a sheer long-sleeved white shirt open at the cleavage and tied right under my breasts. I had my Hisoka star and teardrop shades on, and long drop earrings, and I'd added some heat to my coils so that my soft big afro was doing what it was supposed to do. But that's not why my girls were stunned. It was the makeup.

I'd been examining all the things I'd set aside to differentiate myself from Lilith and my sisters, from the gold digger lifestyle they'd tried to impose on me. I'd come to terms with the fact that there was nothing wrong with what they did as long as their marks were consenting; it just wasn't a lifestyle I had wanted to embrace. Conversations with Devon late at night had helped me realize how I'd repressed part of me to embrace the Oriole persona that had become all I knew.

I had my own style and loved cosplaying, makeup, and dress-up. I could be a trusting softy, but I'd put it aside to present myself in a way that didn't show any gentleness.

"Well, enough of both of you gassing me up. I gotta go." I turned around to pick up my little purse, and Aisha gasped.

"Your behind is almost out," she whispered.

I grinned and strolled out of the room.

"Where you going? Come back here and explain yourself, young lady! You're a married woman now!" Mila hollered, and I cackled.

"Exactly, and I'm going out with my husband. See y'all later!"

———

DEVON'S EXPRESSION was priceless when he saw me walk down the stairs. He rushed to the bottom of the steps and gave me a smirk that told me I would have a good ol' time tonight.

I sorely needed it. I knew things were coming, but it was nice to have a night to just have a good time together. I hadn't known how to tell him that without seeming reckless, but somehow, he'd found the perfect way for me to spread my metaphorical wings and still be safe.

"Bombo..." he said under his breath, ruffling his fresh locs as he slid a hand around my hips and pressed himself against me. He planted the softest of kisses on my forehead when I looked up and grinned at him. I couldn't help myself. Tonight, I wanted to play make-believe. That he was my true husband, and I was his true wife, and all was well in our world.

"Sir, where you goin' with these fresh locs, looking like a snack? You're a married man now." I tangled my fingers in his hair, and he ghosted kisses along the bridge of my nose.

"I refreshed them at Mila's sister's, just for you."

"Mhm, for me, huh?" I grinned. I loved his scent, and now, after us living together for a couple of months, it had changed slightly, a hint of sweetness added to his—our scents meeting and merging. I tightened my hold and tugged at his locs, and his hands trailed down my skort, making me sigh until he found the exposed skin where my ass met my thighs.

"Yes, for you. Is this for me?" He cupped my exposed

globes. "Because you're a married woman now." His rumble made my pulse skitter, and I wanted to stay. This fish fry could be postponed for all I cared.

"It's for me...and for you," I whispered and groaned when he squeezed my ass and bent to trail kisses right under my ear.

"Good. I love that you're letting yourself be all you are and that you trust me to be part of the journey."

This man, ugh, why couldn't he just fondle me and leave it at that? He needed to tug at my heartstrings while making me hot and bothered.

"Excuse me," Aisha sing-songed in a quiet voice that was way too close behind me.

"Listen, we're trying to go before you both make voyeurs out of us. Not that I'd mind because sheeze, the two of you are so sweet and hot as fuck, but we gotta go," Mila explained.

I shook my head in disbelief as Devon maneuvered me out of the way, his laughter booming in our apartment.

"Let's go, sweets."

"Awww, he really likes her," Aisha whispered as she walked past us, and we followed behind.

"Yeah, and he also wants to fuck her bad, so let's go," Mila whispered back, squeezing Aisha's hand and then glancing back to wink at me.

"SO THIS IS DELROY'S..."

"You can say it—mansion."

"Damn, when you said he was in the business, I didn't realize it was this profitable." I stared around the two-story structure. It was a grand house by the 826 with land around it and a full gate separating them from anyone else.

The gate was opened by a security guard that dapped Devon up and nodded at me, calling me "Devon's likkle woman." I swear, hanging out with Jamaicans made me feel like I was smaller than I had ever been. The expansive driveway was enough to accommodate more than the twenty cars currently double parked there. Even with all of that, the house had a wonderfully homey feel to it as we walked into the open floor plan with a double high ceiling with whites and grays. It was probably gorgeous during the day with all the natural light.

"Who lives here?"

"Right now, Carpenter and our cousin Desiree stay here sometimes. She has her own place, but this house is closer to the highway, straight to the strip clubs and the parking garages we manage. D found this spot in foreclosure and got a bargain. He hired a Jamaican-American construction company and remodeled the house for half the cost."

"That's nice. Does Desiree run things right now?" I stared at him as we followed the bass of the reggae music leading us through the modern yet cozy decor and out to the backyard, where about twenty people were chilling.

I knew Delroy stayed attuned to everything that happened outside of prison, but even though he took calls and I'd seen enough gun safes in our apartment to know he had once been way more involved than he felt comfortable talking about, I still couldn't see how Devon could manage all of what this empire probably required.

The smell of fried fish made my stomach growl, and I was glad for my light attire as the heat of the night had stuck close to the ground, the summer in full swing.

"Here's Desiree, and yeah, Delroy wanted me to do it, but..."

"But dance is your thing, I get it." I squeezed his hand, and he granted me that sweet smile that melted me every time. The terrace was huge, with a large expanse of green grass and a lit crystalline pool in the middle. There was wicker furniture in pods underneath umbrellas in corners of the large area, and a gazebo where two men and a woman were frying fish. The woman turned toward us and approached.

"Cousin, yuh late." A beautiful, statuesque woman in a flowy strapless white dress with long braids down to her calves, walnut brown skin, high cheekbones, and soulful eyes greeted us.

"Sal, this is Desi; Desiree, this is my wife, Sal."

I felt Desiree's scrutiny, and I returned it tenfold. Drat, I wish I had my computer to do a quick search. She didn't set my alarm bells off, but I liked knowing people's backgrounds if I could. Desiree seemed to be a badass, and I was ok with that, but I wasn't intimidated by her, so she needed to lower the intensity.

"What's up, Desiree?" I attempted to smile at her even though I knew she was sizing me up. If I didn't know this was important to Devon, I'd have my stank face on, but I didn't want to start that way.

"Mhm, wifey, huh? We shall see. Come, Sal, let me introduce yuh to the crew." For a second there, I was about to stop Desiree and assert myself as Devon's wife, but then I remembered our marriage and probably our relationship had a termination date already prescribed, and I felt an impotence I couldn't process.

"You good?" he whispered only for me to hear, and I squeezed his hand.

'Yeah, I'm alright."

———

THIS WAS the fifth time detailing my Jamaican heritage to one of the crew. Devon had explained through the introductions that all the people here tonight were part of the organization, all from Devon and Delroy's neighborhood in Jamaica. They'd been tight since Delroy was a kid and had risen up with him as he became a powerhouse.

"Every person here is trustworthy."

"Which is why you let me out of my pretty cage today," I teased him in between introductions.

Now his paternal cousin, Oney, called that because of the patch he had on his eye, was drilling me with questions.

"But did yuh motha cook yuh ackee and saltfish inna de mornin' on Sundays?"

Sigh.

"No, more like eggs, waffles, and a lot of bacon."

It was Oney's turn to sigh, then he stared at Devon. Devon grinned and shrugged as he sprawled on one of the large wicker chairs big enough for both of us to sit together. He was having too much fun with the gentle grilling I'd endured tonight.

Everyone had been polite, but nice was a stretch. It was like there was an outer perimeter that kept me away from them, but they slowly were inviting me to open up. Some more than others.

"Here, Oney. This gyal no yardie, Devon went and hook up with an American. A tragedy." Desiree handed a beer to Oney, and Oney shook his head.

"Nah, man, she know where her people from in the

island, she didn't just say 'Kingstan' so there's something there. We can work wit dat."

I avoided rolling my eyes as Desiree and Oney kept up the conversation, which soon changed to who was the better cook in the crew.

"You should have warned me they'd grill me," I hissed at Devon, but he laughed at my annoyance. I sat closer to him, loving the way he rumbled with his amusement. He finished his Red Stripe in one last gulp.

"And miss this fun? Nevah."

"Asshole."

"Mmm, sweets, you keep calling me names, and I'll make you pay later." That sensual, deep voice of his chased away all of my annoyance, leaving me restless.

"We can go now."

"Nah, we staying here tonight."

"Ok, ok. That's cool." I searched around the backyard and imagined the primal possibilities. I didn't dare hope, but this could be so good. I'd brought a bag just in case as he'd suggested. "Is anyone staying tonight?"

"You mean Desiree? Nah, she's going home tonight. Just Carpenter and the security in charge of the house, and he stays in the guesthouse." He nodded at Desiree, who was now sitting on Oney's lap, slowly grinding to the rhythm of the music.

"Is he her man? Aren't they cousins?" I asked curiously. Oney had a grip on her generous hips and looked to be in heaven.

"Yep, together since eighteen. Not cousins; Desiree is my mom's cousin's kid. Oney is my dad's brother's kid. Never married, though. Oney has a few kids outside the partnership, and Desiree has three kids with another man."

"What?"

"Long story. Desiree has tried to drop him several times, but Oney always stayed true to her. They love each other and that's all that matters. We Reid men love hard and love long. We don't let practicalities like divorces or other people's interest get in the way. Don't forget that." Devon stood up and pulled me to my feet.

"Come dance with me, sweets. Then after everyone leaves, I have a surprise for you."

———

Cora and Patrice's gift was waiting in the room we were going to stay in for the night. Devon gestured at the package, then turned around and pointed at another box.

"They rushed that one to my apartment and asked me to hold onto yours till mine arrived. I figured we could use them tonight..."

"What is it?"

"They didn't say, but they asked that we open them separately, so I'mma go to the room next door. Meet you downstairs?" He grinned mischievously, and I was certain he knew way more than he was telling.

"I don't like that smile, Mufasa," I called after him, and he chuckled and closed the door behind him.

Curiosity surged through me, and I rushed to open the black box sitting on the bed. It had a purple ribbon around it, and I couldn't wait to see what it was.

With sure hands, I uncovered the top portion to find light purple tissue paper lining the inside. The gentle rustle of paper crinkled as I hastily parted the layers to find a black bodysuit lying in the box.

"These hoes..." I whispered and pulled out the outfit.

With trembling hands, I undressed and slid into the

nylon and spandex suit. There was a large mirror in the bathroom, and my heart fluttered at the view. I hadn't cosplayed in years; they knew that. I hadn't enjoyed it as much anymore. With the high-key microaggressions in the community outside of the Black creators I hung out with online, I hadn't had the desire to explore this passion of mine for a while. But somehow, my friends had known, and somehow, Devon had gotten involved.

The design was exquisite, everything I'd imagine Alix wearing. It had a zipper in the front and very fine, beautifully curved purple lines swirling around, creating the illusion of a snatched waist and plentiful hips, not that I needed any help in that department. The black collar curved high behind my neck, similar to the Queen in Snow White, creating a dramatic effect as it plunged into the perfect cleavage.

The long, tight legs molded my thighs to perfection, and my ass...damn. They'd even sent a weapon, the gurade sword that I strapped to my back made of firm foam. My idea had been that Alix's battle gear had ways to provide easy access when she had encounters of a physical nature, and they had delivered my vision.

If I followed the curved lines around the hips, I could detach the legs, leaving the bodysuit high on my hips with a V-shape barely covering my crotch, exposing that love handle between leg and belly and my asscheeks to perfection.

This suit was supposed to be unveiled in the next scene when Alix went from just surviving the attacks to actually planning and strategizing how to win the war, a level-up of sorts where Alix figured out she didn't need to be a sitting duck anymore and went on the counterattack using the demons' strengths and converting them into weaknesses.

Devon and I had talked at length about what I wanted to accomplish, and I'd told him I would love to wear a body-suit like this... I reapplied my gloss and darkened the lines around my eyes. I was ready to see Devon, and I already knew what I would find.

The booming sounds of reggae and the selecta's voice were gone, and the terrace was now a symphony of rushing water from the pool and the myriad of insects that took over the outdoors. There were mango trees, royal palms, and shrubs all around in darkened corners in the vast yard, and a tall, well-manicured bush surrounded the space. No one could see Delroy's property, and I understood his need for privacy.

While I waited, I approached the pool area, the illuminated clear water provided a calming contrast to my nerves.

The crunch of grass behind me alerted me to Devon's presence, but my subconscious knew he'd been outside all along. I turned and gasped at how fucking breathtaking he looked in his own Jax costume.

A long-sleeved black faux leather bolero hugged his sculpted arms with a smaller collar than Alix's. The open-style jacket connected across his exposed chest with draped dark chains that started at his neck down to his belly bottom, exposing his abs. The pants were made of the same material as the bolero, with the same purple motifs as Alix's costume, and he had his weapons of choice behind him.

"I had plans for tonight, but now that I see you, I can't even think straight. You're stunning," he said.

I made an 'oh, please' gesture because my words were caught in my throat.

"Nah, you gotta listen. This? What you created? This is your bravery manifested in these costumes. And I can't wait to see the final scenes. When I saw how excited you were about this upcoming passage, I thought of getting the costumes made, but your friends were one step ahead of me and had already commissioned yours. When I reached out to them, they rushed mine. This is my thanks for letting me be a part of your process. I know you don't do that often. And when you're ready to actually put the game out there, I'll be your number one fan."

I took a shuddering breath, too full of emotion to say anything witty. I wanted to hug him, to climb him and attach myself to his chest, and I wanted him to take me hard, and I wanted to let his words fill every little crevice hidden from the world because he saw me. And it scared the shit out of me. He saw me, and even when I wasn't giving him all of me, he got me.

"There's a lot of shit going on around us. A lot of noise, but this? We have this," he said.

"We have us."

"Yes, Empress. We have us. And today, I want us to play, and then we'll deal with the rest tomorrow."

"Ok," I breathed, and I saw his nostrils flare as I squared up, realizing he was standing too close for me to dodge.

"What you wan do, baby?" he growled.

Baby. Oh, that one was new, and it made my legs tremble. Shit. I wanted to hide behind my cloak of badass retorts and cynicism, but I couldn't. Instead, I figured I'd dive into the deep end and just ask for something I hadn't had the guts to ask anyone before him.

"Remember the scene with Alix under the sex demons' influence?"

His intense gaze kept me in place, and I brazened the shit out of the role-playing I wanted to enact.

"I want to be the one under the influence now and for you to be reluctant but fuck me anyway. Because if you don't, then we can't save the world. At first, I'll try to fight you, but then I'll succumb, and you'll take me. Take me hard. Take me even if…"

"You want to do a consensual non-consent scene."

"Yes."

"I need a safe word, Sal, and we need a safe signal," Devon said. He concentrated deeply on every word coming out of my mouth, and I already was feeling malleable, ready for him.

I nodded, knowing he was right. I tapped my thigh three times, then reached for his hand and tapped on top of his palm three times. Then I stepped all the way into him, his scent of sea and citrus enveloping me.

"Convenience," I whispered, and he froze, then guffawed, cutting some of the tension around us and allowing me to breathe.

"Ok, wifey. Are you ready?" he growled in my ear, and I shivered at the promise behind the words.

Then I bolted.

Twenty-Nine

BLADES OF GRASS crackled under my bare feet as I sprinted across the yard. The knowledge of the yard's vastness was nothing to my thigh and calf muscles tensing under the speed required for Devon not to overtake me. I swerved to the right of me, closer to a cluster of bushes, diving in between and past them to slow him down.

His silent pursuit was unerringly sensual. My heart somersaulted in my chest as I finally heard the bushes rustle behind me. The gravel and rocks from the manicured path cut under the skin of my feet, and I felt the connection to the earth beneath me and the vegetation around me so vividly.

"I'm not running as fast as I can," Devon said between calm breaths, a reminder that he could take me if he wanted.

"Fuck you, Jax!" I retorted with a smirk. Adrenaline coursed through my veins, and I breathed loudly. I wasn't sure if the fabric between my legs was wet from exertion or arousal. Maybe both. The end of the yard approached, and I second-guessed myself as I ran past one of the mango trees, their fruit pungent and ripe.

The short pause cost me, and a heavy weight tackled me from behind. Pain bloomed as I stumbled and fell on the soft grass, the aroma of fresh soil mixing with Devon's scent.

"Gotcha!" he said, and I clenched all around at his exultant cry.

"No, you don't."

I shoved Devon off me, flipping us both with the effort. I ended up on top of him, his sinewy muscles cradling my bulk. I wanted to get comfortable. The hardness of his body and the bulge below my ass felt delicious. But another part of me, the part that was trying to hide, disliked the exposure; that side of me propelled me up and out of his hold.

I sat up on his lap, grinding my hips as a farewell.

"Fuck," he groaned, and I got on my haunches, then scrambled away from him closer to the mango tree.

I stood up again and assumed a fighting stance; hands up, palms open in a protective way, feet planted firmly on the ground, knees braced for anything. My skin tingled, and my toes curled in the grass when Devon gracefully stood up, mimicking my stance. His beautiful skin glowed under the terrace lights, his stare heavy with desire.

"If you want me, you're gonna have to come get me," I warned, and he laughed, a beautiful, taunting laugh that made my insides liquefy.

"Oh, I want you, and even though you're not fully with me yet, I'll take you for the good of us both. We both have a pact to save each other from this demon heat, and I'll do what I must," he said, and there were so many meanings that could come of his words that my fingers tingled in anticipation.

Devon lunged toward me, and I swerved, avoiding his charge, pulling my sword from behind me.

So many nights as a teenager and young adult, I'd dreamt of meeting someone whom I could do this with. A rush of elation overwhelmed me as I gracefully twirled on my feet and tapped Devon on the back with the foam sword.

He quickly recovered, turning around and pulling out his two spears, and we engaged in a fun push and shove, our foam weapons thudding against each other.

Devon's dancer physique glided over the grass, his sculpted chest gleaming with sweat under the chains, his eyes pools of desire as we divested ourselves of any social pretenses. We had never practiced, so of course, some of the moves were awkward, but overall, it was thrilling. Exhilarated, I threw my head back and laughed, the balmy air brushing my face.

"Fuck, you're magnificent," he breathed, and then before I could take in his words, air escaped me in a whoosh, and I landed on my back. Devon pinned me to the ground, wrestling me away from my weapon, and I was sure he could hear my palpitations. With a deep breath, he gazed into my eyes before he savagely kissed me, our tongues mimicking our fight earlier. I was soaking wet inside my costume. My nipples rubbed against the material, and I brushed myself against his hard chest, chasing the feeling.

Devon wrenched himself away from my lips, and I whimpered, desperate for more.

"I need you," he confessed as he pushed his knee between my legs where I needed him the most, whining when he gentled the pressure.

"Ahh, Jax...more."

"Fuck, Alix, I'm not supposed to. I—" He paused and

ground his dick against my pussy. It ached; it needed to be filled.

"More," I moaned. I bit his earlobe, causing him to jerk into me.

"No, Alix, we shouldn't." He tried to get up, and I loved the fact that he was getting into it, deep into the scene. I had lost the plot in the fun of the fight for a second, but he hadn't forgotten. Not one bit.

I yanked him back into me and stole a kiss that left us both breathless. When we separated this time, he devoured me with his gaze, and I broke into goosebumps.

"If mi tek you, then mi think yuh wearing too many clothes," he murmured to himself, then yanked at my cleavage, breaking the zipper in the process. My tits bounced out like a waifu's in a fan service moment. Devon bit his lips, then slid his hands under my armpits, dragging me on my ass over the grass until my back met solid wood.

I kicked and pushed, the crunch of dead leaves under my feet, and a desperate yearning bloomed in the pit of my belly.

At this point, Devon was feral, eyes dilated, nostrils flared, teeth bared, and I loved every second of it. When he had me against the tree like he wanted, he got himself into a semi-plank over me, then settled himself to demolish his meal.

I screamed when the sharp edge of his teeth met the soft skin of my areola, and I gasped when he captured the tender flesh with his lips and pulled until my distended breast could yield no more. The coiled hairs of his beard tickled my skin as he pressed his entire face between my breasts, smothering himself with them.

Did Devon Reid just motorboat me?

He took a big gulp and then came up for breath from between my tits, still holding them between his hands.

"You smell so fucking good, and your tits are so *fucking* abundant, and my dick is so fucking hard, and I can't even think anymore. I want to fuck your face."

"Don't ask, do," I pleaded, completely caught up in the maelstrom of our desire.

"A'ight." He jumped to his feet in a smooth burpee-like movement; pain shot through me as he grabbed a handful of my curls and pulled my head flush with the tree.

With one hand, he maneuvered his suit, which must have similar Velcro fastenings like mine. His generous dick bobbed out, slick with precum and mouthwatering. I'd been in close contact with his dick for a couple of months now, but it looked especially pretty tonight under the moonlight with its prominent veins and dark, bulbous head.

Using the same hand and still holding onto my head, he hooked two fingers between my lips to pry them open. Before I could adjust to the intrusion, he shoved his entire length into my mouth. At first, instinct and nature made me scramble, the air caught in my throat causing me to panic. Devon, in tune with me, pulled back, and sweet oxygen returned to my lungs. As soon as I recuperated, he was right back in, but this time, I was ready. I salivated around his salty, smooth skin, inhaling the musky scent of him.

"Bomboclat, Sal, your mouth is— Jesus!" Devon groaned. He took a few shallow exploratory strokes, testing my gag reflex. Tears escaped the corners of my eyes, and I stared up at him in defiance.

The mighty warrior, protector, primal, chains bouncing with the movements of his frame, his muscles all tensed up. Devon's knees bent to line up with my mouth, but he remained at my complete mercy. The gentle dancer, tender soul hidden under the traditional masculine expectations, the easygoing dude his costume when stepping out in the world.

See, the problem with these primal scenes between Devon and I was that we kept stripping parts of us bare for the other to see, and lately, we'd been diving deep into each other, so deep I was afraid. Afraid I wouldn't be able to walk away and move back to my apartment after we figured things out with Juniper's man, unable to turn my back once the three years had passed. He wanted to try, and I wanted to as well, but I knew myself, and I recognized my trust wasn't fully granted, no matter how much I tried to rationalize his trustworthiness.

I pushed the troubling thoughts aside and relaxed my throat, and Devon slid all the way in.

"Woman, you're gonna kill me," he moaned.

I hollowed my cheeks and made his dick disappear with each thrust of his. His curses increased in volume, and soon, he was mercilessly pummeling into my mouth.

"Take it, take it all. Take all of me," he grunted; to the naked ear a command, but we both knew better. I groaned and raked my nails over his clothed ass, disappointed I couldn't feel his flesh under my claws.

The gusset of my costume was utterly saturated, and it would probably wash away in the wave of wetness he created. I swirled my tongue all around his length, my lips stretched to the limit. He was fucking my mouth with primitive abandon, and saliva foamed around my lips, pooling at the corners as he pressed me against the bark behind us.

"Nah, I'm coming inside of you, Alix. I need you with me again."

How the fuck he kept the scene straight in his head was a mystery. Hot air rushed into my lungs the moment he pulled back, his dick coated with the froth of saliva and precum. Our pants were loud in the backyard, mingling with the rustle of leaves from the gentle wind.

I sat back against the tree, gathering my strength for what was to come because I knew he wouldn't take it easy on me.

"Fuck me so hard I come back to you, Jax," I taunted, and he bared his teeth at me. Air swirled around us as he manhandled me like a doll, turning me around. I ended up standing against the tree, hands braced on the bark, ass and pussy free in the hot summer night.

He crushed the high collar down, and with a hand on my neck, Devon's hot length nudged my entrance from the back, the heat of him even higher than the sultry night temperature. He glided inside of me with one deliciously forceful thrust, then proceeded to rock me with rough lunges that promised to make me a Devon fan forever.

I attempted to clamp onto him, to slow him down, but my pressure on his dick only propelled him faster. The strokes were so steadfast my entire body swayed against the tree, tits swinging, hips undulating, ass jiggling; I felt it all. And Devon did not relent.

"Devon, it's too much, please," I begged because he was making me feel with his dick what I refused to feel with my heart.

"No, you're gonna yield to me; give me yourself," he grunted, and I wondered if this was the role-play or more. And as if he had a chip embedded within my mind, he continued, words faltering between thrusts. "I want yuh, Sal. I want di whole of yuh. And I'll give yuh di whole of me."

The smart bastard. I could construe his words in so many ways. He left it to my interpretation, and I whimpered at the impotent feeling of it all. Damn my heart that wouldn't fully succumb even when I rationally understood everything he gave me.

I wanted to yield. I did.

He pounded into me, but never did his thrusts lose finesse. All throughout, his dick slid exquisitely in and out of me, the motion of his hips ensuring he hit my spot every single time. His hand slid from my neck to one of my tits. The other hand went to my clit and, with his index and middle finger, circled my little hood.

Time froze. The leaves stopped moving, the earth shook, and pressure built between my legs, in my chest, and behind my eyes.

"Are you with me?" he groaned into my ear, and I nodded, unable to talk. The faster he rubbed my clit, the more I lost myself, and the orgasm built from the tips of my toes, overtaking every cell in my body and transforming me into pure exultant energy. My legs gave up, and Devon shifted, holding me as the most violent orgasm of my life disintegrated me into pure sensation, and I wet his entire dick as I squirted simultaneously.

My pussy squeezed so hard that Devon roared, and with one last delicious thrust, he unloaded inside of me, his hot ejaculation seeping around his dick and down my costume with the abundance of his climax.

We collapsed to the ground, somehow still connected to each other, me on Devon's lap, the tree miraculously behind us. My thighs still burned, and I would pay for all these calisthenics tomorrow. I closed my eyes and surrendered to the exhaustion that gripped me, but not before hearing Devon.

"That's alright, Empress; you'll give yourself to me soon."

Thirty

Devon

The scene from last night kept filtering through my mind —never-ending snaps of Sal in all her glory, her Alix persona, her Oriole bravery fully displayed as we scampered underneath the moon and cosplayed her video game characters. I was glad to give her this moment because I had to share with her what Carpenter had told me when everyone had left before our play. We'd agreed to meet after I had her safely back at home, planning to infiltrate the dealer's group and flush out the danger to Sal. I couldn't sit back and let her be hunted anymore, not now that they had her full name and location.

Sal lay sprawled belly down next to me, plump cheeks adorned by her freckles, mouth parted. She was snoring big time, the cute ass rumble telling me I wore her out last night. Her big booty relaxed in slumber, and her smooth, thick arms hugged the pillow. Her body was a work of art, and flashes of her groans of pleasure appeared unbidden;

the hot feel of her clamp on my dick, Sal laughing with delight in the dark of the night, her ass and hips rippling in waves while I thrust into her. The memories made my morning wood harden painfully, and my heart accelerated in my chest. Her bonnet had fallen off her head, so I gently put it on again, running my hand over mine, making sure it was still over my locs. Who would have thought I'd be lying in bed with my wife in matching blue bonnets?

"Could you be less sweet?"

I grinned at her grogginess. With one eye closed, she eyed me, then buried her head in the pillow. I rubbed my chest, and the gesture was so like hers, I shook my head in wonderment.

"Sal, I gotta talk to you."

"Uh, that doesn't sound good," she said and managed to raise her head again.

"They got your name now. They know exactly who you are, and this dude put out a call for you to get grabbed. They provided your house and the studio as the main areas to find you."

"So they don't know I'm staying with you?"

"I guess not, but I don't think that will last long."

Her eyes clouded in concern, and I could see the joy of the night melting away, the tension in her returning. Even her booty clenched, and I couldn't help but rub one ass cheek in commiseration. Anger had already taken the best of my thoughts when Carpenter told me last night. I was in planning mode now. I was going to make things right for her and us.

"Ok...I...shit. If I had a shred more information... I don't know if Juniper lied about him or what, but nothing from the little I have about him returns anything solid."

"I know, but we might have other ways—"

She pushed herself up and sat crisscrossed facing me. Her titties were free now, and I had to fight to focus above her chest.

"Eyes up here; you can stare all you want once we fix this. I actually like you staring." She shrugged, and I concentrated again. "So, what are these ways? Do these ways include Carpenter and the crew from yesterday? 'Cause I don't want to mess anything up for Delroy."

Stubborn woman.

"You let me and Delroy worry about that."

" No, no, you gotta give me a chance to figure it out before you go to more drastic measures through Delroy."

"You've been searching for weeks, months really. Ain't nothing working. You've barely been able to do Oriole work because of it. Enough is enough."

I knew I got to her when her face underwent several shifts in mood in the span of seconds. She was pleased I was thinking of what she'd lost but worried and stubborn enough to try to defy me. I wasn't looking to argue right now, so I grinned at her, and she narrowed her eyes.

"Why you smiling?"

"Because you're miraculous, and you're next to me in my bed like a dream come true, and I never thought I'd be so lucky."

Her gaze softened, and she bit her tongue, then rolled her eyes.

"You're too much. My legs are closed for the foreseeable future."

I chuckled, letting her think I was thinking of sex, but we both knew I was not.

"Oh, I forgot to tell you. Let's get that joint bank account," she murmured, then hopped off the bed and into the bathroom, leaving me wondering if we had a chance after all.

———

Two weeks later I was pushing myself in every aspect of my life. Carpenter and I were working on a plan to put this shit to rest, I was rehearsing longer hours now that the showcase loomed near, we were having extra hours of practice with the dance team for an upcoming dance competition in August, and I was attempting to pretend things with Sal were good.

They weren't.

She barely spoke to me, even though we still had sex every night. It was like she saved all her energy for our encounters, and that was the only time she let me fully in.

Sal had retreated to her computer and the urgent need to figure out how to get the mark off her back.

We slept together and ate together if I was home, but being locked up in the apartment was getting to her. Witnessing her retreat was affecting me badly. I kept trying to reach her, but it felt like she'd reconstructed her walls and made them impenetrable.

She'd stopped working on her video game, barely talked to Cora, Patrice, Mila, and Aisha, and stayed either doing whatever magic she did on the computer or working on her commissions. She'd forbidden Mila and Aisha to visit, with the wise thought that if they were waiting to grab her, they might use our friends as bait to flush her out of our apartment.

Our situation lay heavily on my shoulders as I sat at the kitchen counter eating some porridge, having the odd morning off when Sal padded down the stairs with her laptop in hand.

"I want to see Q."

"What does Q have to do with this?" I asked worriedly. It didn't feel right; there was something I was missing regarding Q and her brothers. They'd appeared after the bolo, and now Perez and his boss had Sal's info. Until we figured that out, I wasn't sure she should be around them.

"I don't know, but I've been trying to discover more about my dad, and it's proving to be as hard as finding info on Juniper's boyfriend."

"Mhm," I grunted.

"I'm going to see Q," she said again as she settled herself on the large sofa.

"I don't think that is a good idea, teammate." I swiveled on my seat in the kitchen and smiled at her, holding back the maelstrom of my emotions.

She stared at me for a second and scoffed.

"No smiling, Devon. You don't want me to see Q."

I counted up to ten, then I grinned again.

"Why tell you what you already know?" I felt myself retreating. I tried to stay present. I wanted her to see me so badly, to understand my concerns. Every time I tried to open up, she got spooked. I got it, but it hurt.

"But you also understand how I am." She stared at me and attempted to make the sentence a question, but it was a statement.

"So, what are you saying?"

"I said I am going to see Q," she said with a finality that dropped into the room, creating ripples neither of us was ready to confront.

I kept my frustration in, even though it threatened to

remove my ability to regulate my emotions. Once I found my center again, I attempted to de-escalate.

"If you're gonna see him, I'd like to be here."

"Ok, that...that works." She sighed, and that simple gesture cut some of the tension. Us trying to circle around our needs as individuals and not finding consensus was normal. Marriages probably went through this. I was sure Delroy and his wife had scrapes like this in the past. We could work this out.

Now I needed to convince myself.

———

"I'M GOING to invite Q to come later. Does four work for you?" Sal asked while we both ate breakfast the following day. We'd been careful with each other after the conversation yesterday, and I was still feeling bruised today.

"I got rehearsals until six today. Can we do it then?"

Sal paused, then studied me.

"It's Sunday. The company rehearses today?" It was such a calm question, but there was an added weight to it, and I treated it as such.

"Not the company. I'm rehearsing with my fellow dancer and the choreographer. My turns still need work."

"So you had a half-day rest; you rehearsed yesterday. You ain't letting your tendon rest." She frowned.

"I hear you, but the show soon come; I need to be ready." The same bubble of frustration from yesterday formed in my chest again. I probably hadn't done the best job explaining to Sal how important dancing was to me, and today I didn't have it in me to start. I hadn't let her fully in, even though I'd been urging her to do the same with me. I didn't have space to sit with my hypocrisy today.

"You don't need it so bad that you're gonna run yourself ragged," she retorted, and I tried to ignore the concern, secretly enjoying Sal's gentle nagging style.

"It's important to me, dance. It's..." I attempted to lower my guard.

"Never mind." She shrugged and finished eating her breakfast.

I left for rehearsal feeling uneasy with things unsettled with Sal.

Thirty-One

DEVON

Fuck, I was rushing home after a long ass day. I was an hour later than I'd told Sal, but at least we could call Q once I arrived home. It was still early enough for him to drop by. I felt uncomfortable with us meeting him in the apartment, but I didn't want Sal out and about, and the apartment was the safest space we had, difficult to penetrate without Sal or me approving entry.

I'd moved into this apartment for security, and having Q in our space was testing all the precautions and protocols the building had in case he tried to return uninvited after learning Sal's location. Aisha had vouched for him, but in the end, my instinct had saved my life and Delroy's one too many times.

With thoughts of safety and keeping Sal well, I walked into the apartment to find her across the dining room table from Q.

An insurmountable anger rushed at the sight of him in my space, of Sal's undermining my one request that I be here while he visited. It looked like they were already wrapping up.

"Hey, Devon, what's up?" Q immediately stood up, his imposing presence not giving me any alarm, but I still detected something missing in their story. He approached me, giving me respect in my own home. I suspected he had no idea what I'd asked Sal.

"Hey, man, you good?" I dapped him up but couldn't muster my usual smile. Sal stood up, slowly staring between us.

"Hey, Devon."

"Sal."

"You were late, so I called Q. Sorry you weren't here," she explained, her stance defiant. I gazed at her, and she returned it with a glare of her own. The fuck, was she pissed?

"Hold up, Sal, did Devon ask to be here for me to meet? You know what, I should have trusted my gut. Listen, I want to get to know you, sis, but safety is always first. I don't tell anyone how to do things in their marriage, but please make sure you're both on the same page before you invite me into y'all's space again. I don't want to disrespect either of you." Q's firm tone startled her, and the red on her neck crept up and overtook her cheeks as well. Damn, this man shook even Sal. Impressive.

"Thanks, Q. I...I hear you. I...thanks for what you shared about our father. It helps." She nodded, and Q stared at her for a minute, then shook his head.

"You're stubborn, just like Jardel and me. Joaquim has his own stubborn streak, but it has less of an edge, like your husband's." Q nodded at me, then studied both of us. There was an intensity to him that told me he wasn't someone to mess with, and he recognized the same in me.

"Listen, I don't know what's happening, but don't let our coming into your life cause a strain in your marriage. Can't help the big brotherly advice." He threw his hands up and then nodded toward the door. "I'mma head out. I gotta get to the club."

"Ok. Thanks, Q."

"Later, Sal."

The moment the door closed, we went at each other.

"You said you would be home at six!"

"Rass, Sal? You can't take your safety for granted!"

Sal started pacing the living room, hands clenched at her sides, while I went to the kitchen, needing to stay in my corner for a second before I grabbed her and just kissed her till she saw some sense...yeah, I couldn't go there right now. She paced the floor in leggings and a big t-shirt, the fabric of it rippling as she flapped her hands around her, but no words were said.

"Sal."

"We're supposed to be a team," she finally said, her sad eyes lancing through me. Fuck, I was ready for a fight, not for this.

"We are, but we can't if we each keep things from each other," I said gently.

She scoffed, throwing a hand out. "I'm not the only one," she replied, but it had no heat.

I grabbed a banana from the fruit basket and peeled it, needing to keep my hands occupied.

"I know. But..."

"Yeah, but..." She pulled at her coils, staring at me. Both of us were so used to our masks, so comfortable within ourselves, that this last area to open up was a struggle. And within the words unsaid was the missing link between us.

"Come here," I urged, and she shook her head.

"Come here, Ursula."

She approached with a slow gait, hands on her hips. When she stood in front of me, I put down the uneaten banana, then I ran my hands around her waist and pulled her closer. With tender care, she stretched her arms and slid them over my chest, hooking them around my neck. The feel of Sal in my arms softened all the anger and concern, and everything that seemed impossible a few seconds ago now felt inconsequential. Because I had her in my arms, and all the rest was noise.

"We're a mess, aren't we?" she said.

"Nah, we just newlyweds, ya know? It takes time to figure shit out."

"It doesn't feel like we have time..." she whispered, and her soft curls rested on my chest.

I kissed the top of her head, the smell of our grapefruit shampoo soothing me even further. I couldn't answer her back right away because I felt like I was trying to catch water with a net.

"Nah, I'm gonna fight for you, even if I have to fight you as well."

Sal froze in my arms. I held my breath, releasing it when she shifted, and the soft heat of her lips pressed to my neck. Her wet tongue laved over the spot where she kissed, detonating an explosion of sensation, my arousal sneaking up on me so fast my heart tripped in excitement.

Desperate hunger crashed into me. I searched for her mouth, bumping her face in my need. I didn't breathe again until our lips crashed together, our hands clawing at each other, the necessary clothes removed in order to get as close as we could to each other.

"I need you," I said, the simplest, most efficient way to communicate the depth of my emotions to her.

"Take what you need then," Sal teased, her voice husky in my ear.

She didn't need to tell me twice. I hooked her legs around my waist as both our pants landed on the floor, and in one savage push, I drove inside her.

She moaned, and I cursed as I rocked into her, slow, sensual thrusts that made her breath hitch. Sal's wet heat surrounded me, and I wanted to thrust until there was nothing but her and me in this quiet kitchen, skin slapping against each other, the scents of tropical fruit and Sal's earthy scrumptiousness saturating my senses. I wanted to plunge into her until no anger, no secrets remained, until it was just her and me. My wife.

"Say you're mine, Sal." I grunted in her ear. Her beautiful body undulated over me, and I held her bountiful ass in my hands.

"You better not fucking drop me," she threatened, then moaned when I gave her a hard thrust, making her legs shake around me.

"Say you're mine, Sal." I growled and bit the soft skin of her breast, the bite not as hard being impeded by her t-shirt. She cursed and clawed her nails at my neck.

"Fuck me harder, Devon," she moaned.

I slowed my strokes even more until our hips rolled together, the slickness of our skin making the movements easy. She clenched around me and whined, desperate for more.

"Are you gonna make me beg?" she said.

"I'm not making you do anything." I bit her lip, then licked inside her mouth, and she quivered around me, making me thrust harder and faster.

"You don't play fair, Sal."

"Neither do you, hubby." She laughed as I sped up,

needing to nut, to feel her tighten around me, to make her lose control. Even if only here. Even if only in this.

We lost ourselves in each other, the strength of our strokes transporting us to our own little world.

"Ohh, fuck. Fuck!" Sal screamed, her orgasm taking her away, washing through her. She wetted my dick, stealing my breath away and dragging me over with her.

Everything inside of me poured into her. My legs gave up.

"What's happening—oh shit!" Sal exclaimed.

We slid to the floor, but I managed to still hold onto her. I don't know how we avoided injury, and I was glad my dick was already soft, still inside of her.

"I told you not to drop me." She chortled, and I realized how much I had missed that melodic, throaty sound.

"And I asked you something." I smiled as she snuggled up on my lap. I could stay sitting here with the cold floor underneath my ass if it meant Sal's warm, sweet weight over me. We fell into a lull, both contemplative after our desperate passion. Minutes passed until I realized she was dozing off over me.

"We should go wash up and go to bed." I kissed the top of her head.

With shaky legs, we both got up. I intertwined my fingers with hers and guided her toward the steps. Right before we went into the room, I heard her murmur.

"I want to be."

And her words urged me to keep hoping.

Thirty-Two

Aisha and Mila stared at me from the screen.

"So your dad is a major fuckboi." Mila nodded, succinctly putting into words what I'd just shared with them.

"Oh, he's more than a fuckboi. He's an emotional abuser, from what Q explained." It had been a hard pill to hear how my father had manipulated his kids to believe their mom had left him when instead, he'd gotten her deported back to Brazil, so he'd be able to marry one of the biggest powerhouses in South Florida.

Maya Dorsen was a descendant of one of the first Black millionaires in Florida. Her family reach was vast. And Daddy dearest had positioned himself as a wealthy do-gooder, a star agent, and a serial cheater.

"How are you feeling, babe?" Aisha said in the gentle tone that she felt soothed me. It did, damn it.

"I feel so choked up here. I need air. I need to get out."

"Nah, you don't. You have to be careful. That dude, he's

started hanging out in the parking lot again. He's even followed Mila and me, but don't worry, Devon had someone watching us," Aisha confessed, and my stomach dropped at that news.

"Fuck, I'm sorry. I've really made a mess of everything for everyone, haven't I?" I said in a moment of clarity.

"Nah, you haven't. You tried to do the best you could for women that needed help. Your heart has always been in the right place."

"But was it for the right reasons? Was Oriole a way for me to give a big middle finger to all men?"

"Ah, sweetcakes, why are you doing this? Don't second-guess yourself. You've helped so many women get out of horrible situations," Mila said.

"Yeah, like Lilith. You know, I called her, and she broke down and told me my dad had been abusive. Not physically, it never got to that, but abusive, nonetheless. Toward the end, she was afraid of him. A mark not worth the money, she said." Lilith said it had all been worth it because it got me here. That had been a long conversation, the beginning of healing for both of us, and fuck if I hadn't gotten teary-eyed. I blamed Devon for my excess emotions.

"Oh wow...hold up," Mila said, and her camera jerked as she pulled out of the frame. Shuffling and her muffled voice came through.

"What, it's time?"

Another muffled voice, this one male, responded.

"Yeah, we gotta run. You can follow behind, but Daniel already has Mari in the car. Alright, can you bring the ball?"

Oh fuck, elation sparked. I was a softy for babies. Aisha and I grinned at each other in excitement as Mila appeared back on the screen.

"Oh, my God. I'm gonna be an auntie!" Mila squealed,

teary-eyed. Not gonna lie, I got choked up a bit too. In a sea of messed-up, here was a beacon of happiness, and I wanted to share the moment with my friend.

"What hospital, Mila? I'll meet you there!" Aisha said, and this was how connected we were, the three of us on the same wavelength. Then reality came crashing down.

I couldn't go. Not me.

I was stuck in a dangerous mess, a game of cat and mouse, but I didn't know who the cat was. If I did, I'd have already swiped his ass and gotten rid of the tail. Mila blurted the name of the hospital to Aisha, and we said our goodbyes, Mila unable to contain her excitement.

If things were normal, I'd be right there with her. We would be in that waiting hall, Aisha probably with a million balloons, me with my laptop plotting ways to make sure our new niblings' identities were fully protected the moment they got their birth certificates, Mila probably loving her parents fussing even though she pretended not to like it.

When had my life tilted sideways, leaving me in this dark spot where the only light to focus on was what I had with Devon? How?

In a space with no air and no light, our spark was doomed to snuff out before it had the chance to grow.

I couldn't stay here in this apartment, my thoughts racing through my head. I knew Devon was in rehearsals, and he would never agree for me to go to him.

But maybe, just maybe, I could go to someone else that would make me feel safe.

Sal: Hey Q, can I come through?

Q: You are always welcome. I'm in the club but can head over to my house as soon as you are on your way. Is everything straight?

Sal: Yeah, all is good. I need company, I
can't stay with my own thoughts right now.

Q: Come through. I'll hit up Joaquim and
Jardel. If they're free, they'll be here too.

I nodded. Yeah, this made sense. Perez had been
stalking the studio; he didn't know where I was. I just
needed to wear one of my disguises and I'd be good. I
couldn't drive my car, but I could catch a cab and pay them
cash.

With a plan in my mind, I decided to go and hang out
with my brothers. I'd make sure to be back before Devon
was home, and I'd explain to him once I was safe and back
in the apartment. All would be well.

—————

THE INSTANT I stepped out of the building, I knew
something was wrong. A sense of dread poured over me as I
walked down the calm street to the intersection that had
more traffic so I could hail a cab. I searched up and down,
not seeing anything amiss, just the eerie feeling that
someone was following. I was getting close to the corner of
the intersection when my better judgment kicked in.
Turning back to the building, I pulled out my phone to dial
Q. A car skidded to a halt next to me, and the door opened.

"Salome Blackwell. We meet at last." All the hairs on
my limbs stood up at the sound of the malevolent voice. The
person inside kept themselves hidden in the Lincoln SUV
that had retrofitted limo-style seats. I could only see their
polished shoes and slacks.

"Nah, you must be confused." I pushed away from the
car door, but a blunt cylinder poked me right between my

shoulder blades. I tried to whirl around, but the cylinder moved to my back.

"No, we ain't confused, bitch. You thought you were so smart, giving us the runaround. But we got you in the end."

Fuck, it was Perez. I remembered his voice. How the fuck did this happen? How did they know to find me here? Devon had kept his address private, and I'd made sure to bump up his online security once we married. Even if they'd connected the dots, they shouldn't have found his residence.

"Did you, though? Or did I let you catch me...Perez?" I said, the words blurting out. I sounded sure of myself, and I was glad. I had to bluff my way out of this some way, somehow. If I pretended I was ready for this move, maybe I could gain the upper hand.

"Now, Sal, I doubt you knew we were coming. But that's alright, why don't you come inside and we chat some more?" said the man inside the car.

Time slowed down as he moved into my line of sight. My mouth dried when I saw his face. Without a doubt, I knew who this was. It was like looking at Zacarias twenty years from now, with a lighter complexion similar to mine. My breath caught, blood pumped through my veins, and my flight or fight kicked in. I seriously considered running and taking my chances with the gun behind me.

Somehow, all throughout, I managed to keep my expression neutral, but I was certain if he watched, he'd see my pulse galloping in my neck.

"Daddy dearest," I replied with a smirk, and he smiled indulgently.

"Perez, stand down. Let my filha get into the car. She knows better than to run."

Apparently, the man thought he knew me because we

shared DNA. Great. I got in the car, looking back at the asshole behind me, who sneered at me.

"Get in." He yanked my phone out of my hand as I sat across from my sperm donor and shut the door.

The car sped away instantly.

"So, where's Juniper?"

———

The ride to this train yard were the longest, most nerve-wracking minutes of my life. They'd put a hood on my face to prevent me from knowing our location, and they shoved me around, gravel crackling beneath my sneakers as they guided me.

Hot air flew from my mouth back into my nose, and my pulse accelerated through all my pressure points. Someone's large fingers dug into my arm, keeping me from running, but the thought still circled around my head.

If I ran, how far could I make it? Did Q hear what was said before the phone was snatched away? Was he getting Devon? I really hoped so. Shit, how did I go from being ecstatic my friend was going to have twin niblings to this?

What the fuck was my life right now?

I gingerly followed my sperm donor's instructions as he guided me up steep stairs, and once inside, he pulled the hood from my head, my pupils contracting as I got used to the dim lights of this storage container, which appeared to be retrofitted as their center of operations.

I stepped into a nice air-conditioned space with desks and some lounge furniture. The asswipe kept poking me with his gun at my back, and even though I was petrified, I was still extremely annoyed with him.

Perez would be the first one I'd fuck up online once I

was out of this. Because I would get out of this, right? I had to believe there was a way out of this.

On one wall, there was this huge board with pictures of what I could see were the drug cartels in the city. I assumed that because Devon's brother's picture was up in there, and right below was Devon's. Carpenter and others from the crew had smaller pictures too. Each of the drug groups seemed to have circles connecting them to others, and in the middle was my father's pic, with Q, Zac, and Xavier underneath.

My heart dropped to the floor, and that was when I realized it had been made of porcelain because it shattered on impact.

"See your brothers? I heard they contacted you. That's how I found you, you know? I always make sure my boys are safe. Make random checkups. Make sure no one messes with them."

Julio João Souza was an imposing man. At first, I had seen Zacarias in his face, the handsome features arresting, but he had Q's build and Xavier's sharp mind.

He stared at me for a second, then gestured toward a sofa that I sat on against my better judgment. He pulled a rolling chair from one of the desks and sat in front of me. His dudes all dispersed to corners of the container or exited the space altogether. It seemed an entourage was necessary to get me. Interesting.

"So, you stepped out of that fortress, huh? That was smart of you to align yourself with the one family I cannot touch. The Reids have connections in New York and Jamaica, and all the island players are loyal to them. They might not fuck around with hard drugs and only handle weed, but their influence runs far and wide. I heard a rumor that the head was planning to retire, but here you go aligning yourself with the prince. Smart girl.

"When I figured out you had taken my Juniper away from me, well, I was pissed. At first, I didn't know who you were. But I was glad I had Juniper followed that day. She'd been acting very weird for weeks. So, when my guys took pictures of you, we thought it would be easy to find you. But I was wrong. My man knew where you ended up but not your identity. And your disguise was good enough to throw off the scent for weeks as we followed each person that remotely looked like you that day."

The pieces left of my heart shriveled at the thought innocent people had been put in danger because of me.

"So, I continued the search because, see, Juniper took something she shouldn't have."

"You don't need the money, you fucking dirty cop. You've probably been selling the drugs you bust for years. It's brilliant, actually. And let me guess, the entire crew is other cops and DEA agents? How exactly do you think this is going to stay quiet now that I know?"

"I knew you'd be smart. That's all you can be with my genes. But I know something you don't know. Don't worry; I'll tell you about that later." He paused and sneered, then got up and started strolling around the area, making me shift to follow him. That shit pissed me off, so I just stared at the board with all the pictures. My heart raced as my mind rearranged the knowledge I thought I had of everyone surrounding me.

"Do you believe in serendipity, Salome?" He cocked his head to the side as if this was fucking Sunday brunch and we had met over mimosas. I wanted to wipe that complacent look off his smug face, but I knew everything he said right now was important. So, I shook my head in the negative.

"I wouldn't have either before this, but now, I truly do. See, my wife and I have an arrangement. I do my work, and she looks the other way. I have my friends, and she has hers. But what I cannot do is bring more kids into the world. See, she can't have kids, so the knowledge of my boys is a bitter pill for her to swallow. They were mine before the two of us met, so she tolerates them. But more children...no. And I get it. I mean, look at me; I'm in my prime. I could have as many kids as I like, but out of respect for my wife, I don't. So, imagine my surprise when I look a little into you and realize you're mine..."

I rolled my eyes at the theatricality, but inside? Shitting. Bricks. Was there a way I could get out of this? I studied the exit, trying to figure out a way I could escape with my life intact.

"See, the serendipity part comes in the fact that you helped your own little unborn sibling escape before I could take care of their mother and avoid them ever being born. And now, weeks have passed, and she's probably ripe with my son or daughter inside of her. So, she is a liability, and I need her found." He shrugged.

All this time, I'd thought it was about money and drugs, but *this* was the reason why. He needed to keep his rich wife happy, probably the only person that could bring him all the way down. I shuddered at the calm way he described Juniper as a liability, someone to dispose of.

"You're disgusting." Fuck, my voice shook at the end, but I was so angry. Sad for Juniper and what she must have gone through. I wish she had said something to me, but she was smart. She was in danger and did what she needed to do.

"And if you're wondering, in theory, you're a liability too. But I'm a benevolent father, so I won't have you killed. You're old enough for me to pass off as an indiscretion prior to my marriage if anything were to come to light. And your mother must be smarter than I gave her credit for because she never came to extort me. Maybe she's not so good at what she does after all." Another shrug, and I wanted to scream.

"What do you want, Julio?"

"Oh, so we're talking business now? Ok, I can do that. I just thought you'd find it interesting how this whole story aligned. So, this is what you're gonna do. You're gonna call your little friend and tell her she needs to come back. I don't know why she met with you last, but that tells me you're the keeper of her secrets. I thought I had her all followed and knew all her friends, but I guess I need to up my game. She was such an inconsequential part of things that I probably was too lax with her. Tell me, how did you meet my Juniper?"

Oh wow. He was so fucking sure of himself, of his smarts and reach, that he hadn't put two and two together. He didn't know I had extracted Juniper. That was good. If he didn't know about Oriole, I needed to keep it that way.

"What do you care? She needed a friend, and I was that for her."

"True, it doesn't matter in the big picture, so never mind. I just hate loose ends. When things go over my head. Don't you hate that?" He sat back down in front of me, and I stared at the board again, seeing my brothers, remembering Devon's words of caution. My heart sank, but I wanted to believe there was something I was missing.

"Did you grab me to chat? Listen, I have no idea where Juniper is; I truly don't." That was the honest-to-God truth.

I was so glad we had implemented that protocol from day one. If I lived to tell this tale, I'd tell the ladies.

"Mhm, I believe you. I haven't been an agent for all these years not trusting my instinct. Ok." He clapped his hand on his thighs and then linked his hands together as if in prayer.

"You're married to the prince of the Reid cartel. So, you're gonna get me a meeting with him. See, he used to be involved in the game before, from what my sources tell me, and he apparently might have a trail of bodies behind him. One or two, ten, who knows, but he was his brother's enforcer and number two; that we know from the snitch that got his brother. But somehow, nothing could be pinned on Devon, so the DA didn't prosecute him. He's a person of interest, though." My father smiled as if sinking a dagger into my chest. It felt like it. I wasn't a fool, but all the things unsaid between Devon and me now seemed foolish, that silence and space we gave to each other a trap.

"So if I were to find some of those bodies—and trust me, I can—then what would happen to sweet old Devon? I'm not above planting evidence to get things done. So that is step one. Always gotta think of the business. They could run some of my product, get their hands dirty, and I get that cartel under my control. Win-win. Step two is you're going to bring Juniper to me." The violence of those last words was unexpected, and the pain that bloomed when he pulled me by my hair, making my eyes water, was unexpected as well. He released me with a push, and I scrambled to stand, pacing away from him, my scalp burning in pain.

"Daughter, I'm going to spare you because I'm a good father. Ask your brothers. But what will I do if you don't get back to me in seven days? I will beat your husband up. Isn't he a dancer? Maybe I should fuck up his legs. Apparently, he does therapy daily. I could infiltrate that easily. Then I would have him prosecuted for good measure. And after that, I will go after your mother for disobeying me. Remember that," my father said with a friendly smile that would haunt my dreams for years to come.

THIRTY-THREE

DEVON

NIGHTMARES COULD NOT COMPARE to the utter feeling of dread coursing through my veins. I had received calls from Carpenter and Q just seconds apart, and before even answering the phone, I knew. I knew something was completely wrong, and it was Sal.

Carpenter putting someone outside our apartment had been a stroke of genius. They'd witnessed the entire grab and followed along down south in Homestead. But they'd lost the trail, probably once the people that had snatched Sal realized they had a tail.

I'd reached out to Q as well, and he relayed his own information, then shared he could get her to safety. That shit hadn't inspired any trust, and I told him that. I'd have to deal with the repercussions of that with Sal later. Fuck, if I got her back.

Two hours ago, my entire life turned upside down because Sal was in danger. If I'd had any doubts about my feelings for her, I had none left to wonder. Once I got her back, I was going to make sure we figured this shit out, and fuck it, if it was up to me, we would stay married.

I wanted her as my wife.

I wanted her forever.

Carpenter and the rest eyed me warily as my silence deepened, a sense of determined calm surrounding me as I imagined how I'd kill the motherfucker that messed with Sal. I'd stopped letting my bloodlust drive me a long time ago. It was always short-lived and left me on the other side bruised and haunted. The two sides of my coin didn't match up well, which was why I wasn't in the game. Not anymore.

My apartment was full of our crew, all strapped up and ready but with no concrete place to go. We could all drive to Homestead, but how would that help if we didn't know the exact location? Sal's phone had stopped tracking her, but a few seconds ago, her signal had appeared again on the app.

"She's on the move," I said, then realized she was already here.

The door opened, and she walked in, eyes red-rimmed, expression defiant, hands clenched at her sides. She never looked more beautiful because she was whole. I could tell. She was wearing a long emerald green maxi dress with deep cleavage, gold hoops, a big ass curly wig, and fake glasses. Regardless of how many people were in the apartment, our eyes met right away; her gaze weary, mine relieved.

"I— Why are there so many people in our apartment?"

Our. Ok, that's good. I could work with that.

"I was about to go out and get you," I explained, and Carpenter started unloading his semi-automatics.

"We gwaan leave yuh to it, boss, but mi have extra crew posted around the building, yuh undastand," he said.

Sal's eyes narrowed at the boss reference but nothing else.

Everyone filed out of the apartment, leaving a disturbing silence behind.

"You know, we both need to do a better job at communicating," Sal started, strolling into the kitchen and parking her behind against the counter. I eyed her for a second, then approached her.

The smell of her fear was still present, acrid sweat that I wish she'd never had to endure. But underneath it all was her sweetness, even if she kept it hidden from everyone. I enveloped her in my arms and pressed my lips to the crown of her head, and for the first time in two hours, my heart rate slowed. Her arms snaked around my middle, and she held on tight. We stood there in silence forever. Then she pushed me away.

"So, we've been dancing around this topic, but I want to clarify. You were Delroy's number two, I knew that. But is that still the case? That's what I've never been sure of," she asked, and her hand went to the middle of her chest and stayed there pressed tight.

I wasn't going to insult her with a denial. We had danced the hell around this conversation from day one, and I had foolishly convinced myself she got me, so I didn't need more than feelings and our primal connection.

I knew it took revealing all the layers of yourself to be able to truly be primal with someone, but Sal and I had somehow managed to do it without exposing all the ones in our everyday lives. So here we were, paying the price.

"Yeah to the first, no to the second."

"But you didn't explicitly tell me that."

"It's hard for me to open up about that time in my life, and when I tried... You made sure not to ask."

She nodded silently. The calm she portrayed reminded me of how determined I'd been to kill anyone that stood in my way. That calm was scaring the hell out of me after the realization of the depth of my feelings for her.

"You knew I had trust issues," she said in a husky, contemplative tone.

"And you knew I had issues opening up."

"You right...you right. Guess what? It seems my brothers might have been deep in this before. I'm not sure, but...I'm all turned around." She shrugged, and her pain became mine. She wanted to trust them so badly, and I wanted that for her too. I wanted, no, needed to gather her in my arms again; maybe if I did, I could stop this oncoming train that had no other purpose but to wreck me.

"So yet again, I stand here holding the bag, being lied to and taken advantage of for what? We promised each other transparency...but we didn't give it to each other. I know I'm complicit. I know that. But somehow, I thought with you, I had time. I thought it would be different." She shook her head, eyes red, but no tears gathered there. Not my strong, never pressed Sal.

"I didn't take advantage of you. Everything I did from the day I asked you to marry me was to keep you safe, yah understand? I knew that dude was familiar. I knew I'd seen him once or twice, and I couldn't shake the feeling once I saw him that you needed more than your computer and your hacking. Not everything can be solved like that, not when this game is done in dark corners up close in person. There would be nothing for you to find. But you had me and my resources, and while you used your methods. I used mine."

"So you married me to be my knight in shining armor?" she scoffed.

"I did! For fuck's sake, I did! Why is that so fucking hard to understand? You know I could have figured out other ways to stay here. Shit, there's a process for talented people like me to apply on their own. It's lengthier and probably more cumbersome, but I had ways. I might have convinced myself I needed you to stay for dancing, but we both know what my driving force was. I would never fucking take advantage of you. For what? You're my wife!" I pounded my chest, my voice breaking as I watched Sal's eyes grow colder and colder. I reached out to her, but she reared back, shaking her head.

"Nah, I'm not your wife, not in any sense of the word, only on paper." She almost spat the words out. We both stood there, breathing heavily, a chasm opening between us. Sal chuckled, but it was nothing like that melodic, husky sound I loved.

"You know who Juniper's man is? My father. And he's threatened me through you. So see, you didn't think this shit all the way through because now, you have a fucking target on your back. He's trying to pin shit on you. I don't know how true everything he told me is, but at this point, it don't matter. What matters is you need to lay low. And you need to stop dancing," she said calmly.

My head spun at the implications. Her father? Of all people, the person hunting her was her father. But the last thing she said left me cold.

"What do you mean I need to stop dancing?" I asked, feeling air leave the room altogether. Here I was, potentially losing Sal, and on top of that, she wanted me to let go of my one lifeline. The one thing that took me out of the headspace I was in when I was working with Delroy. Maybe if I explained shit to her, maybe if I finally fully opened up...

"You gotta stop. He's gonna try to come at you however he can. You gotta lay low, stay here, just until I figure this shit out. Now that Daddy dearest has given up his plan, I know where to hit him, and once I do, we can go our separate ways. You do the interview, I move my stuff, and after you get your citizenship in three years, we divorce. It was always the plan, and we should have never thought it could be more than that."

I knew she'd been working her way to this, but I hadn't known how it would hit me to hear her say the words. The room disintegrated around me, and I was adrift. I could reach out, but I had no strength to do so. Sal had ripped me in two, and I couldn't find a way to put myself together.

I should have fought, but I had no voice. I should have begged, but I had my dignity. So I let her walk away, up to her room, without me.

Thirty-Four

Sal

The knock on the door startled me. I'd been sitting in silence, staring at nothing. It had been hours since I last spoke with Devon. I didn't know what else there was to say. I thought my heart had shattered when I met my father, but that had been my pride. I knew now because my heart was actually flesh and blood, and it ceased its functions when I walked away from Devon.

His pain had been so loud in that kitchen I would never forget how my ears rang to the frequency of it. I'd wanted to hold his hand and squeeze until I inflicted pain, enough for us to snap out of this alternate reality where we were walking away from each other, where I was walking away from him.

"Devon, there is nothing else to say," I said to the door, afraid my voice would never go louder than this ragged whisper I'd managed.

"It's me, sweetcakes, and Aisha. Open up, babes." My heart leaped to my throat, and I rushed to answer the door.

In walked my two favorite people in the world...after Devon.

Fuck. The man had turned me into this whiny mess, and I didn't like it.

"What are y'all doing here?" I asked once I let them into the room.

"Devon called us," Aisha explained.

I nodded, a prickle in the corner of my eye making me blink twice. Then three times. Then I was in Aisha and Mila's arms, and tears poured from my eyes, washing away the hurt of the day. But I knew the feeling of release was temporary. I wouldn't ever be the same after today.

———

"So he's a crooked DEA agent. Just snitch on him. You have proof!" Aisha exclaimed after I told them everything that happened today, both with my father and Devon. Once I stopped crying, they urged me to take a shower and brought me sweet tea to drink. I saw the cup and tasted it and knew without asking Devon had made it for me. I wanted to ask who was here for him, but I couldn't muster the energy. But I worried. I knew Delroy was his person outside of...well, me and Aisha and Mila.

He loved his crew, but I could tell they only understood *shotta Devon*, whatever and whoever that was. We sat criss-crossed on my bed all facing each other like in the good old days. As I told them everything, I could sense Aisha's discomfort, especially over my argument with Devon.

"Do I? I just saw things and heard things; it's his word against mine. A man like that doesn't survive this game for this long without having connections inside. Nah, I need something to pin on him, something that hurts him but, more than that, hurts the whole op. I need something big like the pregnancy..." I paced around the room, and I saw the ladies exchange glances.

"Listen, babe...let Devon take care of things," Mila whispered.

"What do you mean by that? What do you both know that you're keeping from me? What is he gonna do?" I stared at her, willing her to tell me more. I'd explicitly asked Devon to stay put.

"Nothing. You want to move on from Devon? Fine. You've lost the privilege to know," Aisha snapped, and the bass in her voice took me aback.

"What the fuck, Sha, what does that mean?"

"Sal, I'm here for you, you know that. I love you, and I know you've gone through some hard shit. And that's just what you've shared with us. But that man out there, even though you just wrenched his heart out as you explained, is preparing to go to war for you. All of his brother's people are willing to take on basically Goliath, based on what you described, and put themselves at risk for you. So yeah, spare me your wounded ego. You gotta stop painting every man with the same brush. Is this worth dropping Devon forever?"

I opened and closed my mouth several times, unable to compute what was happening.

"Wow, you left her speechless. Damn, Aisha, you did good, girl!" Mila nodded, impressed.

I stared at Mila, still shocked at this so-called support.

"I thought you were here to support me."

"We are. That means giving you a bit of a nudge, but I think that was enough for today." Mila looked at Aisha, who shrugged as if she hadn't just come from left field at me.

"Listen, I... I know you both love Devon, but I'm hurt,

ok? I don't know how we walked ourselves into this situation where I wasn't fully aware of the extent of his work with Delroy, but I should have known. When he couldn't talk to me. When we couldn't be fully vulnerable with each other... And I did some dense shit, too, I won't deny it. I've buried my head in the sand about this for weeks.

"But I was afraid, alright? Afraid I'd messed up by ever agreeing to meet Juniper. And look what it caused." My eyes watered again, and I swiped the growing tears, angry at myself for putting myself in this situation.

"Ok, so go through all your emotions, then revisit how you feel about Devon. I think you might surprise yourself." Aisha held my hand, and I laid down, resting my head on her lap, willing for once to let my guard down.

———

Devon had become a ghost these past couple of days. He was out with the sun and back when he thought me asleep. Not that I was doing any sleeping. I couldn't fall into deep slumber without his warmth next to me.

He had truly spoiled me forever and ever.

I wasn't even mad. No, I was mad. I was mad he had made me care so much that I ached everywhere. I was mad that I woke up choked up with tears in my eyes and went to bed with my chest hollow. I wanted to finish the video game, but without him, it felt pointless. I wanted to check on him to see how he was doing without dancing, but I apparently had also become a coward. This whole situation was frustrating. I needed to return to my apartment. We could pretend to be married all he needed, but I didn't want to do it under this roof. Not this way. Not without him next to me.

I was still afraid for him, so I kept tabs on him through the girls. Aisha flat-out ignored my text messages whenever I asked about him, only responding to any other topic, but Mila took pity on me and kept me aware that he was teaching classes and had been doing his therapy. That was about what she could account for. He'd told them both he was gonna take care of the threat against me and to trust him.

What the fuck did that mean? Didn't he understand the danger he was getting himself into, and for me? Me, who couldn't stand the thought of living with him and not fully trusting him? I wouldn't let him squander his future.

I had written down everything Julio said, hoping to figure out where to strike. Every second of the day, I scoured everything I could access about Daddy dearest. His online presence was clean, his DEA connections probably adding to the sanitized version of his persona.

I hacked the DEA database, shaking as I did so, to find out he was up for a promotion to become the Special Agent in charge of the Miami division. That was probably something I could use, but I needed to find more, to connect his criminal enterprise with his work. I found that all his bank accounts were straight. Nothing jumped out, no large sums of money moving around. The man was smart about handling his finances—no red flags for anyone to find.

After the third day of sleuthing, I was an emotional mess. I was upset I couldn't find more and missed Devon so badly. A night of tossing and turning morphed into the early morning. I heard his quiet steps down the stairs as I lay on the bed staring at the ceiling, wondering how I would move on from him.

I rushed out without thinking, still in my tank top and panties, but I needed to see him. I didn't understand the compulsion, and quite frankly, it bothered me. I couldn't just let myself forget him, and here I was, running down the steps to him.

Devon must have heard me but continued peeling a mango on the counter, his sole breakfast.

"Where you going?" I snapped. Shit, I didn't mean to...well, I was in it now.

"Oh, so we're back to pretending we care?" He turned around, and it was a punch in the gut to see him. He looked probably just like I did, disheveled, sleep-deprived, and miserable. We both raked our gazes over each other, me checking for his well-being. He knew, but whatever he saw made him sigh, shoulders dropping.

"I never said I didn't care," I whispered. I wanted to reach out to him but stayed the need. I was just here to...check in and make sure he wasn't doing anything drastic because I knew I was about to crack the case of Julio João Souza. I always found a way. I *always* did.

"Ok. Listen, I don't wanna fight. I'm going to rehears—"

"What?!" I couldn't have heard right. Blood rushed to my head, and I felt dizzy at the thought of him rehearsing.

"The show is in days. I need to do this." He shrugged as if there was nothing else to say. And maybe there wasn't because little by little, he'd shown me these past months how important dance was for him. How transformative. How essential. That didn't mean I had to like him putting himself in harm's way.

"That's what probably kept you grounded, wasn't it? Dancing when you were doing whatever it was with Delroy?"

His eyes widened, then he closed them as if in pain.

"I thought you didn't get it," he said so softly I would have missed it if every atom of me wasn't attuned to him.

"I think I always did, but I stubbornly wanted to show you that you were more than just dance. That if you wanted to do something else, that was ok too. I wanted to support you, but I never took the time to listen."

"What if I never return to being the same? I've always feared that since the accident. But dance is what always keeps me going when the darkness threatens to take over. Even now, I still sleep uneasily. Well, until you... I sleep well when I'm next to you." He grimaced and opened his eyes, piercing me with the intensity of his gaze.

"I'm sorry. I didn't hear you before, but I'm listening now."

"Thanks, Empress," he murmured, visibly emotional. "I haven't ever lied to you, but I haven't been fully transparent. Many saw me and called me Delroy's number two, but that has never been the case. Still, with a close relationship like D and I have, it was inevitable that people saw me as his next-in-command. During the first months after I moved to the States, I helped with the business. And I was his enforcer. That shit was easy for me. I did what I had to do in grateful thanks to my brother because it needed to be done. He was solidifying his hold and couldn't afford any snitches, any mistakes, or any threats to the work he did.

"So, I did what I had to do for the brother that always did his best for me. But when my spirit started flagging, he was the first one to call out that things weren't working out. Sent me to New York away from him so that I could immerse myself fully in dance. And dance restored me. Healed the violence I had to inflict and the orders I made. The three murders and orders to hurt, maim or kill—the pounds of debt— still follow me to this day."

"Oh, Devon..." My heart broke for what he had gone through.

"Empress, I just needed to tell you that. I want to be as vulnerable with you as you can be with me."

My chest caved in at the truth in his words. I hadn't given him that space. I hadn't fully dropped my guard. So, he'd mirrored my intentions, even though he tried a million ways to share himself with me. I just didn't let him, not fully. And he, in turn, allowed me to see just part of him, even though he knew I felt it all. All of him.

"I'm afraid he's gonna hurt you," I said, then a sob escaped me.

"Fuck, come here." He pulled me into him, and I accepted the strength of his hug, not wanting it to end. "I hear you, but I need you to believe in me," he whispered in my ear, making me shiver. I pushed myself into him and felt his hard dick against my soft belly.

The same irrational rush that got me out of bed ran through my veins as my hands shook while I pulled down Devon's sweatpants.

"What are you—"

I silenced him with a savage kiss that made him groan into my mouth. I couldn't get enough of his taste. He pulled at my hair, making me moan, and latched onto that spot between my neck and my shoulder he'd taken to savoring on the nights we made soft love. But I didn't want that now. I wanted it hard. I pushed him away and slapped him, my hand warming with the strength of my hit. Devon cradled his cheek where I'd hit him, then charged at me, picking me up with embarrassing ease. I pummeled his back as he strode to the living room, depositing me ass up on the arm of the sectional.

His nails raked my skin as he reached for my panties, ripping them off me with a growl that made me throb in anticipation.

We were not making love.

This was pure carnal need, anger and desperation.

Devon's dick rammed into me, and I shrieked. I was wet but not ready for such force; still, I welcomed it. I savored the slight pain that radiated through me as he went wild with punishing thrusts. He held my hips as he kept up his lunges, so fast but so fucking good. I was keening now, face pressed against the seat, pussy fluttering around his dick, heart resigned that this might be the last time.

Something must have clicked for him, too, because he paused mid-thrust and then slid out of me, turning me to face him. I scrambled back on the sectional, unable to take in the look of pure, desperate love he gave me.

I wasn't ready to receive it. He had hurt me. He had lied and...

"Devon," I gasped. He pushed inside of me again, this time on top of me. Same need and carnality but with a tenderness that made me turn my face away.

"Nah, sweetness. Yuh look at me while I make love tuh yuh," he murmured, his hot palm grasping my chin, making me turn back to see him. To feel him. To accept a love I wasn't ready to take.

His sensual strokes matched the slow way he dragged the hand on my chin to my neck. There he stayed as he undulated inside of me, sending waves of ecstasy through me. I closed my legs around him, and he released my neck, giving me all his weight, biting my lips until I let him in. Then he ravaged me. Devon devastated me with his tongue, consuming me as his length slid in and out of me. I was now fully drenched, and the sounds of us together were obscene in the quiet apartment.

When he let go of my mouth, I took in a big breath that

immediately left me as he stared at me and said, "I love you."

I clenched around him and scrunched my eyes closed. I tried to cover my ears, a childish move, but I was past caring to put up a front. He brushed my hands away and whispered again, "I love you."

I rocked in pleasure as his relentless strokes, gentleness, and love took me over the edge. Sweet kisses rained over my face, my neck, and my chest as I came so hard I had tears of desire dripping from me. Once I could speak again, Devon gazed at me, and without letting me break eye contact, he held onto my face and spasmed with deep strokes as he found his pleasure within me.

The air conditioner was the only noise as we detangled ourselves from each other. There was a silence that didn't sit right with me, and when I met Devon's eyes as he put his sweatpants on, I knew I wouldn't like what he had to say.

"I love you." He lifted my left hand and stared at my ring finger—the finger that was currently bare because I'd taken off the ring he gave me, angry at it all. He stared at it as all the breath left my lungs. "Where's your ring, Empress? You know, nevah mind. After all of this is done… we will talk. If you need to walk away, know I will wait, and I'll get you back. I know you're scared to trust me, but we're meant to be together. For now, let's focus on ending this."

THIRTY-FIVE

I NEEDED to talk things through. I needed Delroy.

"You look like shit."

"That's how you greet me?" I stood and let Delroy dap me up and hug me.

"Well, me nah gwan lie to yuh."

"Sal wants a divorce after the three years; I think she just wants a reset. To see who we are outside of all the rass-clat drama," I confessed.

"Britta said the same thing." Delroy shook his head. Well, that wasn't a good vote of confidence. Even though they hadn't split at that time, they'd still ended up separated.

"Can we be serious?"

"What do you need?"

"I need advice," I told him.

"I need more details."

So, I told him everything that had transpired these past few days. He nodded along in all the right places.

Then when I finished, he paused and simply said, "You say she needs space after this. Give it to her, then show her how good it could be without all the bullshit. You're here planning to put our crew in danger with a DEA agent when your girl has told you that she can crack someone once she had enough information. Now she has it. Get her more."

I nodded along, knowing this made sense but wondering how I could make it work. We weren't even speaking to each other outside of this morning's tryst.

"You love her, don't you? It looks good on you." Delroy studied me carefully.

"You told me I looked like shit." I laughed with no humor.

"Nah, I was just messing with you; you just look like you're missing your person. Trust me, I know how that feels, so I correctly interpreted the situation."

"So, if I don't get her back...does it get better?" I asked Delroy, hoping he'd say this would stop hurting eventually.

"Nah, baby bro. It never does."

———

I LEFT the prison with an idea of what to do next. I hesitated but knew this would answer more questions. It would help us figure out the next steps to take. But before that, I went home and, feeling like a creep, slipped into Sal's room to get her wedding band for something I had planned while she was taking a shower. Once I dropped off the ring with written instructions at the jewelry store, I went to my second stop.

I parked outside of Q's sex club and asked security at the gate to let him know I was stopping by to see him.

Q came out and pointed toward his house, and I nodded

and drove around. He was already waiting outside of his front driveway.

"How is she?" he asked, and I took in the concern in his expression. I let my instinct guide my words. He was keeping something from us, but I knew he was a good dude; at least I wanted to trust that.

"She's ok, but your father is a piece of shit."

"Fuck, I was afraid he'd come for her." When he said that, I saw red, and Q raised his hands in a sign of peace.

"You better start explaining," I growled, my head pounding at the knowledge he'd so casually just dropped.

"Come in."

I walked behind Q into his home, settled myself on the couch, and waited for his explanation. He fixed himself a drink and pointed a glass at me. I accepted it. Q sat across in an armchair, crossing one leg over his other knee.

"My father tried to groom us for his drug trafficking operation, but we got out of the game before we were really in. We got out because we found out my mother was dying of cancer in Brazil, and he had lied to us about her abandoning us.

"Zac, the bleeding heart he is, said he wanted to help the women my father used and abused. He'd befriended one of my dad's current girlfriends before we realized how fucked up he truly was as a man. He'd been with several women, so Xavier and I agreed to help him. We've been doing it ever since. Atonement, I guess," Q said in a steady voice that managed to calm me even while my world was falling apart.

"Did your mom..." I was afraid to finish the sentence.

"Nah, she didn't make it before we got there." A shadow fell over Q's expression, then he cleared up again.

"We found Juniper just when she found out my dad was planning to frame her for a deal gone wrong."

I froze. Q sipped, then continued.

"Xavier reached out to her just as she was making contact with Oriole. She said she trusted Oriole. They had gotten other girls to safety, people she knew, so she trusted them. We offered to help, but the only thing she asked was to help her get some paperwork in order. That's when we found out she was expecting."

"Damn."

"Damn is right because another thing our father does is ensure none of these women stay pregnant. But he sure doesn't do anything to prevent pregnancy. He offers to pay for abortions, but if the women disagree...he finds other ways."

Fuck Sal's father.

Q sat in silence, letting me absorb the information for a minute.

"So we promised to make sure she could disappear safely and added additional measures to what Oriole had planned. Xavier followed Juniper with her permission to ensure Oriole wasn't a backstabbing individual. So, on the way back, he followed them through all the stops they made as they changed outfits at each one until she walked out of that dance studio as Sal."

"So, you researched who she was?"

"You know that we wouldn't have found much. But Xavier recognized something in her...so we got to more searching. We found out who her mother was and..." Q took another sip and shrugged.

"And you figured it out."

"Yeah, another woman that had managed to escape my father's cruelty. And a sister. The rest—well, we just wanted to meet her. But we knew shit was getting intense with our father. See, we don't fuck with him anymore, not for over ten years, but he still tries to reach out to us, especially Zac. And in one of those calls, he let it slip that he knew Juniper was pregnant."

"That's when she stopped answering Sal's friends."

"Yeah, she needed to be extra careful. We can't know for sure, but Julio has managed to create accidents for women to lose their pregnancies."

"Why the fuck haven't you stopped this motherfucker?" I couldn't contain my anger anymore. A splitting headache brewed.

"Who says we're not trying to stop him?" His expression didn't shift, but the heightened sense of danger was enough for me to understand who I was dealing with. I relaxed back into my seat and grinned, taking a sip of my own. Q nodded in acknowledgment—after all, kindred spirits recognize each other.

"I knew you were keeping something from Sal. I told her from day one."

"As you should have, and we were. We wanted to ease into it, but when I heard her on the phone...fuck." Q scrubbed his face with his free hand, and he let through a distraught expression. I sympathized but was still pissed they'd kept all this shit back. We could have known for weeks who was trying to find Sal.

"Why didn't you say anything?" I couldn't keep the challenge out of my tone.

"Because we didn't know Julio knew about Sal. We thought only we knew who'd helped Juniper. If we had, we would have said something."

His explanation had the ring of truth, but it was so minimal I wanted to punch a hole in his wall and keep on going until I'd caused the same amount of destruction his carelessness had.

"That's not enough. But I don't get to decide that. Your sister needs your help," I told him, putting down the tumbler and getting up. I focused on the reason why I'd come to see him. If Sal was going to knock her pops down, it needed to be with all the intelligence she could gather about him. These three would help her.

"Of course, we'll help. I've been texting her, but she hasn't responded to any of my messages. I was about to deploy Zacarias today."

"She's concerned you might be in with Julio João. He has a crime wall of all the major drug players, and below him, he has your pictures."

"Fucking hell!" Q stormed to his feet and hurled his tumbler against the opposite wall. He closed his eyes and cracked his neck both ways. Then after what looked like a ten-count to calm himself, he opened his eyes again.

"If she'll let us, we will help."

———

Now I needed to convince her to let her brothers in again. Sal had gone through what she saw as betrayal after betrayal from all the men she'd recently let into her heart. When I thought about it, when I let rationality prevail, I understood why she'd pushed me away. I got it. That day must have been one of the worst days of her life. To realize she was the daughter of a dangerous, disturbed man, then find out how her brothers and I had contributed to her current position...fuck, I got it. If I was her, I might have packed my shit and walked out, never looking back.

But she didn't, and I didn't because there was something

there. There was love and kinship and two souls in shadows that had found the light together.

I walked into the apartment and found her in the kitchen staring into the fridge. I could tell her things hadn't changed from the last time she'd checked it, but I didn't want to die today.

"What's up, Devon?" she asked, and her voice was steady. Good; for now, we both needed to be level-headed.

"I spoke with Q, and I think you need to hear them out."

"Oh, now I should talk to them? Hmm, interesting. When I was trusting my instinct, that wasn't ok. What changed?"

"I think it will allow us to figure this shit out without..." I sighed.

"Without you causing a drug war, I get it. I do. And I never asked you to do that. I can't imagine what would—" She shuddered, and I felt her. Felt it all.

"So talk to them, Empress. I know that with the knowledge they can provide, you'll figure this out." Her eyes shone with unshed tears, and I wanted to hold her safe until everything blew away. But it wouldn't unless we did something about it. And after that... Well, after that, I would beg, plead, even get on my knees, but I would get Sal to stay with me no matter what it took.

Thirty-Six

Sal

The apartment resembled a command center. I had Cora and Patrice each on a monitor sharing thoughts with Aisha and Mila, who were on a laptop searching through maps for possible train yard locations. Devon was in the kitchen chatting with Carpenter. The Js were all scattered around the living room on their own tablets and phones. Zac winked at me when he found me staring.

When Q, Zac, and Xavier had come in this morning, we had a long conversation about everything that happened since that fateful day I met Juniper. Devon had stayed in his room, giving us space to talk, but his presence close by was a balm I didn't realize I needed.

During our conversation, incredulity morphed into anger, then tentative comprehension. By the time we finished talking, I could understand where they were coming from, but it still would take time to heal completely. Zac pulled me aside after and asked for a hug, and I realized how much of a goofball he was. There was something so sweet about him I couldn't help but accept the embrace.

"Listen, the three of us? We have our Daddy and Mommy problems, so we don't always think things through from all angles. I mean, don't get me wrong, we're sharp as fuck, but the emotional intelligence...heh. And don't let Q fool you. He is great at helping others, but when it comes to himself?" He shook his head in despair, and I chuckled. Somehow, Zac managed to make me smile—something I still hadn't quite managed to do since yesterday after making love with Devon.

After realizing I loved him even if he made mistakes, even if he messed up, I still wanted him. Always.

Damn.

I looked up to find him watching me intently while Carpenter spoke to him. I turned my head back to the laptop, uncomfortable with how things were between us. Unfinished. Unsettled.

"Hold up, I'm finding something in these financial records from his wife's business. Q, you said you had the exact dates when he would *acquire* new product, right?" Cora inquired.

"Yeah, let me upload it to the shared cloud," Q said, and Cora hummed as she read the dates.

"Wow, it seems he might be using his wife's businesses to clean money."

"Hold up, tell me one of the dates and the business?" I asked Cora. Q got up from where he was, sensing we might be onto something. Devon walked over and sat on my other side, and everyone else stopped what they were doing. Just the scent of sea and lemon and Devon's warmth made me want to rest my head on his shoulder, but we hadn't spoken much since yesterday.

"Ok, so, see here? That large sum of money going into the real estate business in April of 2007."

"That coincides with a big bust he had that month, two thousand pounds of methamphetamine. It was huge, in the news and everything," Q said.

"So he flipped some of the product?" I asked, realizing we were getting somewhere.

"Yeah, it was to this Armenian family; they mostly traffic in Georgia. I remember that deal," Xavier said, face grim.

"So, he kept some of the product and sold it right away. We would have to connect more busts to deposits," I said, feeling a rush of adrenaline kicking in. This was it. This was the way we'd get him.

We all went to work, looking for every single bust in his career and connecting it with a major influx of money that couldn't be explained. We were able to match twenty more busts in the span of five years, all recent.

"Hold up, but this would implicate his wife," Devon said.

"Yes, that's what I'm wondering too. Cora, let me see those financial records again?" I asked.

"It seems he'll stick to one of his wife's businesses for a minute then switch after a few influxes, usually lasting a good year or two with the same business," Patrice called out from the video, and we realized the pattern as well.

"Hold up...one of his girlfriends during that time worked at the real estate office, a Dorsen company. I thought that was grimy as hell," Zac commented, a cautious excitement transferring to all of us. We were close. So close.

"And Juniper worked as an accountant at Dorsen & Co., the jewelry store." I quickly went into Juniper's paychecks, which I pulled up on the big screen.

"Holy shit!" we all exclaimed.

My father would leave me alone. I was sure of it.

THIRTY-SEVEN

DEVON

SAL ARRIVED at the meetup with her father with full backup around her. Aisha and Mila had figured out the location by deduction and some reconnaissance done by Carpenter and the crew. So here I was, sitting in a van with Sal's brothers, waiting for her to deliver her father's comeuppance. He'd really fucked around with the wrong person.

She'd reluctantly agreed to wear a wire that Xavier had obtained to protect her in case shit went sideways. Carpenter and most of the crew were around the yard in other vehicles.

A strange calm settled on me as I heard Sal and her father greet each other.

"So, where is Juniper?"

"She's safe. Her and my future sibling. And you're going to listen to what I have to say. You made a big mistake underestimating me, but it seems, for the most part, you underestimate women, don't you? You use them, but you don't think they're smart enough to catch on to your schemes." Sal's voice rang loud and clear in the van.

Q nodded, clearly proud of her. It didn't touch how I felt. I had a knot in my stomach and a lump in my throat, and my chest was filled with awe at Sal's bravery.

"What the fuck are you talking about? Where is Juniper?!" Julio João barked at Sal. A slight thud of something hitting wood vibrated through the speakers.

"Here. This is all the ways you've siphoned money into your wife's businesses to launder the profits from the drugs you've stolen. All of the money lines up with your biggest busts, some of them newsworthy. Imagine how people would feel about the new Special Agent in charge of the South Florida DEA office profiting from the job? And how would your wife feel about the extra money you've taken out with the help of your girlfriends? Stealing from her, even though she's allowed you to use her businesses for money laundering? Hmm, I wonder what she would think? And let's not talk about the prenup she made you sign when you married her, about children outside of the marriage...so many things to spill."

An eerie silence prevailed, then we heard scuffling, a grunt, and Sal's gasp. I didn't even think I was moving so fast, trying to exit the vehicle and run toward the train yard. Arms grabbed me from several sides, keeping me in my seat.

"You have to give her a moment. If we storm in now, we assure a shootout with his men. You gotta give her a shot," Q whispered.

"The fuck! He put his hands on her!" I bucked against Q's force, but he wasn't playing fair. Xavier was helping him at this point.

"She's ok, Devon," Zac said.

"Fuck, I can't just sit here! I'mma kill—"

The sound of skin slapping skin startled us all.

"Shut up and listen, old man. You could kill me, yes. But I just told you you're a master of underestimating women. Do you truly think that file there is the only thing I have as proof? Actually, that's the tip of the iceberg. I've had interviews with many of your old girlfriends. You fucked with your sons' mother, and she's managed to come back from the grave and yank you to hell. So, if something happens to me, there are instructions for everything that I have, including the interviews, to be delivered to all the major news outlets in the state and the country.

"If something happens to the Js, your wife finds out about her other stepkids. If you touch my husband or my friends, I will torch the earth you and your associates stand on until there is nothing but ashes left. So go ahead. Try me. And if you think I don't have contingencies for everything I just described? Fucking. Test. Me."

———

SAL

Relief and uncertainty. Those were the overwhelming feelings that encompassed me this morning as I got ready for the appointment at the Citizenship and Immigration office. A sense of finality marked every step I took in this room that felt empty without Devon in it.

I showered but couldn't stand using the grapefruit shampoo, quickly deciding to leave washing my hair for when I was in my own apartment.

As I got dressed, I stared around my working corner with yesterday's t-shirt draped on the chair, my lotions and products scattered around the room. Just the thought of having to pack when I returned made the butterflies in my stomach wilt in disappointment.

I walked out and down the stairs to find Devon waiting for me already. He had a backpack with him where I knew he had all the printouts and our wedding photo album, and a traveler cup, which he offered me.

"You ready?" he asked, and I nodded, not having much to say. He'd been looking at me just like he was right now, studying me with an intense regard that made me reassure him last night that I was ok. That my sperm donor didn't define who I was. That my father wouldn't come after us.

For additional insurance, I'd sent an email with some of the proof I had described I would deploy and cc'ed his wife. None of what I shared would get him in trouble with her, just enough to spook them both. She had too much to lose and couldn't afford the stunts her husband might try to pull if I hadn't put her on notice as well.

The ride to the interview location was quick, and the wait was wrought with tension between us. We sat next to each other, waiting for our turn, observing other couples and families awaiting their own case appointments.

"So it has come to this?" Devon said, sadness coloring his tone.

"To what?" I asked, not knowing what else to say.

"To this uncomfortable silence...to resignation?"

I shrugged, not having the words to explain how I felt. How I wanted to talk things through and figure out how we could find a path forward. But I still felt he wasn't sharing everything with me...was I being unfair? To hold onto a standard that I had fallen short of myself?

"Number 345, Reid!" A woman came out of a door at the end of the hall, and a bolt speared through me, making my heart race.

I fell in step next to Devon, wondering what I would have answered if we hadn't been interrupted.

"Mr. Reid, Mrs. Reid? Please follow me." A middle-aged woman with a short afro and a no-nonsense attitude escorted us through a long hall to a small office. The room was full of photos of her with what seemed to be different government and local officials.

"Please sit down. I'm Rose Turner. I'm the case officer for your adjustment of status."

"Nice to meet you, Ms. Turner," Devon said, his polite mask firmly in place. I followed suit, understanding how important this was for him.

Ms. Turner asked for the documentation, which Devon pulled out of his backpack, including the photo album. I stared at the pictures upside down as Ms. Turner went through it and I smiled, remembering how determined I'd been to go back to the apartment to play a video game. There had been a moment during the ceremony when things felt so real.

"Tell me about your wedding?" Ms. Turner asked as she examined the pictures.

"It was a regular day...at least at the beginning," Devon said.

"Yeah, we both went about our day, I think probably pretending things weren't going to completely change." I chuckled.

"But they did, all for the better. I've never had anyone that I felt so safe sharing all of me with, not even my brother. And I never knew I'd find the woman to match me in everything, in mind...soul..." Devon confessed, and she nodded along while his gaze focused solely on me. I kept my eyes on Ms. Turner, the tenderness and love in Devon's voice making me falter. I hazarded a glance at him, and he winked. That wink did things to me that made me wish we were in private.

"I remember during the vows, Devon got really nervous...and seeing him anxious calmed me down because I could see how important those words were for him, as essential as they were to me," I said, a warmth spreading in my chest, a little ember of hope flickering alight. Ms. Turner had stopped looking at our papers and leaned in, face propped up on her fist.

"In friendship and in love...I meant it that hot night in our friend's backyard. And I mean it now, every word," Devon said. He'd now turned his chair to face me completely. "And then, after a few nights together, I told her I was ruined, no other pun—"

"Aht-aht! Ms. Turner, are you gonna approve my husband's papers?" I asked, cutting to the chase. He and I needed to talk but not here, not like this. And what had he been about to say?! He was out of control.

"Oh...yeah, of course. I mean, I just wanted a bit of detail about your wedding day, but you both...I'm not supposed to say this, but I see a lot of fake couples come through, and the two of you're the real deal. I mean, obviously, something was happening when you got here, a little fight maybe? Nothing that a good conversation and maybe more—" she winked at Devon, and he smirked, "can't fix. You both go on with your day. I'll process this immediately, and you will be getting some good news in the mail very soon. Y'all remind me of me and my Desmond. You'll be alright."

THIRTY-EIGHT

DEVON

WE WERE both on some bullshit.

I had been so in my head and my feelings that I was about to let the best thing that ever happened to me walk away. Better than dancing, better than performing, better than the feel of defeating gravity when I soared during my triple turn in the air.

As we walked into our building, a woman emerged from one of the side alcoves.

"Maya Dorsen," Sal said, unsurprised by the stranger.

"I was hoping we could talk, you and I?" Ms. Dorsen exuded wealth and elegance, dressed in a pantsuit with tasteful jewelry adorning her.

"If we're going to talk, Devon can listen." Sal folded her arms over her chest, and she'd never been sexier to me than right now.

"Of course. I understand this is your husband...for now." Ms. Dorsen nodded regally, trying to goad us.

I showed both Sal and Ms. Dorsen the way to a boardroom usually utilized by the real estate agent that sold the unoccupied apartments.

"So, are you here to scare me off?"

"Oh no, honey, if I wanted to do something to you, it would be done. But you, clever one, actually served a great purpose. See, you know enough of everything to put my husband in jeopardy, and I needed someone to check him without showing him my entire hand," Ms. Dorsen said, giving us an eerie smile.

"Listen, I don't need to know all that. I want to be left alone. Are we good with that?" Sal asked. I stood behind her, ready to make a move at the slightest need. Ms. Dorsen had come alone, but I wasn't clueless; her people must be close by.

"Sweetheart, we're on the same side. My husband was a means to an end. I'm in the money laundering business, as I know you've figured out, and I needed someone on the inside. I met him, pretended to fall in love, and then planted the seed for his dirty dealings. He really believes he came up with that shit on his own. Please! What he does is like going to the corner store, and I'm Walmart. He can't touch what I actually do, but he provides enough cover and intel so I know when to make moves. Many dealers use my services; I provide a very important amenity to the community. And your father's negligence and sloppiness were drawing too much attention until you came and put him in his place."

"So, you used me?" Sal asked.

"No, no, not at all. I didn't know this was going down, shame on me. He really thinks I care about him impregnating those women; I don't. That's part of the cover. But once Juniper was loose, she was a liability I couldn't afford. Now don't make that face, I haven't done a thing to that girl. She's safe, for all I know; you did a good job hiding her."

I relaxed once I saw Sal's shoulders do the same.

"So yeah, I needed him to be humbled a bit. That Juniper move he pulled without consulting me, and now look where we are. And by the way, child, your hacking was really good. I have some of the best covering our tracks. If you ever want to work for me..."

"Nah, I'm good," Sal said with conviction.

"I had to try," Ms. Dorsen said.

"So, what is the point of this visit?" Sal asked, the same question lingering in my mind.

"I'm a woman of my word, and I want you to know your father will not bother you. He might not have integrity, but I do. I was raised that way. He and I talked, and he's back in line. I have you to thank, so I'm in your debt. Yours and your brothers, from what I gathered after I did my own digging. He will not bother those boys again either. The things I found out he's done to some of the women I allowed him to date... I've let a rabid dog out there, but that stops today."

Another thug with a code. A fancy one draped in designer clothes and jewelry, but a thug, nonetheless. Like recognizes like, after all, and nothing in Dorsen's face told me we had trouble with her. So, after saying goodbye, she walked out of our lives, additional insurance of a peace we surely would accept.

———

I'D GIVEN Sal time after that exchange. We hadn't said a word on the ride home nor the elevator after the meeting, but there was a different quality to the silence between us compared to the ride there. I smiled when she stared at me as I opened the door for her to walk into the apartment and winked when she looked back to steal a glance when she thought I was busy in the kitchen.

Sal was never hesitant, but she had stayed quiet, waiting for my move. I, in turn, needed a second to collect myself because if I'd approached her with the strength of my feelings right after the interview... It wouldn't have gone well. We wouldn't have made it home unscathed.

Finally, we were free of the concerns of her father and the worries about my papers. Finally, we could see what we wanted from each other without any commitments beyond that.

I left the bedroom, no longer feeling like it was mine after staying in hers for so long. Any space where Sal was, that was where I found my comfort. That was where I wanted to lay my head and spill my secrets, trusting that she would hold me tight, hold me whole.

I was about to knock on her door when I got a text.

Sal: *A gif of a room full of candles*

I busted the door open, the wood cracking under the pressure.

Sal sat in the gamer chair I'd gotten her hoping that maybe, just maybe, she would feel comfortable enough to let me in. Her luggage lay open on the bed with a few T-shirts inside but otherwise empty.

"You're not going anywhere." I shoved the suitcase to the floor, the shirts flying out and fluttering everywhere.

"Says who?"

"Me."

"And who are you?"

"I'm your husband, Sal. That's who I am."

She nodded once, sitting wearing a pair of those shorts

that barely covered anything and a tank top that said *Empress* across the chest.

"Tell me you're mine. Tell me you're my wife." My heart hammered in my chest, my palms itching to hold her, but I didn't dare. The gif, the tank top, and the crinkles by her eyes told me what was in her heart, but I had trusted all those signs before...

"I would think the top and the ring on my finger would be a good indication?"

"Did you read the ring inscription?"

"I did...you're such a goofball." She smiled, and her eyes glistened with unshed tears.

"I mean it, though. *In Friendship and in Love.* Mine says *Teammates 4evah.*"

"Oh my God, can you stop with the corny shit and just come and fuck me?" She rolled her eyes but couldn't help the smile that shined through.

"Nah."

"No? No?" Her eyebrows pushed in together, and she crossed her arms under her chest.

"Nah, I gon' mek luv ta yuh."

She moaned, and I took that as all the invitation I needed, jumping over the bed to land in front of her. I didn't bother with niceties. Holding onto the handles of the chair, I hovered over her, her pink lips calling mine to her. Our mouths met, and twin sighs of relief flowed out as I tasted Sal, sweet and tart. Our tongues melded in a pas de deux as we sank into the kiss. Kissing her was all I needed. Tasting her had been my full desire. Having this opportunity again...

"Oh, Devon," she moaned as the kiss grew in intensity. There wasn't one muscle in my body that didn't ache with the deep need to be inside her.

"Yes, Empress, yes. I'm going to make it all better, I promise," I vowed. I yanked her tank top off her, her gloriously ample breasts coming free. I paused for a second to admire how fucking gorgeous she was, then I snatched her shorts off. "There's no need for all dem clothes."

"Aht-aht, hubby, I'm gonna need you to reciprocate," she protested, so fucking lovely sitting there naked, her thighs already wet with her desire.

"That's no problem," I said and wrenched my sweatpants off.

"Oh yesssss," Sal whimpered.

"Dis what yuh want? Dis dick that's weeping fah yuh?" I stroked my length, stopping at the head, teasing my frenulum with the precum that was seeping out.

"Mmmm, ok. Can I say? The dirty talk is really doing it for me, but can we try that like tomorrow or something, because right n—"

Tomorrow. I didn't even blink. I flipped the chair knob until it reclined as far as it went, startling a whoop out of Sal. Then before she could react, I grabbed her legs, hooking them on the armrests, fully opening her up to me. What a beautiful sight—Sal, pumpum wide open, throbbing pink, wetness glistening between her generous thighs. Belly folds and ample, soft tits flushed in red with the cutest hard nipples. And the most impressive scowl mixed with a deep, soul-calling love. The sight filled me with such amazement. I was so fucking lucky. Even with the things I'd done in my life, I'd managed to find Sal. And she'd found me.

I lined up with her, the scent of her sweet earthiness still carrying some of my salt and sea, my dick following its true north into the tightest, wettest hold. My hand glided from her clit up her belly between her breasts, where I rested for a minute as I pumped her full of my dick, staring deep into her brown eyes. Then when I couldn't take it anymore, I clutched her neck and ground my dick into her welcome heaven.

She never stopped gazing at me, she didn't close her eyes, she didn't look away. She reassured me with her lips and her sighs and her moans.

My legs shuddered as her monitors and all the stuff on her desk shook, making a ruckus as I rammed the chair into the furniture over and over. My spine tingled, and my balls tightened, and I prayed I could take her to the finish line.

"Oh fuck, oh fuck, oohhh..." The grip of Sal's punani took me away, her orgasm glorious as she keened in my ear. I finally closed my eyes as our lips met again, our tongues tangling in a decadent dance, and still, I gave her a few last strokes, helpless to stop.

———

THE SCENT of grapefruit wafted through the steam as hot water washed away the lather I'd made in Sal's hair. We stood in the large shower, her plush behind pushing against my hardening dick. But I ignored my body's reaction to her because if I let my primal needs drive me, she and I would never get out of the bedroom. I'd never let her leave my sight again.

"Need another round or ready for conditioner?" I asked her as I finished massaging away the shampoo, white lather running down her back and disappearing under the rivulets of water.

"Conditioner."

I grabbed the bottle, poured a bit out, and saturated her coils with the product. Sal pushed back into me and nestled my now fully hard dick between her yams.

"No more dick for you until we talk."

"Booooo, you're boring, Mufasa." Sal rested her head on my shoulder.

"Sal."

"Ok, well, I'll go first. I let my trust issues keep me from the fact that I had finally found my person. You told me at the beginning it was hard for you to open up, but you never hid from me. It takes time to share the things we've both learned about each other in the span of four months. I get it. I just...when I feel betrayed, I short-circuit. I need to know all the important things. We have time for the rest. And as long as you don't hide from me, no mask on in these four walls...we'll be good," she said, brown eyes staring at me, her beautiful freckles dusting all over her nose and cheeks.

"Close your eyes," I ordered and started massaging her scalp.

"I'm a shotta."

"You were," she corrected.

"I don't know if you ever move away from the kills you did or ordered. I won't sugarcoat any of it. Even though Delroy isn't dangerous, he is in a business that can be treacherous. And I owed him so much..."

"I know, you don't have to explain."

"I do because—" I paused to gather my thoughts, loving the way Sal's languid body rested against mine, all trust. "When you asked me to scale back my dancing...I felt..."

"Misunderstood. And I'm sorry for that. I just wanted to make sure you knew you had options, that you don't have to run yourself ragged just to perform again, but I get it now."

"Dance taught me who I am, and then when I needed it the most, it saved me all over again. Reminded me I wasn't defined by the actions I took..."

"I get it." Sal sighed, and I started rinsing her hair.

"I know I could do other things. And I appreciate that you see all that I am and all my possibilities, but this...this is what fills me. You fill me, then dance. If I ever had to give dance up for a reason..."

"I will never ask you to do that again. I don't promise to stop asking for you to take care of yourself, though. And I promise to let you know if I feel disconnected from you."

"And I promise to do the same." I stroked her clean curls, enjoying the moment of stillness. "I also promise to fuck yuh hard, chase yuh around, and make you cum on my dick or my mouth and my fingers. And if you ever want to squirt for me..."

"Now you're talking my language," Sal said, pushing her ass out, and I slid into her so perfectly.

"Ahhhh, I love you, Devon. Oh god, yes, I..."

Damn, I knew this woman would ruin me for all others. And I loved every minute of the wreckage.

Epilogue

A year and some later...

Sal

He still took my breath away. Devon's performance as Conrad in *Le Corsaire* was the most anticipated of the season, and he didn't disappoint. In this variation, Devon soared through the air, his feet acting like soft springs that barely needed to touch the ground before lifting again in sautés and jetés that elicited gasps all over the theater.

I sat in the second row with Aisha, Knox, Trinity, Delroy, and Mila. My circle was all here to support Devon in his first principal role since the accident now that he had fully recovered. An additional year of therapy and smaller roles and a lot of TLC at home had him back in top shape.

The ballet finished, and a standing ovation roared in the theater as Devon walked out with the other principals, looking gorgeous in his costume. My heart filled with pride as I hooted and hollered with the rest of my friends.

"Cheese whiz, he's amazing!" Aisha exclaimed as we stood in the vestibule watching people filter out of the theater, everyone in awe of the performance.

"Cheese whiz?" Knox smiled down at her with a look of adoration and slight puzzlement, and Trinity burst out in giggles.

"It feel good to see him ina di stage again," Delroy said, and I gave him a nod.

"It really is." I raised an eyebrow at Mila, who seemed to be staring somewhere behind our circle out of my line of sight.

"If y'all want to head out, I know tomorrow is Thanksgiving, and things are busy. I'm going to wait for Devon."

"Wow, I never thought I'd see the day. Look at you, babe, you look so happy!" Aisha smiled.

"And that nomination for Alix the Badass? You doing good things, Sal. That's why you my favorite." Knox winked at me and then flinched, expecting violence from Mila, but she was still looking around.

"Yo." I pinched Mila, and she jumped. What was wrong with her?

"What? What, yeah, he did so good, danced beautifully," she said, and we all stared at her in confusion. What the fuck? She was always ready with a comment.

"Mila, that you?" A deep voice sounded behind me, and I turned around to see a handsome caramel-skinned man, tall with yummy, kissable lips. I stared at him, and something tickled in the back of my mind. I knew him. He had something to do with Mila's sister, but what? Shit, my memory was usually better than this.

"Oh, hey, you! Hey, Tariq, hey." Mila tapped his arm, and right away, we knew something was off. I stared at

Aisha, who looked back perplexed at Mila while she fumbled her words around Tariq. Ohhh, I knew who he was —Mila's cousin's ex...

"Empress."

A shiver ran from my hair to the bottom of my feet. I turned around and saw my beautiful, kind, gentle, dangerous husband.

"Hey, hubby." I slid my arm around him, and he tucked me right into him, planting a kiss on the crown of my head. Even today, I felt the warmth traveling all over, and I smiled at how soft he'd made me.

"You ready to hit the road?" he asked.

"It's like none of us are standing here, amazing," Mila said. Clearly, she had recovered the ability to compute.

"That's alright, my likkle sis-in-law has my brother sprung. As it should be," Delroy said, and Devon dapped him up, then greeted everyone else. Then he stepped right behind me again, sliding a hand around my waist and squeezing my hip.

"Mila, you can come for me when you can string words together beyond 'hey, you, hey,' alright?" I said, and Aisha burst out laughing. Mila pretended not to hear me, and I shook my head. I'd find out what was happening once I returned from Jacksonville for Thanksgiving. After a lot of conversations, some productive, many not, Lilith and I were in a much better place. Understanding her point of view had been important for my healing.

After saying our goodbyes, we started walking to the door, but Devon pulled me backstage toward the dressing rooms.

"Where we going? We gotta hit the road if we want to make it at a decent time. Lilith will wake us up at the crack of dawn regardless of what time we went to bed to help out in the kitchen."

"I know, but this will just take a couple of minutes." He palmed my ass and squeezed it for good measure. "Did I tell you I love this dress? I could just pull it up a bit and..."

I started to feel air caress the bottom of my cheeks.

"Don't play with me unless you gonna deliver, Mufasa."

"Oh, I can deliver," Devon murmured in my ear and bit my earlobe.

He led me into his dressing room and yanked up my dress, pulling me into him as we stumbled toward a chair.

A half-hour later, I attempted to pull my dress down as Devon kept nuzzling my neck and dipping his tongue into my cleavage and wondered if I could change my panties or if I should just ride to Jacksonville commando.

"Devon, if you don't stop, we're gonna go another round, and we will never get out of here." I pulled his head out of my chest.

"Fine, Empress. I know the trip to your mom's has you a bit nervous, so I made us something comfy to drive up in. That's why I brought you here."

He pulled out two pairs of sweatpants and hoodies and opened one up for me to see.

The back of the hoodie had a beautiful illustration of Alix and Jax; I recognized Joaquim's art immediately. The sweatpants had Alix and Jax's initials on them, then right below, Devon's and mine.

"Oh, so we're doing corny shit now?" I choked out.

"Yes, we are, to celebrate your nomination and to make sure you're comfortable on the ride up, not that I have any issues with this dress." He ran his hand over my décolletage, and I shivered again.

"Ugh, you know I love you, right?"

"Yeah, you scream it in my ear when I'm pounding your pun—"

I shut him up with a kiss. And an hour later, we finally headed up to Jacksonville in our matching outfits.

Like fools in love, and I loved every minute of it.

THE END

Also by A H. Cunningham

The Firecracker Cousins Series

Alight

Ablaze

Embers

Toying with Temptation

Holiday Shorts

'Tis The Season to Release

Anthologies

Current: An Anthology for Jackson Mississippi - Vol 1

Wicked Moves Series

Plié

Check out the A.H. Universe website to see how it all connects!

Acknowledgments

Acknowledgments are hard because I want to write five pages of 'thank yous'. After all, writing might feel like a solitary endeavor, but it has never felt that way for me. I am so grateful for all the book content creators who have rode with me from the beginning, those who joined the ride after the Firecracker cousins, and those new to the ride since Plié. Thanks for trusting my words and for amplifying my work. I'm so thankful for the community.

My beta readers are the heroes of A Turn in the Air, Meka James, Gabrielle Brown, Lynell (Weekendreader), and Kaitesi Tiba. Each of you took the work with love and care and immediately understood Sal and Devon.

Thank you!!

Seeing Devon come to live under Afro Anime Senpai's art and then witnessing the cover design by Brynn Harbon made my entire month.

DeAnma Cooper @hentaigirl82, thanks for being so open to sharing your experiences as a Black Cosplayer. Your spirit came through during our talk, and Sal is better because of you.

Kaitesi, thank you for your earth brain that understands mine! I can't wait to continue the partnership! All the tweets are bookmarked for the future :)

To the Mr. it all matters. Every word, every encouragement, every evening you sit next to me and watch me type. It all matters.

To my children, one day, I'll be able to take that month with you and spend all the quality time. May these words be the way.

About the Author

A.H Cunningham is an introvert that weaves lovey-dovey contemporary romance and erotica. Her characters are Black and Multicultural adults, trying to navigate their grown folk lives while contending with all the horny feelings and falling hopelessly in love in their journey. In her writing, you will find a deep love for the entire Black Diaspora and all the ways we connect through our heritage. When she's not writing, you can find her reading, snacking at odd hours, dancing some Panamanian song, and playing the metaphorical Tamborine as her family navigates a new move.

Join A.H's newsletter to get all the latest updates!
http://www.ahcunninghamauthor.com